Praise for *A Life* ... novel:

'Jim Rush is a charmer and a liar who comes at you from somewhere between an Elmore Leonard low life hustler and Patricia Highsmith's loveable, homicidal hero, Tom Ripley. A compelling read.' *Liverpool Daily Post*

'One of the classiest thriller writers around ... Grant-Adamson's amoral charmer has a charmed life, and it is her considerable skill to explore this in depth, and make it both enthralling and credible.' *The Sunday Times*

'This unusual thriller stands comparison with Patricia Highsmith's Ripley novels.' *Today*

And for Lesley Grant-Adamson's previous novels:

'She knows how to create an atmosphere of unease and incipient horror.' *P. D. James* (*Patterns in the Dust*)

'Grant-Adamson is certainly among the top crime writers of our younger generation.' *The Times* (*Curse the Darkness*)

'The book grips as tightly as the rope around the dead man's neck.' *Woman's World* (*Curse the Darkness*)

About the author

Lesley Grant-Adamson was born in north London in 1942 and spent much of her childhood in the Rhondda in South Wales. She worked on provincial newspapers before joining the staff of the *Guardian* where she became a features writer, then worked as a freelance journalist and television writer while establishing herself as a novelist.

Dangerous Games is her twelfth novel. Her first, *Patterns in the Dust*, was published in 1985. Her most recent is *The Dangerous Edge*.

She is married and lives in north London but does much of her writing in her cottage in a Somerset village or – in the case of *Dangerous Games* – in Spain.

Dangerous Games

Lesley Grant-Adamson

CORONET BOOKS
Hodder and Stoughton

For David and Dorothy Dry

Copyright © 1994 by Lesley Grant-Adamson

First published in Great Britain in 1994
by Hodder and Stoughton
A division of Hodder Headline PLC

First published in paperback in 1995
by Hodder and Stoughton

A Coronet paperback

British Cataloguing in Publication Data

Grant-Adamson, Lesley
Dangerous Games
I Title
823.914 [F]

ISBN 0 340 62872 3

Typeset by Keyboard Services, Luton, Beds

Printed and bound in Great Britain by
Cox and Wyman Ltd, Reading, Berks

Hodder and Stoughton Ltd
A division of Hodder Headline PLC
338 Euston Road
London NW1 3BH

1

The bullet ripped into the lintel above his head. He dropped, swinging away, scrabbling for the deeper shadow of the bushes. His own noise seemed immense: sharp intake of breath, scuffle of shoes on paving, crushing and crunching of stiff-leaved shrubs as he thrust in amongst them, and then the rasp of his uncontrollable breathing.

He clamped a hand over his mouth. The hand smelled of earth and sweat and fear. The hand fell away. Around him hibiscus blooms bobbed, greying blobs whose hot colour cooled with the last of the tropical day. Their stems creaked. He grabbed the nearest and stilled it.

He listened, with every nerve he listened, desperately, not expecting to hear anything. Until the shot he'd believed he was alone. There'd been no sounds in the evening air, except for the soft movement of his own clothes. And then, without warning, it had happened.

He waited, not knowing how long he waited. His left leg grew stiff. It was held awkwardly, bent beneath him. He tried to move it without disturbing the leaves. An inch, a pause, another inch.

As panic subsided, he began to feel foolish. It was absurd: a quiet prowl to an empty house, and very nearly a bullet through the skull.

He waited. Far off, monkeys began to shriek in the giant bamboo. All around, the stealthy sounds of night creatures cautiously resuming activity. But nothing made the sounds of a man, of a man with a gun.

A stab of cramp forced him to a decision. With care he manoeuvred until he was poised, on palms and toes like a sprinter on a starting block. Then he eased forward, risking exposing his head from the cover of hibiscus, trying for a view down the path to the road, and praying his pale face didn't present the target his attacker was awaiting.

He didn't doubt the man *was* waiting. No one had come to the house and rooted among the bushes; and there'd been no footsteps receding on the path, no click of shoes along the harder surface of the road. Of course not, the gunman was waiting.

He withdrew into the foliage. *Where? Where was the man waiting? Where had the shot come from?* The answers remained hidden in the darkness absorbing the island. Soon there'd be no shapes, only the warm black velvet. Escape became more chancy by the minute.

And then a faint sound reached him from the direction of the road. A shoe scuffing a stone, perhaps, or something heavy being set down. Anyway, a sound made by a human being. An indistinct something of a sound, but it was enough.

Immediately, he was at his imaginary starting block again, toes and hands speeding a crouching run. He broke from the bushes, cleared the paving in front of the house and skidded round the side of the building. As the gunman was near the road, escape lay in any other direction he could get away. If he were lucky, there'd be a path behind the house. If not, he'd blunder through the forest until he reached one. He could get lost, but not seriously lost if he kept the song of the sea on his right.

He'd taken three paces into the dense blackness of the trees behind the house when he became suspicious that he'd got it wrong. He wasn't alone. Someone was hiding, directly ahead. His eyes caught a glimmer of light clothing, a shape whisking aside. Retreating to the house, he concealed himself in the dark angle of two walls, and he waited.

The figure in the trees was moving gradually to the left. He could see it working its way round towards the house and could hear the sigh of the leaves it stirred. Then, for a while, there was nothing. The glimmer faded, there was silence. Tempting to hope the man had gone away, found a route out of the garden and taken it. But then it came to life again, moving more carelessly and quickly, loping towards the building.

It was coming straight for him but he wasn't going to stay until it slewed to a stop, raised the gun, aimed the shot he mightn't live to hear. No, his instinct was to hurl himself on his attacker.

He rocketed out of his hiding place, slammed into the gunman sending him flying, recovered his own balance and was poised for renewed assault when his brain unscrambled words from the confusion and he hesitated.

'Don't shoot!' he heard. 'Please don't shoot. I wasn't doing anything. You've got to believe me. *Don't shoot.*'

The voice was English, southern, a soft country drawl. Terror raised it way above its normal level.

He peered down at the pleading man, said quietly: 'I don't have a gun. Where's yours?'

'Mine?' The voice was a squeak. 'Don't be bloody daft.'

3

He stood back and let the Englishman rise. The man was trembling, gabbling.

He cut him off. 'If neither of us fired that shot, then the guy who did is still around. I think he was on the road.'

'Who are you?'

'What?'

'I'm Martin Peters. Who are you?'

'Jim Rush. Look . . .' He wanted escape, not acquaintance. He didn't conceal his impatience.

Peters said: 'I mean are you the police?'

'Police?' An ironic laugh.

'I thought maybe . . .' He'd guessed wrong but didn't sound altogether disappointed. 'You're American, right?'

Jim cut in again. 'That guy could be on his way round here right now. I'm not hanging about to check it out, OK?'

He dashed towards the trees, aware that Peters was sticking close. Jim planned to streak away from him once they reached a path. He was younger and fitter, especially now that Peters was winded from the fight. But Peters said he knew where the path was and once they were on it he kept pace and he kept talking.

His talk was repetitious and tiresome, picking over the drama they'd just lived through. But he had a torch and he knew the way. Jim grunted occasional agreement and didn't attempt to outstrip him.

The path ended in a clearing. Off to one side were a few shacks where happy voices chattered in patois and cooking spiced the air. Below lay the harbour town, a few narrow streets of shops, houses and all the usual unexceptional things, winding up the hillside until it met the forest. Its stone quay was drawn in yellow lamplight. Within its protective arm, smaller dots of light indicated a few boats

4

waiting with furled sails for their crews to return from the Green Parrot bar, which was a splash of orange light at the end of the quay.

Jim got the question in first. 'Where are you staying?'

Peters used the torch beam to point to the left of the town. 'Bamboo Lodge, they call it.'

They dropped down. When they were close to the town they sheered off along a road that curved round the flank of the hill. The torch played on great shrubs garlanded with flowers, on massive trees draped with creepers. Peters gestured again with the beam of light. 'There it is. Down there.'

A soft pool of light showed the lines of a long, low Spanish colonial-style building. It lay in a garden as lush as Eden, on the edge of a palm-fringed beach.

Jim saw him properly for the first time when they entered the lamplit garden. Martin Peters looked about 40, was stocky with a squarish face, and was losing his hair. It was the bushy, wavy type of hair. He wore it slightly longer than was fashionable, which emphasised the thinness on the crown and the receding temples. He was dishevelled and had walked unevenly; perhaps, Jim thought, the temporary effects of the evening's adventures.

Peters' lightweight jacket and trousers were standard casual wear for the average Englishman on a jaunt to the sunshine. He had a friendly, cuddly look about him, except for his eyes. Martin Peters' eyes were sharp. While he was saying something, they would be saying something different. Whatever he was, Jim concluded, he wasn't the average Englishman come to soak up the Caribbean sun.

'Police?' Jim asked him, making a joke of it, once they were in his hotel room.

Peters laughed too much and slopped the drink he was pouring. The room was a *cabaña* in the garden. There was ample space for two but he had said he was staying there alone. A woman would have liked it: pink hibiscus flowers in a vase; nuts and bananas in a plaited basket; floral-patterned fabrics; and the drifting scent of pink and gold frangipani blossom through a louvred shutter. A ceiling fan cooled the humid air to comfortable.

'Police! It's true though, Jim, isn't it? You can never find one when you want one.'

'What then, Martin?' Jim accepted the glass.

Peters gulped down a mouthful of rum, brushed his lips with the back of his hand. 'Holiday. What else?'

Jim shook his head in gentle admonishment.

Peters laughed again. 'All right, then. Seeing as you saved my life. I mean, I'd have run straight into that bastard with the gun if you hadn't stopped me.'

He flopped into a rattan chair, the twin of the one where Jim sat. 'All right,' Peters said again, his soft country voice growing confidential. It was a pleasant voice now it had calmed to its normal pitch, a gentle sound with purring 'r's.

'I'm a photographer, Jim. But that's not for everybody to know, mind.'

Jim didn't grasp the point. Everyone else at the hotel, everyone at *all* the hotels, was humping cameras. He queried with a narrowing of the eyes.

Peters downed the last of his drink. 'The sort of pictures I take, well they sell all over the world. Celebrities.'

'Film stars?'

'And royalty. That's the big money-spinner. Royalty.' He rolled the word round his mouth, greedily.

Then: 'I'm not saying I wouldn't touch anything else if it came my way, a nice bit of voodoo or a shipwreck, but basically royalty is what I do.'

Jim thought: *Me. He'd do me if he knew I was the guy on the police posters in London, wanted for murder. Or if he knew I'm the one who pulled off the impersonation of the millionaire orchid dealer and made a packet from it. He'd do me, except that he'd never make the link.* Even while he dismissed the risk of Peters identifying him where the police had failed, his scalp tightened. The unworded thought was that Martin Peters was dangerous company.

Raising the bottle, Peters offered a refill. Jim held out his glass. He seldom drank much and wouldn't now but he didn't want to part from Peters yet. He'd been around but he hadn't met anyone quite like him. Right from the outset, he had that impression.

'Now you understand,' said Peters, 'why I don't want it to be common knowledge. If the target, the subject, gets wind of it, I'm done. I might as well pack up and go home.'

'Diana. That's who you've come for.' Jim savoured the smooth warmth of the rum, the tang of the lime.

Peters admitted it with a slight bow. 'Simply the best.'

'But she's not here. Wrong island, Martin.'

'Oh come on, you don't think they'd let me book into the same place, do you? It's private, that island. Owned by the almighty Lord Something of Somewhere. There's a lot of places like that around here. But you take a look at the map, Jim. This is about as near as I can get. It's the way I work, you see. Get near enough and then make forays.'

7

Jim looked doubtful. 'It's still a long way.'

'No, it's ideal.' He stretched back in the chair, hands clasped over his thinning crown. 'I get out there, I do the business, and I put my film on a plane to a newspaper. Easy.'

'How close do you manage to get, working like that?' Jim was thinking of all the hazy not-much-good shots that newspapers were prepared to use.

Peters took a folder from a drawer in a chest and flicked through it as he replied. 'Not close at all, hardly ever. All right, I could try something fancy. Say I get myself hired as a waiter over there? Not that anyone would hire me in the first place. But supposing they did, that I wormed myself on to the right island. What then? How do I get out? I mean, getting out is as crucial as getting in. No, I prefer it this way. Less risk of bumping up against the security people.'

He handed Jim a photograph, one of the hazy not-much-good shots that newspapers published. This one showed the back view of a group of people. A woman with short fair hair was sitting on a beach with her head lowered. Two young boys were a blur, running towards the sea. Someone else's leg, female, stuck into the photograph on the left and a slab of a man's body filled the lower right. Peters was proud of it.

'From a plane,' he said. 'The only photograph of her on that island, so far.'

Jim thought it such a poor shot that it took a leap of faith to identify the woman as the Princess of Wales. He passed the print back.

'Ever get caught, Martin?'

'Not now. Once or twice, in the early days when I was young and reckless. But you have to take chances in the

8

beginning, to get your name known at the picture desks. Dedication, that's what you've got to have. After a bit, the picture editors come to you. If you're any good, that is.'

Jim wanted to know what had happened when he was caught. Peters said not much, all they did was tell him he was a naughty boy and send him away.

'I've been bawled at by the royals at Sandringham, but that was in eighty-one when Diana came into the frame. We were all being bawled at then. She was whizzing around in that little red Metro she had and we were all whizzing around after her in case, just in case, she was the one. It stood to reason, he was going to have to make his pick, he couldn't leave it much longer. *Somebody* was going to have to be the next Princess of Wales, why not Lady Di?'

'Did you get your picture?' He'd been to Norfolk, knew Sandringham House was surrounded by hundreds of private acres. If Peters claimed athletic feats, he'd be sceptical.

Peters patted his slight paunch. 'I was fitter in those days. I was on the roof of a furniture van and I got her in the grounds. The driver thought I was a nut when I flagged him down but once he saw the fistful of fivers he became quite reasonable.'

He had started another story of those days, about sneaking a shot from a window overlooking her flat in Coleherne Court, when several people ran past the *cabaña*, making the kind of cheerful noise people make when they're on the verge of being drunk.

Peters looked over his shoulder, making believe he could see them through the wall. 'There they go again. Every evening, a bottle of rum in one or other of their *cabañas* and then a race to the bar. After that, they'll giggle all the way through dinner.' He shrugged. 'Well, I suppose we're all entitled to enjoy our holidays the way we want.'

Except princesses, Jim assumed. There was no intended irony in Peters' remark.

Jim stood up and set his empty glass on the low rattan table. He wasn't sorry Peters had been interrupted because the story threatened to be a long one. Peters, he fancied, was lonely and envious of the boozy camaraderie of the holidaymakers.

'You going, Jim?' Peters eased himself out of the chair. He rubbed his leg. Although he'd brushed at it with his hands when they'd arrived, there was a patch of earth on the material. He was stiffening already, he'd be bruised by morning.

'I have to, Martin. Thanks for the drink.'

'A pity. I thought we might have had dinner here, if you weren't busy.'

'I'm sorry.'

'No, it was just an idea. I'll call you a taxi.' Peters used a telephone Jim hadn't noticed because it was sitting on the floor beside a sofa. Then: 'Jim, they *said* ten minutes, but you know how they are about time. Another one while you wait?'

Jim shook his head. There were questions they'd both been avoiding, which was odd. He'd been holding back so that Peters would ask but Peters had preferred to tell him that keep-it-to-yourself stuff about chasing Princess Diana. So Jim asked, after all, in a playful way.

'What were you doing at the house this evening, Martin? And I won't believe you if you say you were snatching pictures.'

Martin Peters' eyes grew evasive although he smiled and

agreed that yes, even for him, the conditions were unfavourable.

'Just nosing,' he added. 'I've seen it from the road. Great old ruin, nobody near it. I went for a walk, up through the woods and out in that direction thinking I'd take a closer look at it. Of course it took longer than I expected and of course it got dark. But that's the way it goes here, isn't it?'

Jim said that was pretty much his own explanation for being there. He was lying. Peters was lying. They both knew. Jim said: 'A plantation house, wasn't it?'

A shrug. 'It's got a great view from up there. Seems a waste, letting it rot.'

They walked through the garden and met the taxi. 'Which hotel?' Peters asked Jim as it drew up.

'I'll go to the harbour.'

This puzzled Peters. There were no good hotels close to the harbour and Jim didn't seem the type to be doing the West Indies on a shoestring, staying in cheap guest houses. Jim looked too smart for that: expensive clothes, good hair cut, the confident demeanour that isn't acquired by nervously chasing the pennies. 'Where are you staying then, Jim?'

'St Elena.'

Peters' eyebrows shot up. 'St Elena? But that's . . .'

'Sure, I know.' Jim told the taxi driver he'd like to go to the harbour. The man reached over and flicked a catch to open the rear door.

Peters said: 'But that's right next to . . . They're your neighbours.'

'I know.' Jim got into the taxi. 'See you around, Martin. And thanks again for the drink.'

As the cab pulled away, Jim turned to wave. Martin

Peters was gaping after it, hands clutching at the bushy hair on either side of what would soon be his bald patch.

Jim stretched out on the lounger by the pool and closed his eyes against the yellow light. The island heat lay on him like a blanket. This was morning, later it would be ferocious. He hoped the others would think he was asleep. Then he began to count the minutes before one of them disturbed him. Guy, probably. Guy had been a bore in London and was more of a bore now. Laughing at his own puerile jokes, always demanding attention and never being worth it. Jim sighed and shifted his position, then wished he hadn't. Sleepers don't sigh, not like that, he'd given himself away. He willed the others to ignore it. Lucinda would, she didn't bother him much. Nor did Charles. He and the scrawny Lucinda were too wrapped up in each other to bother anyone about anything. Jane was the one most likely to come to him, lure him back into the group.

'Hey,' said Jane, close. 'Are you asleep, James?' She had a low, caressing voice. Without looking he could see the midnight eyes, the long hair like black silk, the mischievous smile that had attracted him to her.

'Yes.'

The lounger tilted as she perched on the edge of it. 'We're going down to the beach. You will come, won't you?'

'When?'

'Now.'

He opened one eye. 'I'll follow you, OK?'

She began to tickle him, very lightly, her fingers barely touching, just enough to send ripples of delicious feeling through his whole body. He sat up abruptly and grasped

12

her wrists, so quick she didn't have time to move. She gave a yelp that was half alarm, half pleasure.

Guy appeared beside them, a tubby figure wearing a ridiculous sun hat and carrying a battered tennis racket. His shadow blocked out their fun. 'Come on, you two. Don't keep the captain waiting.'

Jim released his grip and Jane stood up. She fetched a long loose shirt from one of the other chairs and pulled it on over her bathing suit. Neither of them said a word. Jim knew she sometimes resented Guy and his heartiness, or at least the way he used it to interrupt any fun they were having. But Jane didn't admit this. She was ambivalent but uncritical. Guy was one of her set, they stuck together no matter what. If there was to be criticism of anyone, then it lay in what was *not* said rather than in the snappy aside.

Jane had risked a lot for Jim, easing him into her circle in London and then whisking him off on this protracted St Elena holiday exactly when London had grown perilous for him. She'd saved him from the police who wanted to ask him about a death that had been an accident although they believed it to be murder. She was his lifeline and his love but her friends appalled him. And here he was, incarcerated on a speck of rock with Jeremy, Lucinda and Charles, and the especially awful Guy. Still, it was improving. There were fewer of them than there had been. After several weeks, a handful of others had gone home to work, or else they'd touched base briefly to swap swimsuits for skis. Postcards had arrived from the trio holidaying in Klosters. Later the same three checked in from the Seychelles.

The islands were a place of comings and goings, which is what they'd always been in one way or another. During

Jim's stay, a series of Guy's friends who were living or holidaymaking elsewhere in the Caribbean made briefer visits. For a time Piers and his brother had stayed. Piers was run of the mill, the brother so languid even his exclamations of surprise or pleasure seemed interrupted by a yawn. Presumably he was capable of livening up because this was the marquis, the one who disappeared from his country estate the night a village girl's body was discovered in the house.

While he was on St Elena, someone brought a London newspaper that devoted a half page to the case and the way it had foundered. It was exactly two years since the killing and throughout tabloid newspapers had been unstinted in their condemnation of the Missing Marquis, egged on apparently by a police force resigned to lack of co-operation from his friends who saw no advantage in applying the law to one of their own. By contrast, the girl's parents, tenants on the estate, were invariably cautious in their comments.

The article concluded with a quote from an elderly, famous and rather dotty writer who'd lived all her life in the world of the well born. 'Gentlemen no longer go into their libraries and shoot themselves when faced with disaster. They run orff and rely on the silence of their friends for protection.' She seemed to have as much distaste for this falling-off of standards as for the murder of village maidens.

The newspaper was passed quietly round but not openly discussed. A young man would finish reading it and turn to his girl with a lifting of the eyebrows and she would reply with a moue. Jim imagined his own presence contributed to their reticence, but of course never knew.

When it was his turn to read the newspaper he read it all and learned that the press hadn't forgotten him, either. It amused him to calculate the odds against St Elena harbouring at the same time two young men, Jim 25 and the marquis two years older, both wanted in Britain for murder. But the presence of the Missing Marquis was worrying because if the police came, brazening Guy and arresting the marquis, might they not notice Jim too? He wondered what powers the police would have on the island, whether it was British or whether it was covered by an extradition treaty. He couldn't ask, it was too pertinent a question, and whatever else was permitted, pertinence was out. Life on the island was deliberately playful.

'Life is a dream,' breathed Lucinda one day, her sharp elbows jutting out like handles from the lounger where she sprawled.

'No, a film,' suggested Jim, missing the reference to the Spanish writer Calderón and his play of that name. In his mind he developed his own point about life's jump cuts and plots and the way you could edit it to please yourself. Too cold in London? Then jump cut to a Caribbean beach. Not enough to do on St Elena? Then pop in a storyline that speeds the action, moves it away from the claustrophobic rock. Claustrophobia? *Class*trophobia, why not? A film makes up its own language too.

Aloud he said: 'Dreaming, you have no choices.'

But they didn't want to discuss it, they just noticed he'd missed Calderón.

He hadn't admired them in London, with their mistaken notions of superiority and their wealthy negligence, although a few were talented and a number held down responsible jobs. Charles, for instance, was something with a London auction house. Once they'd reached the island, however, there'd been an outbreak of infantilism. Even Jeremy, quieter than most and occasionally to be found with a book in his hand in London, had revealed a taste for gaudy clothes and a penchant for practical jokes. Possessions had been hidden, keyholes had been gummed up, fake telephone messages had been delivered, that sort of thing. Fortunately these jokes were usually aimed at Guy, Jim hadn't suffered unduly. And anyway the phase had passed, Jeremy had run out of inspiration.

Jane had smiled on indulgently, and after Jim shot her a look that expressed 'how *could* they?' she made a point of explaining, privately, later: 'Darling, you have to realise that beneath that veneer of frivolity lies an impenetrable band of exactly the same thing.'

The rich lead less interesting lives, they have more certainties. Jim had reached that conclusion weeks ago but he had no one to discuss it with. In fact, no one to discuss anything with because Jane's friends weren't talkers, not in that way. They played verbal games. They made preposterous statements that were the opposite of what they believed; or they skirted around answers to simple questions; or they used any device to confuse and mislead without telling the lie direct. Providing one knew the rules, it worked well enough as a means of keeping safe the club secrets. Jim wasn't a member of the club. Jane had infiltrated him only to its outer edges. Of course, they made allowances for him, being American.

Their clubbiness was comical to him. There was the club for those who'd been at prep school together, others for the public school pals and college cronies. What was extraordinary was that school wormed its way into conversation every day, as though a cog had jammed and stopped their emotional development. And it wasn't as though the school memories they shared were the least interesting, they were standard stuff about incompetent staff and boisterous boys. One evening, when Guy was behaving especially like Guy, Charles roared at him: 'Guy, you were a beastly little bugger at school and you haven't changed a scrap.'

Guy was delighted by this and they plunged into another round of reminiscence. One of the stock characters whenever they told these stories was a boy Jim came to think of as Smith Minor. In fact, Charles and Jeremy affected not to remember his name and Guy refused to divulge it. This boy had a terrible term with Guy accusing him of rule-flouting, then failing to notify him of a new rule so that he was punished for breaking it.

Charles revived the Smith Minor business when he wanted to tell Guy, in a jocular way, to stop being bossy. He'd put on a squeaky pubescent voice and chirruped: 'I say, Guy, I'm not that skinny boy whose father makes black pudding, you know.'

'Gosh,' said Guy. 'I thought you were.'

Jeremy said: 'Faggots, surely?'

Actually, said Charles, his family were major share-holders in one of the food industry's biggest businesses and the black pudding was only Guy's joke.

But how they'd enjoyed it, enhanced it, enlivened their schooldays by taunting the little Smith with it. He'd also made the mistake of being clever. Unforgivable!

Tiresome though they were, the school stories taught Jim much about Guy's personality. In all the escapades there was a lack of moderation. Once he was in charge, he didn't know where to stop. Not only did Guy need to be centre stage but he needed a victim. Early on, Jim realised Guy had cast him in the role of Smith Minor. Jim's ploy was to refuse to let Guy see he'd noticed this.

Guy had taken a dislike to him before they'd met, telephoning Jane's London flat to say: 'I don't believe we know him.'

'I've known James for months, Guy. So have Charles and heaps of the others.'

'Months? That's what I mean, Jane.'

She'd patched over Guy's resistance, making foolish promises that they'd take to each other. Then she'd played the card that said, *without* saying so, that if Jim didn't go to St Elena then neither did she. 'I want him there, Guy.'

'Well, if you really think so.'

She hadn't wavered, she'd laughed away Guy's doubts and made up, for Jim's sake, an alternative meaning for the conversation he'd half heard. Jim pretended to believe her. Months later, he and Guy continued to prowl around each other, distrustful, Guy attempting to intimidate and Jim continuing to behave as though he had absolutely no idea.

They were going to the beach to play the island's own version of bounce, which they assured Jim was a derivative of beach cricket. It involved a tender tennis racket with Elastoplast on the handle, and a bright red rubber ball that had come in on the tide. Guy and Charles argued a lot about the exact rules, several of which had been defined by Simeon, one of the Klosters and Seychelles trio. One day they argued with such intransigence that all they could agree on was that it was imperative to telephone Simeon for a ruling. He was roused from his bed on the other side of

18

the world. He told them to adapt the rule to suit prevailing circumstances, and he retaliated by telephoning St Elena several times the following night with fatuous enquiries. Everybody declared it hilarious.

Jane and Jim walked behind the others through the palm grove on the water's edge. Guy, in front, suddenly whirled round and yelled: 'Look out.'

This was a cue for them to run. One of Guy's games was inventing island hazards the rest had to be afraid of. He deemed the palm grove a danger zone because of falling coconuts. Lucinda, who was always all elbows and giggles, shrieked and fled. Charles plonked his hands on his head and chased after her. Jeremy obligingly scampered behind them, hitching up a pair of cerise and yellow shorts that threatened to escape. Jane started forward but Jim held her back, swung her up and carried her.

'Too slow,' Guy shouted. 'Come *on*.'

'Can't you see? She's been knocked out by a coconut.' Jim feigned staggering under Jane's weight, then set her down and they walked on. Guy had turned away and was running after Charles, Lucinda and Jeremy who were moving out over the glittering sand.

Jim thought: *A mistake, Guy. Now Charles is going to choose the pitch and you won't like that one bit.*

He looked forward to Guy's discomfiture, or at least he looked forward to being proved right about it. The confrontation itself would be tedious. Guy would never come right out and say what he felt, neither would Charles. They'd each pretend compliance and niceness while not budging an iota. It would be left to one of the others to tout the virtues of a different pitch altogether, and that's where the game would eventually take place.

God, if only it weren't all so predictable, so boring, Jim thought.

Charles was scraping the sand with a stick. His shadow was stumpy although Charles himself was lanky with broad shoulders. The doubt in Guy's voice drifted back towards the palm trees. 'Here, Charles?'

The reply was lost because Charles was bent over marking out the lines.

Guy said: 'Well, if you really think so.' But he didn't mean that, he meant that Charles had made a stupid choice and should be considerate enough to change it.

Precisely as Jim had foreseen, the pair of them wrangled. He steered Jane off to the right, along the rim of the bay. White sand was darkened with the shadows of tossing palms. Turquoise sea sucked lazily at the shore. Beyond the coral reef, a yacht skimmed by, its sails the same shade as the pink-lipped shells of abalone and conch that lay scattered on the beach.

Jane said: 'James, remember what you were saying the other day? About going away for a while?'

'I must have been crazy.'

'No, it would be good. We could charter a boat and sail up and down the islands. They're all different, that's what's so wonderful about the Antilles, you can never feel you've seen it all.'

Hundreds of islands, the peaks of a submerged volcanic mountain range, endless coastlines and reefs to explore – you could sail for ever. When he'd mentioned sailing away, almost a week ago, it had been no more than a wish born out of boredom. He dared not go, it would put at risk the little security he'd gained. Also he'd meant he wanted to go alone. But going with Jane? Wasn't that better?

He said, tilting his head in the direction of Charles and Guy arguing and Jeremy and Lucinda splashing in the surf: 'Unfair on them though. The others have gone home and if we wander off too . . .'

'Not at all. Reinforcements are on the way. Camilla's coming out for a week.' She paused to see his reaction.

He made sure there wasn't one. Being mistaken for a friend of Camilla, whom he'd never met, had given him his entrée. Then he'd met Jane. She'd guessed but she'd protected him.

She said: 'And Tadpole's bringing a couple of his friends. We won't be missed, I promise.'

The prospect was so tempting he wanted to agree to it there and then. He was confident that, perhaps relying on Jane's support, he could fob off Camilla. All he had to do was fake astonishment that she wasn't, after all, the Camilla he claimed he'd met in Washington. In her world it wasn't a rare name. Yes, if ever they came face to face, that's what he'd do. Simplicity was always preferable. Danger lay in elaboration.

Jane misinterpreted his silence. 'I'll handle Camilla.'

'There's no problem about Camilla.'

Jane swung back her hair. 'Good. I thought you were afraid we'd look as though we were hiding if we sailed off alone.'

Across the beach the argument was reaching a new level. Lucinda, who'd been reticent until now, could be heard above Guy and Charles. In a moment they'd let her prevail and the game would be allowed to begin. Jeremy was already with the others, chipping in but not trying to dominate.

'I wouldn't at all mind hiding,' Jim said to Jane.

She mocked him, saying it had become part of the game, this tussle about siting the pitch. 'You can't believe they're serious, surely?'

'Oh, no.' How could he? They weren't serious about anything.

Lucinda won, looked up, and made a beckoning wave. Charles obediently dragged his foot across the sand, scrubbing out the lines of his labour. Guy detailed Jeremy to mark out the new pitch. Then, suffused with conqueror's pride, he jerked round in search of his missing players.

'Oh come on, you two. Captain's waiting, you know.'

With an excellent attempt at enthusiasm and good humour, Jim hurried over to join in the game. There was, he calculated, an hour of it to endure before one of the servants called them to lunch, or carried lunch to the beach if that was what had been arranged. He asked Jane, jogging beside him, which it was to be.

'On the terrace, I think. You're not hungry already?'

'Anticipating,' he said.

And she thought he meant they'd go to their room afterwards and make love. It was easier when they lunched at the house, they could slip away whenever they liked. If they were on the beach, they had to tolerate Guy's inanities when they announced they were going back to the house. Guy liked everybody to do everything together, a jolly little gang with no spoilsports. Worst of all were the days when Guy decided to stroll back to the house with them, convinced he'd have no more fun on the beach because they'd broken up the party.

'Over there, Jane,' Guy shouted, pointing a couple of hundred yards to her right. She trotted off. 'And Jeremy, can you draw in a bit? You know what Lucinda's like, the ball could go anywhere.'

'Cheek,' Lucinda called back. She made a motion of swiping him with the tennis racket, stopping in mid swing as Guy wheeled to see what was amusing Jeremy and Charles.

Jim stood where Guy placed him, near the water although the chances of Lucinda striking the ball that far were slight. Guy always put him on the edge, of everything. Jim assumed this was a way of demonstrating that he wasn't quite one of them: he was to be obliged to play their games but not allowed to participate fully, and never, of course, to win.

'OK,' Guy yelled. 'Everybody ready?'

He was going to bowl the first ball himself, probably a unilateral decision like most of his others. No amount of playfulness could disguise his bossy nature. Jim didn't watch. He gazed up at the island rising above him. It was a very few miles long, with its white sand wrapped around it like a ribbon on a cake. At the other end the land rose to a hill. There was a stream, some forest, fertile soil where fruit trees flourished and rows of vegetables were planted out, there was safe bathing and a nicely protected harbour. If you set out to invent the perfect island in miniature, you'd probably come up with St Elena.

A shriek went up and Jim dropped his eyes to see Jane and Charles scrabbling after the red rubber ball and Lucinda tearing up and down over the sand while Guy waved his silly sun hat in the air and counted. At that moment Jim hated Guy. St Elena was perfect except that Guy came as part of the package. Guy's cousin owned the island, it was thanks to Guy that any of them were there. Jim hated being indebted to Guy but he was.

He stayed in his place while Guy rearranged his fielders and gave them a pep talk. Someone called for a dope test because of the dramatic improvement in Lucinda's form. Someone else claimed to have seen her practising through the night, racing up and down the sand in her nightie. Lucinda said she was ready for the next ball.

Jim daydreamed again. He glimpsed the house through the trees and it set him thinking of the old plantation house on the bigger island, the one where he'd been shot at and then discovered Martin Peters.

That was two days ago and he'd spent a good deal of time mulling it over. It amazed him he hadn't realised someone was there ahead of him. He'd approached the house in silence, missing the significance of that: birds and other creatures had already been scared away. Another curious thing was that comment Martin Peters had made, about the house having a wonderful view. Well, it didn't. Not from ground level, anyway. Bushes and trees screened it from the road and behind it lay the forest. If Peters had enjoyed a view, then he'd been upstairs, perhaps as high as the roof.

Peters had carried his torch with him, not his camera. Jim didn't believe the man had been caught out, as he'd claimed, by the swift-falling night. All along, Jim had suspected Peters was lying. He'd have to watch out for him. The man was a self-appointed snooper, he could prove a nuisance.

Suddenly there was a hullabaloo, the ball came flashing towards the sea. Jim lurched back to the present and flung out an arm. Useless, the ball was many yards away. But he was the nearest fielder, it was his duty to retrieve it. He paddled out until the water was up to his thighs, then set off in a slow crawl in pursuit of the red dot.

Sink, he willed it. *Sink, damn you, and sink Ghastly Guy's ghastly game*.

But the ball had floated into their lives and it would continue to float. Besides, Guy would never be short of a ghastly game.

Jim was in no hurry to reach the ball. Throwing it ashore would only start off another round. Then he heard shouts of encouragement and responded with a few quicker strokes. But he made a mess of tossing the ball, letting it slip and splash so that he had to swim after it again. This wasn't intentional, it was clumsiness. Guy groaned. Lucinda was still running when Jim looked back, but Guy was remonstrating with her and the fielders were in dispute. Jim threw the ball properly. There was a flurry of cerise and yellow silk as Jeremy scooped it up from the sand and did whatever fielders were supposed to do when they had the ball. But no one was paying attention.

Jim turned on to his back and drifted. The heavens were blue, the day was glorious. He considered Jane's idea. Charter a boat? Sail around the islands? Bliss. Expensive bliss? He had money, enough for a while, but he didn't have the unfathomable supply Jane's friends enjoyed. He wondered how far she trusted in his stories about his business in New York, in Connecticut. She hadn't mentioned any of that since they'd arrived on St Elena weeks ago. In fact, she had never done so unless a friend asked her directly who he was and what he did. Jim had overheard her repeating tales he'd told her, improving on them. Whether she realised the extent of the deception, he couldn't guess.

The splendid thing about Jane was that she made her

own decisions about what mattered and what didn't. Until now, whenever there'd been a choice, she'd chosen him. Her family and friends had disapproved but she hadn't been shaken in her judgment. She was far from stupid, it was simply that she did what she wanted.

On the beach everyone was squabbling away, oblivious of him. He struck out for the headland, not many yards away across the diminutive bay. Then he saw the boat. He'd noticed it several times before, passing quite close to the island. Plainly it had started life as a fishing boat and now it had a big cabin as well as a wheelhouse. The interesting thing was the contraption fitted on the stern. Not fishing gear, although he couldn't imagine what else it might be.

The same two men were on board, one olive skinned and dark, the other a big man with red hair and skin the sun and sea air had whipped to an unhealthy pinkness. Jim couldn't see them clearly but the last time they'd come by he'd happened to be on the hill with binoculars and they'd provided a little entertainment until they rounded the point.

Jim made a few rapid strokes after the boat, pretending it was possible to catch up with it and assuage his curiosity. Then he came ashore on the headland. This was no more than a few rocks and a tumble of surf, enough to cut off the view of the next bay. Everything about St Elena was small scale, contained. Having grown up in the wide open spaces of the hawkeye state, he felt he'd stumbled into a dolls' house world. For weeks it had been enchanting, after months it was frustrating. He felt constrained, restless.

From the slight elevation of the headland he watched the boat and looked for a clue to its destination. There was no reason for it to travel so close to the next islands in the chain if it wasn't calling at either, yet he'd never seen it moored in any of their bays. Sometimes he took the St Elena yacht, the *Mariposa*, out on his own although usually Guy saw to it that the whole jolly crew went. The last time he'd gone alone was when he'd offered to fetch some supplies and had stretched it into a trip that ended up at the old plantation house.

He'd lied to Martin Peters. He hadn't been mooching around the hill sightseeing. No, he'd begun by trailing a man he'd thought he recognised, a limping man who'd nimbly side-stepped trouble that time in the cays and skipped with the money, a man who'd be appalled to find himself cornered by Jim Rush. But Jim had lost him on the road, a half mile below the old house. And anyway, by then he'd worked out that he was wrong, he'd wasted his time prowling after a stranger.

After leaving Peters, he'd slept on board in the harbour and sailed for St Elena at first light, hauling the sails up fast before they were thrashed by the trade winds chasing down from the high hills. He'd raced the wind and he'd won. It blew him away, with a breath perfumed with spice.

That outing hadn't made him popular. Lucinda had persuaded herself the yacht and Jim were sunk. Charles was cross that he'd spent a sleepless night because Lucinda was fretful. Jeremy smoothed his parrot-coloured T-shirt and was silently disapproving. Guy's annoyance was palpable although all he said was that he was very, very pleased to see Jim and the yacht back safely and that he'd known, of course, that everything was all right. Only Jane had been undismayed by his failure to hurry back. She understood he needed time to himself.

Jim wished he could just take the *Mariposa* and go. Anywhere. Anywhere at all. He pictured himself sneaking away while the argument about the beach game was still in full flood; chasing over the empty sands and casting off. If he sailed south they wouldn't see him go. He could scour the next islands for the old fishing boat that had the peculiar thing attached to it, and if it wasn't there he could sail away after it, trailing it through the archipelago. Better, he could . . .

Voices broke in on his daydream. He jogged back to the beach, switching on the sunny smile that made him agreeable company.

Guy appeared to have won the argument. He had a victorious glow about him again, Jim could see it in the strut of the fellow. Then Guy concentrated on Jim. He whipped the tennis racket under his arm for a crutch, bent one leg up behind him and roared: 'Aha, Jim, lad.' He was rewarded with howls of laughter that left Lucinda giggling helplessly on the sand.

'*Robinson Crusoe*,' said Jeremy, who seldom said much and when he did was usually wrong.

More noisy mirth as several voices corrected him. '*Treasure Island*.'

Jeremy was taken aback. 'Are you sure? Wasn't that the one with the footprints on the sands of time, or somesuch?'

Jane saved Jeremy by pretending his confusion of Defoe's *Robinson Crusoe* and Longfellow's *Psalm of Life* was deliberate. 'Don't tease, Jeremy, or Guy will have us searching the island for Man Friday. And we won't find him, of course, because Defoe used Tobago.'

Guy was still doing *Treasure Island*, although all he could recall of it was 'Yo, ho, ho and a bottle of rum' and 'Aha,

Jim, lad.' He did them both several times, in a fanciful eighteenth-century kind of voice, vaguely West Country and distinctly guttural.

Charles said that actually there was none of this 'Aha, Jim, lad' in the book, it came from the film. Guy said, 'Shiver my timbers,' and addressed Charles as 'matey'. Jeremy said that surely what Guy was doing was Tony Hancock's sketch, not the film and not the book. He was correct this time, but as he was usually wrong no one considered it. And, anyway, before they could consider anything, Guy's performance was enhanced by a parrot flying out of the shoreline palms.

'Captain Flint!' cried Charles and Jane.

Guy hopped after it, pleading with the parrot to perch on his shoulder and squawking at it: 'Pieces of eight! Pieces of eight!' While he was doing this a servant came down to say that lunch was ready.

Jim joined in the badinage over lunch and gathered that Guy's new joke was unlikely to die: they were going to go on calling him Jim. They thought it rather witty they should do this, having no idea that only Jane and her friends had ever called him James.

Later, alone in their bedroom, he decided to tell her she was right about acquiring a yacht and taking off for a while. She was in the bathroom and he was trying to use a mirror that was her height not his. He was no more than average height but he had to stoop. He ran the comb through his hair, its fairness lightened by months of sunshine. Concerned that it looked more like artifice than accident, he fingered strands, letting them fan out and fall back into place. The angle was awkward. He stepped back from the mirror and bent his knees, then fiddled with his hair again, wishing she'd come out of the bathroom where mirrors were tall and a person's height made no difference.

When she came, her hair sleek and coiled up high on her head for coolness, he told her of his decision. 'I'll make some phone calls, see what's available.'

That evening he mentioned four possibilities. 'I'll go take a look at them.'

'Where are they?'

He named three different islands. Her face fell. 'That will take days, seeing them all.'

'It's not smart to choose over the telephone. A boat can sound great and when you get there it's an old tub.'

'Yes, I was being impatient. Of course we must examine them. It's just that . . .'

'What's the problem?'

She gave the slightest shrug. 'Guy won't be keen. He was so tight lipped when you didn't come haring back last time, I'm afraid he'll find a reason not to let us take the *Mariposa*.'

'Then we'll hire another boat to go looking for the one we really want.'

He concealed his dislike of Guy beneath an encouraging smile. He knew he'd given Jane the correct answer: that every problem could be solved if you spent money on it.

Jim cornered Guy in his room early the same evening, when Guy was drowsy from sun and affable from drink. Also, Guy had enjoyed rather a good day's fun, much of it at Jim's expense. Perhaps that's what Guy had in mind when he replied to the request with: 'Aye, shiver my timbers, Jim, lad. Ye shall sail abroad in the good ship *Mariposa* and ye may lay to it.'

Guy slumped in his chair, acting the drunken pirate and

30

singing 'Yo, ho, ho and a bottle of rum'. The magazine he'd been reading when Jim entered fell to the floor and Guy unwittingly kicked it aside with a booted foot.

Jim said: 'Cheers, Guy,' and went out of the room.

He met Jane coming out of theirs, caught her hand and drew her back in. He kept his voice low. Having grown up in a wooden house, he knew they didn't guarantee privacy. 'Guy said yes. I'm leaving right now, before he changes his mind.'

'Oh. Now?'

He went past her, opened a cupboard, and reached for a bag. Above it his clothes hung neatly, with equal spaces between the hangers. Jane watched him pack. She usually chided him about his extreme neatness. This time she said nothing. He looked over his shoulder, paused. Perhaps he was doing the wrong thing. If he were, he'd expect her to tell him and help him get it right.

She stayed where she was, her arms folded. She was running her tongue along the edge of her teeth, a trick she had when she wanted to give herself time to think before she spoke.

Then she said carefully: 'I thought we'd go together.'

He knew that. She'd talked about it as though they'd both go. He said: 'Wouldn't it be better if you stayed? Company for Lucinda, if you like.'

'Lucinda has Charles.'

'Ah.'

'Look, James, Guy can be a rotten tease. Every time you go off without me . . .'

'I'm sorry, I hadn't thought.'

He went to her and kissed her. Of course she would sail with him, she was his talisman.

* * *

Jim anchored for the night in a bay on an island to the south. Alone, he'd have gone further, keen to put distance between himself and the St Elena set, but Jane wanted to stop. She was competent on a boat but no daredevil. Even so, he liked sailing with her, partly because sailing was something he did especially well and he enjoyed her admiration.

They spent a pleasant night with no company but seabirds, inquisitive fish and land crabs. Otherwise they were alone. No one made appalling jokes. It was wonderful.

Jane spotted the crabs' burrows when they anchored and promised to show him them, although they came out only at night. She and Jim sat on deck while the moon silvered the coconut palms and the island was veiled with dusk. Then she used the boat's spotlight and held one of the big white crabs still, using the beam of light like a stick to pin it down.

'That's how they catch them to eat,' she said. But the people had gone. The coconut plantation was abandoned, fallen nuts rotted in their husks. A few trees lay where the last hurricane had flung them, roots grappling the air and great scoopfuls of earth torn out. Beauty and violence had always gone together here.

'Let it go,' Jim said, sorry for the poor trapped creature, free and yet not free.

When light broke, Jim was up and making ready to move off, eager to take advantage of the usual dawn squall. But Jane was sluggish, needing a dip in the sea to freshen her and a cup of coffee to warm her. She delayed them long past the brief tropical dawn but he didn't mind. They'd escaped, they weren't being pursued by Ghastly Guy, they were free and would be until they chose to turn for home.

As they moved down the coast, the wind streaming into their sails with a great smoothing of canvas, the converted fishing boat appeared ahead of them. It seemed to materialise out of the hilly coastline.

Jane said: 'They call it a hurricane harbour. It's almost landlocked and when you're in, you're protected from anything that's going on out here.'

'Like the one on St Lucia?' He hadn't seen it for himself but Marigot Bay was reputedly the best hurricane harbour in the West Indies.

'A baby version of it. We sailed in there once, oh, years ago. Look, that's where you go in.' She was pointing at the kind of gap you miss unless you know what you're looking for.

The fishing boat was dawdling along. Whipped by an offshore wind, the *Mariposa* was gaining on it.

'Know what that is?' Jane was pointing again. 'On the back?'

'What?'

'It's survey equipment. They're surveying the seabed. Something to do with prospecting for oil.'

'My God, you're full of information this morning.'

Even when she was shouting above the creak of rigging and the swish of the sea, her voice was musical. She laughed, delighted by his surprise.

'I met them last year, a couple of escapees from England. They'd got into a mess, fouled an anchor or something, I can't remember exactly. Anyway, the crew of the good ship *Mariposa* sailed to the rescue. Then they had to be nice to us, poured beer into us and swapped sailors' yarns.'

Jim let the yacht lift with the breeze, sent her flying down the coast. Soon she'd be clear of the island and he wanted the benefit of this breeze while he had it. He chased after the other boat.

As they drew near, the man with the olive skin and dark hair waved. Jane shouted a greeting, standing on the lee side of the sail so it would throw her voice, but the wind snatched her words away. Then the *Mariposa* had left the boat astern and was past the island. Wind and current were different. Jim swung the tiller to aim squarely at the next grey shape rising from the sea.

From time to time he looked back, at the wash, at the flashes of pink and silver as the climbing sun glanced off the water, at the streaked sky, and at the old fishing boat that was following him. He decided she *was* following. When he set his course for a harbour on the western headland and then changed his mind and opted for one on the east, his pursuer altered direction too.

Oil? It was possible, he thought. There was oil far south at Trinidad. But if there was oil in the Antilles archipelago, enough to make it worthwhile going for it, then it would have been discovered long ago. And it would have been discovered by one of the big American oil companies or by a government, not by a couple of guys in an ordinary little boat with a thing, whatever it was, hanging on the back.

The boat followed the *Mariposa* into a rundown harbour and moored. Jim preferred to drop anchor and use the dinghy. The water was flawless, the bottom coral. Eddies stirred up pink sand as he paddled ashore. The dark man was waiting and held out a hand to offer Jane unnecessary help. She took the hand.

The man said: 'It's Jane, isn't it?'

Recognition pleased her. 'And you're Mike. Hello, again.'

She couldn't recall the name of the other man, the redhead with the pale northern skin spoiled by wind and weather. He reminded her he was Drew. It was unclear whether this was a first name or a surname. Introductions completed, they all went aboard the old boat. Water was boiled, instant coffee was made. There were pleasantries about the joys of island sailing and the sleek lines of the *Mariposa*. Before long Jim was able to slot in a query about the surveying equipment.

Mike Rooney took him over to look at it. Apparently what they did was lower the contraption on the stern into the water so that it scanned the ocean floor. A screen on a console in the wheelhouse could then show what the equipment was looking at down below.

'Mostly fish and coral,' suggested Jim.

Rooney said that was about right. 'Of course, what we get's a rather crude impression. There's smarter gear around now, this isn't the latest. On bad days Drew grumbles it's like looking into one of those bag-check machines at airports.'

'Mike, you haven't said what you use it for, but I guess it's neither fish nor coral.'

Drew called out that there was more coffee if anyone would like some. Rooney turned away from the equipment, obliging Jim to follow.

Rooney told him: 'We check up on pipelines, cables, that kind of thing. Whoever has something down there that needs to be looked at, we do the looking for them.'

Jim had known large survey vessels used for such work. Once again, the boat seemed wrong although it *was* tempting to believe the story: everything else in the islands was miniature, why not the survey equipment? And if it were true, what a splendid job Drew and Rooney had invented for themselves.

Jane had told Drew about their quest for a yacht they could sail around for a few weeks. When Jim joined them Drew was listing possibilities. He and Rooney weren't mere holidaymakers, they lived on their boat and they used the harbours. They knew what was available and what was worth having.

Rooney mentioned one particular yacht twice, drawing special attention to it. The *Caramba*, she was called. She was kept on the same island, a couple of miles down the coast, and belonged to a friend of his. Or maybe it was a friend of a friend.

Drew interrupted to say: 'She's for sale, Mike. Not charter.'

Rooney flicked him an impatient glance. 'OK, but if she won't sell maybe Jock will hire her out. What's he got to lose?'

Drew took the point. 'I suppose it's worth asking, if she's the kind of thing you want, Jim.'

Jane sat quietly listening to the exchanges. No one asked her opinion. When it was arranged that they'd go and look at the yacht, she was disappointed to discover she was to be left behind. She sat in the cabin of the *Mariposa* for a few minutes, then decided to go ashore and wander through the village. She wondered whether there'd be a market, the usual kind of thing: tumbles of fruit, sour sop, dasheen, yams, bananas and water melons in their seasons; miles of batik-dyed cloths; flurries of chickens, and unfamiliar odours. But no, the harbour would be crowded on market day and it wasn't. She'd hear the sounds from where she was, and there was nothing.

She decided to go ashore anyway, pick up some food and perhaps have a drink at a café. But when she went on deck the first thing she spotted was the *Mariposa*'s dinghy tied up a hundred feet away across the water.

'Oh, no!'

Her exasperation was momentary. With a laugh and a shrug, she tossed her purse on to the table and sought the suntan lotion. There was a comfortable space on the roof of the cabin. Jane climbed up and lay there, to think about all the places she wanted James to take her. To Martinique with its smart international gloss. To the green fortress island of Dominica, mysterious in its rainforest, the island where the last of the Caribs lived in a reservation, sadly on the Atlantic side where the weather was windy and unkind. She'd never seen a Carib. The nearest she'd come was a few broken pots in a display case in a museum on a touristy island. The note beside them said, somewhat confusingly, that the Caribs of the islands were less aggressive although given to cannibalism, while the mainland ones cultivated manioc and hunted with the blowpipe. She suspected that, after years of holidaying in the area, she was lazy not to have learned more than that.

Aboard the fishing boat, Jim was trying to persuade Rooney and Drew to open up about their surveying. Each time he worked the conversation round, they sheered away. Drew, in particular, avoided discussing it. Jim was amused by the play. It confirmed his suspicion that they'd lied. Twice. He didn't doubt Jane's story that they'd mentioned oil. Perhaps they'd realised how improbable that was and switched to pipelines. Pipelines were better, not much but better.

Pretending he hadn't noticed their reluctance, he followed up one of his questions with: 'What are you working on right now?' Unless they were going to claim an impromptu holiday, they'd have to give him something.

'Telephone cable,' said Rooney.

'Gas pipe,' said Drew simultaneously.

Jim's blue-eyed gaze was unwavering. 'Where?'

Drew looked at Rooney for leadership. Rooney said: 'North-east from Venezuela.'

Drew winced.

Jim said: 'That's a lot of ocean.'

He was convinced they knew he didn't believe them. Rooney was avoiding his eye. Then Rooney and Drew again spoke at once, changing the subject. Jim let them change it.

The *Caramba* was moored at a ruinous jetty by a coconut grove. Barnacles encrusted some of the jetty's beams, shipworm was devouring them. It was a disregarded place, where seawrack and driftwood fringed the beach, not a place where tourists came or fancy boats put in. A woman with a brown and yellow scarf twisted high on her head stepped from behind a pink shack to stare at the newcomers.

Beside the boat they'd come to see, there were two others, a launch and a fishing boat, both scruffy. The *Caramba* was all right. Her lines weren't as beautiful as the St Elena yacht's but Jim doubted he'd be fortunate enough to find another to match that.

He leaped ashore and picked his way carefully down the

jetty. A man on the launch said good morning and kept an eye on him. Jim boarded the yacht. Mike Rooney joined him.

'Jim, she handles better than she looks. She has a way of lifting over the water, not labouring through it.'

'You've sailed her?'

'Oh yes, I've sailed her a bit. A while ago, mind. Three or four years. Jock, who owns her, well, he was going up to Martinique one time. Come along, he said. So what could I do but go? If you're in the islands and you're not sailing, then what on earth are you doing here?'

Jim gave him a wry smile. 'Hunting wrecks?'

The remark stopped Rooney dead. His face took on a guarded look, something in the eyes, a twist to the mouth. He tried to speak but there were no words and he let out his breath in a rueful sigh. Then: 'Is it that obvious?'

Jim lifted his shoulders slightly. In fact, he felt foolish not to have worked it out sooner. If they were searching for wrecks, then everything about their boat fitted. The crew were the right types, the out-of-date equipment and the cheap old boat were exactly what people like that could afford.

'Where is it?' Jim asked.

Rooney said they hadn't struck lucky yet, they were only at the stage of searching for a wreck. But over the next half hour, prowling around the *Caramba*, ostensibly discussing her merits, Jim winkled it out of him. Their wreck lay off one of the smaller islands of the archipelago, she was a Spanish galleon called the *Gloriosa*, and further work was delayed until a friend arrived from Canada.

Jim wondered: 'Can't you get anyone else? A pity to waste the good months.' Already it was hot, later there'd be hurricanes.

'He's a partner in this. He's putting in cash and effort, so we have to wait.'

'Does he say when he's coming?' Jim was picturing a deskbound, snowbound executive in Toronto, dreaming of his escape to the sunshine isles but doing nothing to make it come true.

Rooney shook his head. 'Keeps changing the date. Business commitments, family problems... A string of reasons he's still there instead of here.'

Jim murmured sympathy. His imaginary executive was running out of money as well as time.

Yet Rooney sounded sanguine. 'I'm sure it will work out.'

Jim said he was sorry they'd become stuck. 'Especially tough when you're dealing with buried treasure.'

Rooney hadn't been specific, for all Jim knew the ship might have contained nothing valuable when it sank. Besides, it had almost certainly been searched before now and stripped of anything interesting. But there was a chance that it hadn't been found, that the force of the seas scouring the ledge where she lay had shifted and exposed her fairly recently.

Quickly Rooney said they didn't know exactly what she'd been carrying. She'd sunk when attacked by pirates on her way from Trinidad to Spain.

Rooney continued to be sanguine. 'If we're lucky, she's rich. If we're unlucky, we end up poorer than we started.'

It was a risk, a gamble. Jim loved risk, he thrived on it.

He envied Rooney and Drew the chance and the hazards. He couldn't help himself, he wanted a part of it.

Casually, as if it hardly mattered one way or the other, he said he'd like to see the galleon. Mike Rooney agreed to it, just like that.

Just like that. And it shouldn't have been. There should have been refusal, coaxing, wavering, reluctant agreement. There was none of that. Mike Rooney agreed.

So then Jim knew. He wasn't fooled by Drew's tight-lipped annoyance when Rooney explained that Jim was going out to the wreck with them. Jim had them taped: Mike Rooney the guy with the dark looks but the open Irish heart who was the talker, the chatterer, the one who made the plans and oozed information; and Drew who was tighter, took time to make friends and share with them. But Rooney was the leader, he got his way. What he wanted was Jim Rush's involvement.

They were back on the fishing boat when they all three talked about the wreck. Jim was wary of appearing eager but was anxious to fix a time to go out to her. Of course, it was Drew who put up objections that had to be kicked aside before plans could be laid. Rooney broke off to go down into the cabin and fetch the telephone number of Jock, the owner of the *Caramba*.

There was a moody silence. Jim ignored it, faked interest in the softly swinging sea. Somewhere out there, fabulous fathoms deep, lay a treasure ship from the age of romance. He looked dreamily off to the horizon and waited for Drew to speak.

Drew cleared his throat. He spoke quietly, apparently hoping Rooney might not overhear. 'The thing is, Jim, she may not be anything.'

Jim grunted, continued to seem preoccupied. 'Hm?'

'We want it to be the *Gloriosa* because she went down somewhere around there, but when Mike says . . .'

Jim gave him his attention. 'You haven't positively identified the wreck?'

Well, that was unsurprising. Their scanner would hardly have revealed her identity, that was too much to ask. And as wrecks were plentiful, mistaken identity was a distinct possibility. Some Caribbean wrecks were ships raided for the treasure they were carrying home to Spain from Mexico or Venezuela; others went down in sea battles involving the British, Spanish, French or Dutch; hurricanes, storms and bad seamanship accounted for scores of others. Jim knew it was easy to believe you'd located one ship when it was actually another.

Mike Rooney reappeared with a slip of paper on which he'd written Jock's telephone number. 'He's usually around in the mornings, Jim.'

Instinctively, Jim looked at his wrist watch. 'I'll try right away.'

'There's a phone at that bar.' Rooney pointed to the pink shack.

Jim took the slip of paper and stood up. He wanted to leave them something to think about while he was gone, so he asked: 'How are you going to make sure you have the right wreck?'

It wasn't really a serious question, more a way of saying he had to be convinced of it himself before he tipped money into the project. Then he sprang on to the jetty, skipping over the crumbling planks, and headed for the telephone. He expected them to talk of nothing else while he was gone.

He was smiling broadly. They'd plotted to snare him and

42

were thrilled at how easily they'd done it. Secretly thrilled. While he was with them, they had to restrain their jubilation. But he wasn't the least puzzled by the whoops of laughter echoing down the jetty behind him.

He wondered how many other attempts they'd made? How many other people they'd approached? Anyone would have done, anyone who appeared rich enough to squander money on a romantic dream. Simply because Jim had sailed with Jane, whom they knew, on the *Mariposa*, which they knew, from the privately owned St Elena, he'd become their target. He didn't entirely believe in the deskbound, snowbound executive in Canada, but he did believe that Rooney and Drew intended to bleed Jim Rush dry, and that he could have a lot of fun before they saw the error of their ways.

Jim ran the last few yards to the bar. He felt light, happy. Life was becoming more interesting.

2

Jim put on a passable English accent when he made the telephone call to Jock. He drawled a bit, the way Jane's friends did. Jock was a Canadian Scot, no expert on upper-class English accents. Jim told him he was a friend of Mike Rooney, that he was staying on St Elena and was interested in buying the *Caramba*. Would it be all right if he were to take her and put her through her paces? Oddly, Jock said that would be fine. Jim didn't even have to fetch Rooney to the telephone to vouch for him. Very odd.

Jim sauntered back, amused by this little triumph. It was a slight stroke in the game he was playing with Drew and Rooney but every move counted. Not only would they fail to trick him but they'd discover he'd outdone them at every level. He didn't, though, understand why Rooney was keen on him using that boat unless it was because it put a little business the way of a friend.

Quite soon Jim was casting off. He took her away under engine power, preferring not to manoeuvre an unfamiliar yacht under sail where space was limited. She made good speed. In fair weather she was fast.

Jane was delighted with his find and made no complaint about being abandoned.

45

'James, she's wonderful.' She poked around inside, flipping open lockers and exploring nooks and crannies.

'She'll do. I haven't sailed her yet, mind.'

He realised this was rather silly. He'd gone in search of a boat to sail around the islands and returned with one that was untried.

Jane didn't notice. If she had she might have wondered what else he'd spent the time on. If he hadn't been seeing whether he liked the way the boat handled, what had he been up to? Fortunately, her mind was on practical matters.

'How are we going to manage this, James? We have to return the *Mariposa* . . .'

'But not yet. Guy expects us to be gone a day or two.'

Whatever the new boat was like, he couldn't bear to part with the St Elena yacht yet.

'What we're going to do now,' he said, 'is sail the *Mariposa* round this coastline until we come to the restaurant Charles and Lucinda told us about. Remember? We should make it in time for a late lunch.'

That appealed to her. She liked it when he made plans. In London it had been the other way round. Jane had squeezed him into her busy social life, including him in visits to nightclubs or taking him to the country at weekends. He'd shared in her life, she hadn't shared in his, and for reasons he could hardly tell her: the squalor of his room in the suburbs, the fraud he was carrying out at a London hotel. Jane's busyness and lack of curiosity had made the relationship work. In the islands, they were more equal. He, bored and restless, was the one who dreamed up outings and treats. Lunch at the Charles and Lucinda restaurant was to be a treat for Jane. Jim didn't care about it himself. He had more interesting things to speculate about than the menu of a fanciful chef.

There were tables dotted beneath shady palms and an open-fronted dining room where fans cooled the air.

'Inside or out?' he asked Jane.

'Out, please.'

The question was a formality. For her, one of the chief advantages of being abroad was that one could eat beneath the open sky and not die of it. He teased her but she didn't waver. As usual they sat outside.

After they'd ordered, and had nothing to do except sip their drinks and take in the surroundings, Jim felt himself stared at. A figure at one of the dining room tables seemed unable to stop looking at him. His scalp prickled. He was scared he'd been recognised, and he was a young man who'd left behind him a number of people he never wanted to see again.

Jane was saying something about the restaurant, its reputation and Dominican chef. She'd had a tussle choosing between the land crabs and the crawfish in pink peppercorn sauce. There'd also been a moment when she'd virtually settled on the mountain chicken, a big frog served in beer batter. Unlike scrawny Lucinda who picked at her food, Jane invariably had an enthusiastic appetite.

Jim murmured a reply but his mind was entirely on the figure in the dining room. He could see now that it was a man and not a woman, but he could see nothing distinctly. He felt a tightening in his chest, a fear that threatened to choke him.

The worst thing always was having to sit still, to stay when his instinct ordered him to flee, to appear relaxed when every nerve was screaming. He imagined himself running away, pursued through the garden but racing the *Mariposa* out of the bay, escaping. He almost believed that if Jane hadn't been beside him he'd have done it. But she was there and he was stuck. Like a butterfly on a pin he was fixed. The man in the shadows of the dining room continued to watch.

Jim wiped a sweating palm on his trouser leg. There'd been that trouble in Florida, in the cays. He'd escaped in a boat that time, too, although not literally chased by a man. Was it possible someone from those days had recognised him? Or was he the victim of unlucky coincidence? Had a police officer from London fetched up by chance on the same Caribbean island?

He shook his head, trying to clear his mind of complicated nonsense. It would probably be all right, it was probably . . . What good was probably?

If the wrong face emerged from the shadows, everything was lost: Jane, the protection of her circle, his shiny new life. Wherever he went, whatever he did, whoever he was with, he could lose it all in the split second an accuser's eye met his.

Jane's voice broke through the confusion in his head. 'James?'

'Sorry, I wasn't listening.'

'I was asking you whether you thought we ought to . . .'

He was gazing off to her left. She turned her head. In the dining room a man was rising from a table.

Jane was agitated. 'What is it?' And when Jim didn't answer her: 'Who is he?'

Jim managed a weak smile of bewilderment. 'I don't know.'

And then he did. The man reached the doorway, the sunlight. Their eyes met. The man was Martin Peters.

Jim's pent-up breath escaped in a laugh of relief. He recovered fast, was on his feet and greeting Peters, then introducing Jane. Peters had lost his dishevelled look. His clothes were clean and neat and his bushy hair had been brushed. It was a pity about the bruising on his face, the stiffness in his gait.

Because the two men stood and Jane continued to sit, she was partly excluded from the conversation. Peters dropped his voice to tell him: 'The target has lunch here some days. That's why I'm here.'

'Oh?' Jim looked around. He saw no hint of Princess Diana's presence: no discreet security men, no rubber-necking by other diners.

Peters said: 'My contact was wrong. She isn't here today. None of your neighbours are.'

Jim thought it comical that Peters had been put to the expense of a lavish lunch on the wrong day. He said: 'You've had a wasted afternoon, then, Martin. And travelled a long way for it.'

'Well, you can't expect it to be as simple as staking out the San Lorenzo in Beauchamp Place, can you?' He added that he'd spoken to several of the restaurant staff, he'd made good contacts and those always paid off in the long run.

'What's more, Jim, there's a girl in the village a couple of miles from here who used to work in your neighbours' kitchens. I'm going to look her up before I leave.' He turned slightly so that Jane was included again. 'Nice to have met you, Jane.' He patted Jim's arm. 'See you around, Jim.'

'Sure.'

Jim sat down and pulled the kind of face that said how strange people were.

Jane was intrigued by Martin Peters. 'What an odd man. He sounds like John Arlott but furtive.'

'Who?'

She enjoyed his ignorance. 'One of the best-loved English voices, James. A cricket commentator, died a few years ago. Your Martin Peters sounds the same, has a Hampshire accent. He sounded lovely but what was it all about? And why wasn't I meant to hear?'

'Martin enjoys being mysterious.'

She refused to be fobbed off and rattled questions at him. Behind her smiles lay a determination to know all there was to know. He reached across the table and squeezed her hand. Then he teased her with a version of the truth.

'You'll never believe this, Jane, but I saved Martin Peters' life when he was being fired at by a madman with a gun. That's how Martin got those bruises, by me knocking him down to stop him running into gunfire. Martin's business is snatching photographs of sunbathers, but he doesn't like people to know about it. That's why he was muttering behind his hand, so you couldn't hear.'

Jane was laughing. 'You're right, James, I don't believe a word of it.'

He feigned hurt feelings. 'Honestly, it's true.'

'Nonsense.'

'You really don't believe me. But why?' He was doing wide-eyed innocence now.

'Entertaining nonsense,' she argued, freeing her hand and slapping at him. 'For one thing, there wasn't any shooting. You'd have told me if anything as exciting as that had happened. You couldn't have kept it to yourself, no one could.'

'Hm.' Jim appeared to concede the point.

'And as for him snooping about with a camera, well, he looks too clumsy for anything like that. He'd trip over or he'd forget the film or something.'

'Hm, maybe.' He let her win that one too.

'Now come on, James. Let's have the truth.'

But he kept up the pretence that he was sulking because she'd challenged his story.

Soon her crab and his juk-up fish, char-grilled strips of jack fish in garlic and coconut sauce, were brought to the table. They talked of other things: where they might sail and how they'd return the St Elena yacht. On a fair day, Jane said, she'd sail singlehanded; but she was nervous about doing that in less than perfect weather. Although she was competent and willing, she claimed to have done little sailing for several years.

'Then we'll pray for fine weather,' he said, and put the problem to the back of his mind.

He was more concerned about how he was to get out to the wreck of the *Gloriosa* without Jane. It didn't do to tell her much about his adventures. He'd managed to make her laugh off the Martin Peters business but that trick couldn't be used again, or at least not often and not soon.

Jim imagined he was safe from Martin Peters for a while, possibly for ever, but the wretched man was waiting for him outside the restaurant when he and Jane eventually left. Peters stepped forward from the shadow of a casuarina tree.

'Hello, again.' Peters was hot and anxious, his cheerful greeting an immense effort. The cheerfulness didn't reach to his eyes. They stayed angry.

'Still here, Martin?' Jim hoped he looked merely startled, not annoyed as well. He felt his hand tighten involuntarily on Jane's and wondered what she was making of the reaction.

'My boat's cleared off,' Peters said. He indicated with a sweep of an arm the bay that was empty save for the *Mariposa*. His camera bag was on the jetty close to her, a clue to his eagerness to board her. 'I told him to stay, paid him up front, everything. What does he do?'

Jane was sympathetic. 'Oh, what bad luck. I'm afraid that sort of thing's always happening.'

'Is it?' Jim hadn't heard of it before.

She said: 'Actually, the mistake is to pay in advance.'

Peters retorted that the man had refused to stay unless he was paid in advance. 'Pretty well said he didn't trust me. Cheeky bastard. What did he think I was going to do? Turn native and settle here?'

He smoothed his hands over his hair, emphasising the soon-to-be-bald patch. Then he looked out at the bay, as though there was a chance, a glimmer of a chance, that the missing boat was going to come swinging in, that the jolly, loose-limbed boatman would be waving and grinning and apologising for keeping him waiting. Unlikely, though. The islanders didn't measure time that way. There might be grinning and waving but there'd be no apology.

Jim started to ask why Peters hadn't used the restaurant telephone to summon another boat, but Jane interrupted. 'Where do you have to get to, Martin?'

And so it was Jane who suggested they take him there

52

aboard the *Mariposa*. She was tiresomely full of bright ideas. Her next was that, now they were three, it would make it easier for them to return the St Elena yacht. They had to go in that direction to take Martin Peters to his hotel.

Jim hated it, he wanted to hold on to that boat for days yet. She was a beautiful plaything and he wanted to carry on as though she were his. But Jane's logic was unassailable. Even when Peters confessed he was no sailor, she spotted the solution. He was to take the new boat under engine power, which he was happy to do, and Jane and Jim were to sail the *Mariposa*.

With misgivings, Jim fell in with her plans. At first he kept looking back, checking that Martin Peters was staying afloat. But then he forgot about the man and concentrated on enjoying what he was doing himself. That was what the sea did for him: it made him live in the present, tested him.

Paradoxically, it was the limitations that freed him. A motor boat demanded nothing but when he sailed there was the challenge of harnessing winds, denying the dominance of the sea, and overcoming failings in a boat's design. The result could sometimes be magic.

They were nearing St Elena and the wind, as always in the lee of the island, was puffy when Jane called to him: 'Do you think Martin's all right?'

The other boat lay off one of the last islands they'd passed. She seemed to be drifting gently on the tide.

Jim groaned. He feared it would be just like Martin Peters to ruin the engine or sink her. The man was accident prone, a nuisance.

Jane called: 'Perhaps the engine's packed up.'

When he was inshore in smooth water, Jim slackened off

the sails until the *Mariposa* was barely moving. He wasn't willing to go back and investigate, especially now he'd guessed what Peters was up to.

Jane clambered across to stand near him. 'Martin did seem a bit dubious about whether he could do it.'

Dubious? It hadn't struck Jim that way at all, the man had been positively eager.

He said: 'There's nothing wrong with that engine.' To his own ears he sounded dogmatic, fed up.

Jane tensed as an unpleasant thought occurred to her. She was barely audible as she said: 'It was true, then. What you said about him spying with his camera.' She clamped her lips together to prevent herself saying any more.

Jim hated to see her distress. He tried to put an arm around her shoulders but she slipped from him.

She blurted out: 'It's despicable, what he's doing. And we've made it possible for him to do it.'

Her colour was rising. Jim had never seen her this angry. She was usually too cool and ironic for that kind of display. He'd known her annoyed, exasperated, irritated but always controlled. Now he knew her to be capable of a raging temper, too. It was in the flashing eyes, the stance, the set of the jaw. Jim was frightened what would happen when she next got close to Martin Peters. Without consulting her, he sailed on.

As they walked up the track in the direction of the house, Guy's voice wafted down to them. No words, only his spuriously hearty tone followed by a yo, ho, ho.

Jim hesitated. 'Jane, I don't think we need mention Martin Peters to the others.'

She looked at him as though he were an idiot to suggest

there'd ever been any question of mentioning Peters. 'Certainly not,' she snapped. And she bit her lips again and hurried ahead, spurred on by fury.

Jim dropped back. He could do nothing. She wouldn't be calmed or consoled. Whether she was most cross at him, or at Peters or at herself, was debatable. For his own part, he was wishing he'd let Peters run into gunfire after all.

From the hill, Jim watched Peters arrive. With a heavy heart he walked back down. Peters was so full of his own success that he ignored Jim's lack of enthusiasm.

'That was terrific. I mean really terrific, Jim. You know what I told you, the other day? Well there they were, the Neighbours, all on the beach. Princess Mum, couple of kids, Lady This and the Honourable That. *All* of them. Not such a wasted day, was it?' He aimed a playful punch at Jim's arm.

Jim looked at the camera bag on the deck. He imagined Jane flinging it into the water, flinging Martin Peters in after it.

He said something polite, something that sounded interested and uncritical.

But the tone was wrong. Peters broke off his gabbling. 'What's up, Jim?'

'Everything's fine.'

Peters looked around, scanned the hillside and the cove, then studied Jim. 'Girlfriend trouble?'

'Jane's gone up to the house. That's all.'

'Ah.' Peters smoothed his hair back. 'Look, I know you offered to take me to Bamboo Lodge . . .'

'And I will, unless you want to be dropped somewhere else.'

'No, the thing is, I was wondering if there was a place I

could stay here. I mean, I want to get over to see the Neighbours again tomorrow.' With a jerk of the head he indicated the island where he'd scored a direct hit on his target.

Jim said it wasn't such a great idea. He knew he sounded stiff, unfriendly, but Peters was a pain. He'd upset Jane, and Jim's relationship with her was already delicate.

Peters ignored his remark. 'I saw cottages on the south of the island. Know what they are?'

'Staff cottages, I guess.' Jim had never walked up to them. There were various buildings on the island apart from the main house where Guy and his party were staying. The island was like a country estate: people who worked there had to have housing, and there were boat sheds and farm buildings dotted around. Some of these were dilapidated, others not.

Peters stashed his camera and hoisted the bag on to his shoulder. 'You didn't see me, OK? You don't know anything about me.'

'*Martin!*'

But Martin Peters was on his way up a narrow path through the trees, going vaguely south. He raised a hand in farewell but he didn't look round.

During the night Jim crept downstairs to the room that Guy, for the sake of one of his games, had dubbed the library. It was a small sitting room with a writing table, a painted bookcase and a view of a shrub being smothered by a yellow vine. Among the books put there by Guy's cousin, the owner, were several about the Antilles or the Caribbean in general. The rest were novels or biographies, reading matter for days when it was too hot for scampering on beaches or too wet and blowy to do other than nestle in an armchair.

Jim pulled out several of the books on the West Indies and settled down to skim them. He'd come silently, without, he hoped, disturbing anyone. Jane was sleeping heavily and hadn't stirred when he eased away from her. With luck he'd be back in bed before she missed him. Without luck, one of the others would come to investigate the lamplight and then he'd be forced to explain, to justify, to endure jokes about it. Of course he'd say he'd been unable to sleep and had come to read. In most households that would be enough, but it wouldn't do here. It would make him the butt of another round of jokes; it would point up his differences; and once his differences were exposed, then so were his companions' suspicions. As always, Guy would be the most malicious, the most accurate.

Several of the books referred to the numerous wrecks around the islands, only two provided detail. The *Gloriosa* that Jim was concerned with was mentioned in both. There'd been another more famous ship of that name and she too had been a treasure ship wrecked in the Caribbean, although not in the Antilles. The coincidence of names was initially confusing. Like most seafaring nations, the Spanish had no objection to recycling names. Only in modern times did shipowners balk at launching, say, a second *Titanic*.

According to one book the *Gloriosa* lost off the Antilles was sunk in battle with a pirate ship captained by a notorious Englishman. The other book said she went down in a storm south-west of St Vincent. Unless one of the authors had made a hash of it, the discrepancy indicated that the fate of the vessel and her cargo wasn't known precisely.

Jim flicked through the rest of the books, gathering up snippets of information about the turbulent history of the islands. The writers liked to begin at the beginning, with Rodrigo de Triana sighting landfall from the forecastle of one of Columbus's ships, the *Pinta*, in 1492. They recounted how Columbus discovered islands and a new continent; parrots, tobacco and hammocks. But he didn't discover gold and as it was gold he'd promised the sponsoring Spanish monarchs, he was destined to die a discredited failure.

Accounts of the first two voyages were lively but not relevant to Jim who skipped through them, pausing only to enjoy Columbus's own descriptions of 'fish like bright roosters'; 'breezes from the hills laden with the sweet odour of flowers or trees'; and the wind that 'blew gently once more, filling all the sails of the ship, the main course, the two bonnets, the spritsail, mizzen, topsail and the boat's sail on the poop . . .'

He picked the story up in the Antilles, in the hands of an author who liked to start even earlier, with Caribs moving from the mainland and slaughtering the Arawaks who inhabited the islands. Comeuppance came with the arrival of an astonishing foe, the white man with his great galleons and his guns.

Jim flipped over the pages, prospecting for gold. Treasure was found on the new continent and the world changed. Stories popped out of the pages to waylay him, tales like that of the treasurer of Santo Domingo who became so rich he lost his mind and filled the salt cellars with gold dust for a banquet.

He skipped on, through the years when the Spanish ferried home the riches Cortes had seized in Mexico after the death of Montezuma, and Giovanni da Verrazano, a Florentine sailing under the French flag, became the very first pirate. Verrazano's haul was gold, emeralds, pearls, exquisitely carved objects, masks encrusted with precious stones, rich cloaks ornamented with figures of birds and flowers worked in feathers. After this, the seas were infested with pirates.

Sometimes they were purely freelance, more often they worked for king and country because only the Spanish monarchs accepted the Pope's decree that all the New World was the rightful property of Spain. Sometimes pirates . . . But he tore himself away from their adventures.

St Elena was seldom mentioned in the books, except for a story about confusion of its name and corruption of the spelling. In another part of the world the island would have merited a page or two, but where history meant drama the few acres of rock had done no more than share in the fortunes of the archipelago. It hadn't had a volcano blow up or a hurricane kill every living soul.

Columbus had noticed St Elena during his third voyage, in 1498. He'd sailed on south to the trio of peaks he named Trinidad; and on and on until he reached Venezuela and what he believed to his dying day was the Garden of Eden. Neither the French nor the Dutch nor the British had risked life and limb to seize St Elena when larger spoils were to hand. It wasn't rich, not strategically important, not worth it.

Jim wondered how to get fuller information about the *Gloriosa* and the events surrounding her last voyage. He needed to be certain Drew and Rooney's wreck was indeed that ship, and that nobody had yet dived down and salvaged her cargo. If they'd truly found a Spanish treasure ship, then he meant to have a generous share. They'd got so far, but needed money for equipment and another diver. For once, Jim had money. He didn't trust them. He didn't intend to take their word for anything. But how could he check without giving away his interest? If he went around the islands asking questions, someone else would step in and claim her. He was stumped.

He put the books back on the shelves, turned off the lamp and, once his eyes had adjusted to darkness, tiptoed out of the room. Jane moved towards him as he got into bed. He stroked her absentmindedly, thinking about ships and treasure and about becoming permanently rich.

Jim considered how it would change his life. One immediate thing, it would change his relationship with Jane. In England she'd assured her friends he wasn't hers for ever: she'd called him a beautiful stud, and a beautiful snowman who'd melt away when his season was over. The friends had been mollified: Jane wasn't going to throw herself away on a mysterious young American who wasn't one of her kind, and probably not the kind he said he was either.

But with real money? That could alter attitudes. Money usually did. Perhaps Jane would take a longer view, and perhaps her friends would think she'd been courageous rather than reckless.

He pondered the likelihood of being able to buy himself one of these pretty tropical islands. Perhaps the Antilles was too high to aim but there were the Virgins and the Caymans, among others, that came on the market fairly regularly. Would he actually like it, though? When he'd stopped visualising the yacht he must buy to go with the island, he grew doubtful that a hunk of rock fringed with sand would keep him interested. He didn't fancy splendid isolation, the life of the castaway. Poor old Ben Gunn had had treasure, and what use had it been to him?

Jim stuck on the problem of whom he could choose for company. Someone content with self-imposed isolation, of course. Lots of people fooled themselves that such an existence was paradise. But after a week's package holiday on a touristy island they were desperate for traffic jams, supermarket queues, the noise and press of humanity.

Jane was a non-starter. She had more friends than anyone Jim knew. All her life she was either with them or on the telephone arranging to be with them. In a car, in a restaurant, wherever he'd gone with Jane in England, she'd whisked out her telephone saying she simply must ring so-and-so and say such-and-such. This had irked, he'd felt he seldom had her full attention. On St Elena the rules were different. They were all there courtesy of Guy, and it was natural that Guy commanded attention. Jim disliked the man, but he wasn't in the least envious of him.

He refused to think about Guy. Once again he imagined the treasure – doubloons, bars of silver, gold trinkets, pieces of eight . . . And his mind was back with Long John Silver and with Guy. *Pieces of eight! Pieces of eight!*

For a while longer he lay awake, listening to the sounds of the tropical night. Crickets. Frogs. A buzz that might be a mosquito, hated symbol of the darker side of tropical life. Moonlight fell through the slats of the shutters. He fell asleep among its silver bars.

Jim woke next morning to see Jane coming out of the bathroom, pale and with a packet of tablets in her hand.

'Headache,' she said, and sat on the side of the bed while

she washed down the tablets with a glass of water. Then: 'James, would it be awful if we didn't sail off today? I hate to be a spoilsport but I really can't face . . .'

He patted her hand, said it was all right. 'We have all the time in the world.'

Jane went back to bed. She asked him to open the window because she felt fresh air would help her. He let in the scent of white blossoms, a happy marriage of tuberose and gardenia. Then he plumped all her pillows and left her to watch humming-birds, surf breaking on a coral reef, and an overloaded ferry boat carrying islanders, animals and fruit to market.

Jane's absence was convenient for him. He skipped breakfast, and possible queries about night-time footfalls, and hurried down the track to the cottages below the hill on the south of the island. Although he'd been powerless to prevent Martin Peters staying the night, he intended to get rid of the man rapidly.

When Jim came in sight of the harbour, his heart faltered. The *Caramba* was missing. Immediately he grasped what had happened. And he cursed, violently. He stood there, outraged, unable to decide what to do. Then, as if it had been waiting for him to be in position to watch, the *Caramba* came into the bay.

Jim turned down the footpath to the harbour. He was struggling to control his fury. There was no point in saying half the things he felt like saying to Peters. The sensible course was to take the man back to his hotel and lose him there.

Peters was delighted with his escapade. This time the smile reached up to the eyes, there was no contradictory message. 'Good morning, Jim. Didn't think you'd mind, and I couldn't really come up to the house and beg permission, now could I?'

'What makes you think you'd have got it?'

Peters threw back his head and laughed. The twin bushes of hair bounced. 'Perhaps I didn't.'

'Well, was the journey worth it?' He didn't care what the reply was, he was speaking automatically, thinking only about getting Peters off the island.

'Depends how you look at it. I got something, then I was chased off.' He held up his camera, as if eyesight could pierce the case and study the image captured on the film.

Despite himself, Jim was interested. The very nerve of the man was impressive. And to think Peters made a career of it. Jim had no wish to encourage him but was bound to ask what had happened.

Peters was on the dock now, fondling his camera while he described the encounter. 'There's a swimming pool on the beach. The Neighbours' place isn't like this, it's flatter. Well, I'd been thinking it over for a while, the best way to go about it. Then I thought, hell, everybody knows she swims every morning, at home at Kensington Palace or wherever she's staying. So I thought, why break a habit? She'll be taking a dip first thing every morning here, sure to.'

Jim nodded as though he too had known the swimming habits of a princess.

Peters went on: 'I tootled down there and took a look around. And out she comes! But of course she's too quick for me, she's dived in the pool before I've got my finger on the trigger. Once she's in the water I can't see a thing. Well, I took a shot or two of the beach and I was working out what to do next when, suddenly, out of nowhere, there's a launch coming right for me. Security men, no question. So I took off.'

'Straight back here?' Jim hoped the answer was no. If Guy and his guests were asked about the intrusion, he could be in trouble. He hated talking to detectives about anything, ever.

'No, the other way. I chased right round the island before I could swing up this way.'

'How far did they follow you?'

'Not far, just far enough to make sure I was leaving.' He pulled a handkerchief from his jacket pocket and carefully wiped over the camera. 'So, Jim, I got something but it's the wrong thing. What I should have got was that dive. It was a beauty, went in like a sword. That's what I should have got.'

'I guess that's the way it goes.' He was about to say Peters should get straight back on the boat and he'd ferry him to his hotel.

But Peters said: 'Yes. Lose today and win tomorrow. If you want to win in this game you've got to keep at it. Dedication. Didn't I tell you that's the name of this game?'

'Oh, now Martin, you can't do it again.'

Peters missed the meaning entirely. 'I don't say it'll be easy. Not now they've spotted the boat. They were on me so fast I reckon they logged me yesterday when I swung inshore there. They were ready for the *Caramba* to reappear. I'll have to think it out, exactly how I do it next time.'

'Look, Martin, I'm saying there can't be a next time. Not for the *Caramba*. If you want to hire a plane again or swim out there, that's your affair. But you don't take a boat from here and you don't involve St Elena.'

Peters looked startled, then disbelieving. 'You wouldn't prevent me getting that picture.'

'You don't understand about the people here.'

But Martin Peters knew. He trotted out their names. Their names, their ranks and their lovers. 'Don't ask me how I know, let's just say it's my business to know.'

Jim was dumbfounded. Peters told him: 'I'm not a beach photographer, Jim. I'm a journalist. You mightn't think much of what I do, I don't suppose your friends up at the house do. But I'm the sort of journalist whose work sells papers. If I take a picture of Princess Di diving like she did this morning, I'm in the money. She's a great swimmer, she won cups for swimming and diving at school. Her dive was perfect, not a ripple, the other kids called it the Spencer Special. That's what I saw this morning, Jim, and I missed it. Of course I'm going in again.'

Feebly, Jim said it didn't seem right.

Peters laughed again, this time holding on to his hair so it didn't spring about. '*Right?* Look, she's public property. And the public got enough of that stuff showing her patting kids on the head and stroking old ladies' hands. They like to see the private moments in public lives. And don't forget, Jim, Diana wasn't born royal. She chose it.'

Despite his laughter, Peters was het up. His voice had risen, become harsher. Like a man who's frequently called upon to defend himself, he was all attack. The argument was an old one but not one that Jim cared to become involved in.

He shrugged off Peters' intensity. 'I guess you chose your life, too, Martin.'

Peters touched Jim's arm, not exactly apologising for raising his voice but as a way of signalling that the subject was closed. Jim reopened it, saying he'd take him to Bamboo Lodge.

'Oh, *Jim.*' Peters sagged beneath the weight of great stupidity. 'I'm not even asking you to do anything, just turn a blind eye for the rest of the day. Come on, you can do that.'

Jim needed to dangle a more appealing alternative to shift Peters. If he simply ordered him aboard to be shipped out, the man might dodge him and hide on St Elena, then sneak out with the boat again next day. For a moment he wondered about letting that happen and, once Peters was buried in the undergrowth, removing both the boats. It was a poor solution. A marooned Peters was no less of a nuisance. More perhaps if he believed he could get help up at the house, or, and this was equally undesirable, if he stole one of the craft used by the servants.

Instead, Jim played the bold stroke. He offered to take him to spy aboard the *Mariposa*. Peters, he explained, would keep himself hidden and snatch his photographs unobserved while Jim pretended to flounder with the sails. As the yacht was well known to the people Peters referred to as the Neighbours and to their security men, there'd be no trouble.

Martin Peters thought this wonderful. He still thought so after Jim had explained that, because of other commitments, he couldn't delay until the following morning, and that they'd have to set off right away. Peters muttered a few times about not catching the dive, but Jim made it obvious that terms were not negotiable. They went to look in on the Neighbours.

It was easy. The royal party was sitting around the pool where a tall, fair-haired young woman was teaching a boy to dive. Jim grappled and struggled and put on a good performance of incompetent seamanship. Then he warned Peters the game was over, and he let the sails fill and carry them away.

'I owe you, Jim.'

Martin Peters was sprawled on the seat in the *Mariposa*, one arm stretched along the rail, the wind lifting his twin bushes of hair. Having got his way and his shots, he was all affability and charm.

'Sure you do.' Jim too was relaxed. He'd peeled Peters away from St Elena, denied him any excuse for returning to the area and now the photographer was free to fly to London and peddle his wares. Fascinated though he was by Martin Peters, he'd had a surfeit of him.

'Jim, now I'm going to do *you* a favour.'

Peters waited until Jim finished toying with a rope and looked over his shoulder at him.

'What favour?' He couldn't conceive of anything Peters might do in return, but the man didn't appear to be joking.

'Those guys with the old fishing boat, Drew and Rooney . . .' Peters left the sentence hanging while Jim scrambled across and sat down opposite him.

Jim hoped he was showing average interest, not urgent need of knowledge. He couldn't gauge how far he was succeeding. Peters had an open, friendly face but not one that explained what was in the man's mind.

'Go on.'

'They're not right, Jim. Normally if it's none of my business I keep out, but I owe you this much. You saved my life and you've helped me this morning. Well then, as a favour I'm telling you you'd best steer clear of those two.'

Peters was embarrassed, as people are when they say too much or too little. His eyes shifted from Jim to a frigate bird riding the swell.

Jim laughed, to ease the moment. 'Hey, if you really want to do me a favour, you have to explain.'

He expected Peters to warn him the wreck wasn't the *Gloriosa* and the wreck hunters knew it. Or else that it had already been searched and cleaned of anything worth taking. Or else that Drew and Rooney made a habit of fleecing people who believed they were investing in a dream of raising sunken treasure.

What he didn't expect was for Peters to say: 'They're running arms.'

'*Arms?*' Stupid to echo, he knew what was meant.

'Sub-machine-guns, rifles, maybe hand grenades.' Peters brushed a wisp of hair from his face with the back of a hand. 'Looks like it's been going on a while, and it also looks like they're being watched.'

'How do you know this, Martin?'

He was having trouble imagining it. Drew and Rooney seemed too lightweight. Arms trafficking, like drugs trafficking, was a serious business. Some islands depended on the twin trades for their economic survival and political protection. Why should the high-powered men who ran the business tolerate a couple of outsiders like Drew and Rooney dabbling? They'd be minnows in a sea of trouble.

Peters said: 'A contact.'

'Police?'

'Journalist. He mixed me up with another photographer, someone whose surname is Martin. This other Martin was supposed to be flying down from Washington to work with him on a magazine piece about the Caribbean arms trade. Before we'd sorted out his mistake, he'd told me a few things he now wishes he hadn't.'

The wisp of hair was over his face again. Peters grabbed at it and tucked it behind his ear. Jim asked him to explain how Drew and Rooney came into the story.

'Well, from what this reporter said, Jim, your pals bring the goods ashore. They meet a ship out at sea and crates are handed over to them. Anyway, that's what the law thinks.'

The method was neat. The ship needn't interrupt its voyage, and there were too many boats in and out of the islands for there to be any pretence at surveillance and security. But Drew and Rooney?

Sceptical, Jim said: 'Well, OK, Martin, let's say it's true. Where are the crates being landed? And why haven't Rooney and Drew been pulled in yet?'

'I can't say but there's a big police operation planned for the not too distant future. Which is why the magazine writer begged his office to send him down a photographer. The magazine wouldn't have the pair of them sitting around like that unless there was something in the offing.'

Jim fiddled with the line again. Then he asked whether Peters was certain they were the two men the reporter meant.

Peters said he was, adding that the reporter had hinted at a hidden cache. 'As a matter of fact, it was because of a few things he said that I went up to the old plantation house the other evening.'

This was too much. Surely Peters wasn't claiming he'd gone after the cache single handed and unarmed? But, in effect, he was.

'Nosiness,' he said, with a self-mocking laugh. 'Call it an occupational hazard, Jim. I'd been sitting around doing nothing all day, and I was thinking that one morning I'd seen a man who could have been Mike Rooney on the path near the old house. It was early, I mean very early, and I was out just running off a film for the hell of it. Pretty pictures. Dawn over the headland, that kind of stuff.'

'You say it *could* have been Rooney.'

'It was Rooney, Jim. No question. I've got him on film. Then one or two things the reporter said fell into place and I thought, well, if I were obliged to squirrel away something illegal, I might do a lot worse than conceal it up at the ruined house. It's reasonably remote and from the upper storey you've got a decent view over the town and the harbour.'

Jim enjoyed the faint pleasure of being proved right. Martin Peters *had* been upstairs in the house, as he'd supposed.

'What did you find?' Presumably if Peters had discovered a stock of arms he'd have declared it by now but Jim was compelled to ask. Where Peters was concerned, it was hard to take anything for granted.

'Nothing much. A few sticks of furniture, a chair by an upstairs window. I flicked the torch around for a while but it didn't seem I'd walked into anybody's hidey-hole.'

'That window, was it at the front?'

'In the centre. I could see the harbour lights and the town. In daylight there'd be a terrific view.'

Neither of them spoke for a few minutes, Jim noting that Peters wasn't pressing his case against Drew and Rooney. Peters trailed a hand in the spray. Eventually he gave a lop-sided grin and said: 'Of course, if I hadn't seen someone coming up the front path I'd have prowled around more and I might have found conclusive evidence.'

He raised a hand to the bruise on the right side of his face, the side that took the brunt when Jim attacked him. Jim felt his pulse check. He was back on the path hearing nothing but his own gentle movements; then he was at the door; and then a bullet was smashing into the lintel. Now he knew that in the room directly above the door Martin Peters had been flashing a torch.

Jim went to adjust some lines. A fort made a jagged outline on a rock, backwash from the island beyond it set the yacht tripping in her stride.

He thought: *All this rubbish about me saving his life and how grateful he is. He nearly had me killed!*

He asked who Peters had seen on the path. The answer was no one, only a shadow, a mere movement. Trees and shrubs had made it too dark for more. Peters said he was going out of the room when the shot was fired, and he ran and hid where Jim later found him.

This story lacked the ring of truth. Peters had raced for cover into trees close to the path by which he'd arrived, yet he hadn't run away.

'Martin, why did you hang around?'

'Camera.'

'But you told me you hadn't taken one with you.'

'A lie. Wicked, eh? Obviously I had a camera, when do I ever move without one? OK, I'll tell you when. It's when some crazy bastard starts loosing off bullets. I got out of the house fast, the camera stayed.'

Jim understood the rest but Peters told it anyway. 'I played hide and seek in the garden until it seemed safe to go in and rescue it. But then what happens? *You* happen.'

The camera had remained in the house. Peters abandoned it rather than risk being shot while fetching it.

'Jim, I never said I was a hero. Hell, I'm not even over here for that arms story. Celebrity pics, that's me.'

'But if you'd taken a shot of an arms cache you'd have turned it into dollars anyway?' At their first meeting Peters had told him he'd cover any big story that came his way.

'The minute the story broke.'

Peters glanced round. The sea was frothing white around rock. They were cutting in close as they headed for the harbour. He stood up, one hand keeping tight hold of the lifeline.

'See it, Jim? The scene of the crime.'

On the hill above the harbour town the old plantation house stood, cloaked by trees. Part of its roof was visible, that was all. The scene of the crime – which could mean the place where a man fired at them in the dark, or a staging post in the illegal traffic in arms. Martin Peters believed it was both.

Jim went with him to his hotel, the Bamboo Lodge. Peters had offered him a meal and Jim discovered he was very hungry indeed. Until then he'd forgotten he'd skipped breakfast rather than face Guy and his chums.

A hotel servant delivered lunch for two to Peters' *cabaña* and set it out on the table on the terrace, a shady corner sheltered from onlookers by sweet-scented frangipani. Jim wished life could be like this. Beautiful. Comfortable. Assured. With someone else to take care of the details and clear up the mess.

For him it never could be. Even when he was a part of it, as he was with Jane Logan, he was conscious that he was only Jim Rush playing a role. That's what his life was, a series of roles that didn't exactly fit, roles forced on him by fate. He imagined Fate as a bossy character, though not an unhelpful one.

'Jim, things look tough. Better drop out of sight for a while, get an ordinary kind of job like an ordinary kind of guy.'

'Damn. OK, Fate. All right if I fix television aerials?'

'Sounds good, Jim.'

'Jim, necessity demands you join the leisured classes.'

'Right.'

'And try not to look bored, do try.'

'Sorry, Fate.'

Martin Peters broke off eating to fetch a photograph, a colour print. At a glance it was a competent study of shafts of sunlight through trees. Then Jim's eye was drawn to the figure in the middle distance, a man walking out of the trees and on to the path. The man was looking to his right, not quite facing the camera.

Jim said: 'It could be. I can't say for sure.'

Peters passed him a magnifying glass. 'Try again.'

This time it was easier to share Peters' conviction. Either the man really was Mike Rooney or else it was his double. The olive skin that was partly natural, partly suntan; the slight hook to the nose, probably the result of a break; the height and the build, they were all right.

Jim decided he recognised the jacket too, although jackets were hardly unique. The photograph encouraged him to believe Peters, but, as so often, there was room for coincidence. And anyway, a walk in the woods?

Peters read Jim's mind. 'Where he's coming out, that's the access to the garden of the old house.'

There was satisfaction on Peters' face, something else in

his eyes. Jim didn't return the print immediately. He put it down beside his plate and from time to time switched his attention to it. Peters was questioning him about St Elena, and Jim used his apparent preoccupation with the photograph as a way of avoiding giving answers. But Peters kept probing about St Elena and Jim's friends.

Friends. Jim never described them as that, it was Peters who called them his friends. Jim regarded them merely as people he happened to be spending time with. Except Jane, naturally. That relationship was altogether more complicated.

For Jim, friends were people you picked carefully and dared to trust a little. He had few, none truly close, and had no wish for more. Friends would make demands he couldn't fulfil, would pin him down when he needed to float free. He was a fine companion, could insinuate himself into any company he chose and blend into any background; but he wouldn't be tied down. Friends liked to tie you down. Not because they necessarily believed it best for you, but because they themselves needed the safety net of a group of friends. Without them they were less certain of their own worth, their identity. And that was part of his objection: a friend always had other friends, wanted to show them off, flaunt the ability to make friends.

Jim refused to make them. Acquiring friends was a positive act. People who were good at it were good because they worked at it, usually unconsciously. Jane Logan, for instance, chasing from party to party or on her telephone keeping in close touch with so many friends that Jim had early on ceased to bother to remember who was who. To him they were interchangeable anyway. They came from the same background and class. They had to, because maintaining this exclusivity was what kept the social barriers in good repair.

Jane had taken a risk when she picked him up. Or she would have done if she'd realised what she was doing. Her risk-taking came later. At the time she'd made a mistake. Another girl, drunk at a party, had mistaken his credentials and misled her. Jim occasionally wondered what would have happened if he'd met Jane under different circumstances. Nothing, probably, although maybe that was unfair. She'd told him once that they were both people who enjoyed a risk. The difference, which he understood even if she didn't, was that Jane did it for fun whereas the risks he took were a matter of survival.

Here they were, then, together in the paradise islands of the rich. Together still because he'd needed a place to hide and Jane, in her heart, appreciated that he wouldn't linger in her life long enough to become a problem.

Martin Peters was asking another question about St Elena. 'Who's coming out, then, Jim?'

Jim kept his eyes on the photograph. On the pocket of the jacket, as seen through the magnifying glass, there was a badge. He must look for it in future when he saw Rooney. If he found it, it wouldn't be proof positive that the man in the shot was Rooney but it would encourage his belief that it was.

Jim said, without looking up: 'Nobody I know.'

Across the table Peters shuffled in his chair, impatient. 'Well, do you remember who they said?'

Peters was fishing, not casting a fly lightly on the waters and praying for a bite but trawling, forcing results. Jim looked up. The hardness in Peters' eyes confirmed this wasn't chitchat.

Jim resigned himself to answering. 'A man whose nickname is Tadpole is bringing his friends. Five of them, I think.'

'Tadpole?' Peters mused on the name.

Jim suppressed a smile. The only reward for Peters' fishing trip was a tadpole. As for himself, he'd learned several very useful things that day.

He leaned forward and studied the screen. Bag-check quality, Drew had once called it. That was about right. Jim made out dark shapes and pale shapes, rounded shapes and straightish lines but mostly amorphous lumps. Coral and shell clusters disguised original forms.

Mike Rooney was closer. He drew a line across the screen with a fingertip. 'That looks like a section of the deck.'

To Jim Rush it looked like nothing at all, one of the paler streaks. Rooney offered identification of a few more of the shapes. None of them was convincing, except that it was obviously a wreck because what else could it be but a wreck?

'OK?' Drew called. Against the blue of sea and sky he looked hotly coloured with his ginger hair and flushed skin. Also his pale eyes and sparse feathering of eyebrows gave him an unfinished look that Jim found repulsive. When Rooney called back yes, Drew moved the boat on, circling, and stopped again. They looked at the new pictures being bounced to them from the sea floor. A long smudgy shape was deemed part of the underside of the hull. If any of these declarations were accurate, then the vessel had settled on her starboard side.

Rooney watched Jim Rush watching. Then he said:

'She's reasonably intact.' He sounded pleased, and couldn't help gushing on. 'Of course if we'd known where to dive we'd have found her with a swim search, she's lying on a ledge, not too deep and waiting to be picked over. We didn't really need this box of tricks but don't tell Drew I said that, he loves it. If we'd found a totally buried wreck then this would have been brilliant for giving us an outline of what was below the surface. You know, the way they found the *Mary Rose* off Spithead.'

Jim could barely make out a ship let alone a reasonably intact one. He'd come for proof and felt he wasn't getting it. Perhaps a man used to interpreting grey shapes from the watery depths would be satisfied, but he hadn't attempted this before. Neither did it seem a good moment to question how practised Rooney and Drew were.

Rooney stabbed at the screen again, explained more of what Jim was supposed to be seeing. He sympathised with Jim's hesitation.

'It takes a little while to get used to, I know. When I worked on my first one, off Florida, I found it hard to believe what I was being told. Everyone else was going crazy, shouting they'd got it, they'd really got it. And I was looking at a blur on a screen and thinking, well, I haven't, not a thing. But you get used to it.'

'Florida?' The word quickened Jim's interest. He'd read the other night about the American teams who'd dived on the treasure ships, eight of them, lost between Merritt Island and Fort Pierce. They'd used a machine, a massive cylinder, to blast sand off the ocean floor and uncover the treasure. But that was long ago, in terms of technology. That story began in 1961.

Rooney said: 'Yes, Florida. There were six of us,

working in shifts, all hired by a rich banker with a hunch. That's where I learned this business. Got the bug, if you like.'

'Did his wreck look something like this?'

'Something like. Similar encrustation but she was lying at a different angle.'

'More upright?' If Rooney's interpretation of the screen images was correct, then the port side was partly buried and the hull tilted over. Even if she were burdened with riches it might be impossible to locate them.

Rooney admitted his Florida wreck had been at an easier angle. Then there was a pause during which he sensed Jim's enthusiasm ebbing. He glanced across at Drew who was in the doorway of the wheelhouse. Jim caught the look that passed between them, triumph on Drew's face and dejection on Rooney's.

Jim turned from the screen. 'I guess she looks more encouraging from down there.'

He was toying with them, loved it when his remark made them swap looks so that suddenly Drew was the one who seemed cheated and Rooney the winner.

Not long after that Rooney and Jim were in the water. Jim had done a little diving for pleasure, and decided it wasn't one of the great pleasures of his life. But given a choice between going down and taking Rooney's or Drew's word for anything, he went down.

He didn't much care for poking around the wreck. It was all right moving about among the parrot-coloured fish but the ship was frightening. As Rooney had tried to show him, it was partly buried in sand and tipped over on its side. Most of the pale shapes and dark shapes of the screen were transformed into heaps of debris and rearing spars frosted over with coral. One part of the wreck had been exposed for less time and coral was only beginning to colonise. He was alarmed to think of the power of the seas that had scoured the ledge and raised her from her sandy grave, but these were waters where hurricanes blew, where tidal waves engulfed islands, and islands could turn into erupting volcanoes.

Rooney swam ahead of Jim, gesticulating for him to note certain things that would be explained later. Then Rooney's arm swung up in a 'follow me' movement. Jim swam after him.

He was glad he wasn't first, because being first meant being the one to disturb some quite alarming creatures. In particular, he was nervous of meeting an octopus. He'd heard the scary stories of how the only way to save yourself was to let the octopus entwine itself around you and when it had no free arms left, you stabbed it between the eyes. He was on the look-out the whole time for an octopus. He didn't spot one but the rest of the wildlife was distracting, that and the diving equipment that was too unfamiliar to be comfortable or ignored.

Sand, purple coral, shells, there was hardly a surface that wasn't hiding something else beneath it. Jim thought you'd have to know a lot about ships to be confident you were dealing with a particular type, let alone an individual wreck in an area that was dangerously rich in wrecks.

But mostly he didn't think. He looked where Rooney pointed and he struggled to remember and to understand. There'd be ample time for thinking later.

Rooney swam out again, Jim trailing close behind, not daring to lose sight of the froggy outline. He really didn't enjoy this at all. After a few more minutes Rooney made the gesture Jim had been praying for. They rose through the water, to safety.

When eventually Rooney flung the mask back from his face his first words were: 'What do you think of her? Isn't she great?'

Jim gulped fresh air, feared his relief at entering the real world was all too apparent. 'Great.' His voice was thick. The real world looked wonderful, never so beautiful.

'Any octopuses?' Drew asked.

Rooney said: 'We didn't tangle with one. Isn't that right, Jim?'

Jim cleared his throat and said they'd seen a great many fantastic creatures but no octopuses. 'Oh, and a wreck,' he added as a comic afterthought.

While they talked about the wreck, Jim stripped off his wetsuit. If either of them suggested a return trip, he didn't want to be dressed ready to go. Then Drew made them coffee, instant coffee with a bitter metallic taste. Jim drank it gratefully.

For a while they looked again at the sonar pictures, Rooney pointing out features he'd shown Jim down below. At last, when Jim had run out of questions and Rooney had run out of guesses, Drew started the engine. It rumbled like an old-fashioned bus and filled the air with a stink of diesel.

Drew took a channel where water churned between islets, then he made a sweep around a bigger island where the chart showed dangerous shoals. Throughout, he was making in the general direction of the one with the hurricane harbour where they usually anchored. Rooney said they never took a direct route, preferring to keep people wondering where they'd been.

They were living on the boat. They told Jim they'd left England to risk almost all they owned in their wreck-hunting venture. It was simplification of a story Jim was to learn later. After Rooney had become hooked on treasure hunts during his months diving off Florida, he'd coaxed Drew into it. This took considerable persuasion because Drew had recently bought a new holiday home in the south of Spain and was packed to go there when Rooney diverted him. Drew was the ideal partner. He loved to tinker with engines, he chose the boat and he had a redundancy cheque to pay for it. Rooney, it appeared, had nothing like that to offer, just contacts, hunches and enthusiasm.

And the third man, the Canadian executive in his Toronto office? Until Jim asked after him, they didn't bother to mention him at all.

'A disappointment,' said Rooney. They let it go at that.

Later, sailing alone to St Elena, Jim took stock. Nothing he'd seen or heard that day, or any other day, substantiated Martin Peters' allegations about Drew and Rooney. Everything he'd learned confirmed his own feelings: they were a couple of chancers, living on next to nothing plus hope; they were luring him into handing them money to pay for equipment and men to raid the wreck or even, as Mike Rooney suggested in one of his wilder flights of fancy, to *raise* the wreck.

From what he'd seen, raising it was out of the question. It was partly buried, especially heavy because of its coral carapace, and they couldn't say how much of the starboard side remained intact. People with sophisticated equipment might well be able to work it out but not Rooney and Drew. That sort of expert advice would have to be paid for. They'd expect Jim to pay.

They hadn't discussed with him that kind of investigation for this particular wreck, all their talk was general, concerned with methods of bringing ships or their contents to the surface. Heavy items, they'd explained, could be raised by attaching clusters of balloons to them, then filling the balloons with compressed air pumped in from a surface compressor. As pressure was increased, items lashed to the balloons roared to the surface. They cited massive marble sculptures salvaged from Greek waters in this way. The same principal applied to the wrecks themselves. Again, Rooney and Drew had neither expertise nor equipment. They gave Jim to understand this was another of the aspects their Canadian partner was to have financed.

All in all, Rooney and Drew looked like a very bad bet. Unless . . . And always it came back to this: unless the ship actually was the *Gloriosa* and her tiptilted hull concealed a treasure hoard. If only he knew. If only there was a way of finding out.

Jim seethed with frustration. When he planned his own scams he was thorough, did his homework. But here he was trapped without access to libraries or other records, unable to ask around for fear of raising suspicions that a rich wreck had been discovered. Rooney and Drew were all talk, especially Rooney. They told him a document led them to the wreck, a chart pinpointing the site of the *Gloriosa*, but they didn't show it to him. Whether it existed or not he'd have wanted more.

He was nearing St Elena, puffs of cloud heralded evening. He glided the *Caramba* up to the dock. The *Mariposa* had gone. Jim felt a spurt of anger, he loved her and was possessive about her. Then he smiled at his inconsistency. That morning he'd felt a similar flare of annoyance because she'd bob there all day and no one would sail her.

He began to wonder about Jane. She'd been off colour for several days. He wished she could be better. He didn't like it when she was unwell and he could do nothing to help her.

The house was empty. Jane had written him a note, left it on their bed beneath the white film of the mosquito net. It was very brief, written in a hurry, her handwriting slurring one letter into another. They'd gone to a party, she said. She named an island he'd never been to. 'Back tomorrow,' she wrote. She added a question mark after the tomorrow.

Jim sat on the side of the bed, holding the note. He didn't know exactly what it meant, but was afraid it meant more than it said. His fragile world rocked.

Then he rose and wandered through the rooms of the house. Exquisitely decorated, lavishly furnished in that slightly shabby English style, it was a rich man's version of simplicity. He pretended it was all his. Why shouldn't it be? After all, it only took money.

Immediately, he was less certain. Money plus something that wasn't easily labelled. Confidence? Confidence was required to live in this house. The house made statements. One thing it asserted was that the owner was a sociable person. Why else all those bedrooms and bathrooms? Or the dozens of this and that?

Jim heard footsteps and froze. A servant appeared through a doorway. 'Good evening, Mr Rush.'

'Good evening, Claude. Looks like we have this place to ourselves.'

Claude smiled. He was an islander, older than Jim, dark and smiling with fluid movements. Jim supposed being a house servant on a private island might be a decent job, in an area where the choice was emigration or service. He never had enough conversation with any of them to find out. A few words more than necessary to one of them, and he'd been chided for his egalitarian American ways.

Claude said, with the friendly politeness he always showed: 'If you're wondering, Mr Rush, they left here about three.'

'All of them?'

'All of them. In the end.' The smile contained the suggestion of arguments, resistance, capitulation.

Jim had to do with that, it would be wrong to ask Claude for a rundown although he longed to know with what measure of reluctance Jane Logan had abandoned him. He was neither piqued nor jealous that she'd gone. It meant she was feeling better and that was pleasing. But if she'd deserted him lightly or without thought, then it mattered. She was his future. He might lose it.

He told Claude he'd want only a light supper and until then would be in the room they called the library. He didn't go to the library, he continued his prowl through the house. The partygoers had given him an opportunity.

Guy had chosen a corner room for himself, a room with exceptionally fine views. Through one window trees and glowing shrubs were darkening. Through the other, the sun was glinting low, making silhouettes of a clutch of islands.

Jim examined a bedside table, a cupboard and a writing desk without finding anything to detain him. The search was quick, the room tidy. No telling whether Guy was a neat fellow or not, the servants put everything straight in any case.

There were two easy chairs and a table. He remembered

Guy sitting in one chair, drowsily malleable when Jim had called in to beg use of the yacht. For a second the memory was as vivid as if Guy were really there.

This echo of Guy's presence intimidated him. He twisted his head away, then stared again at the chair. Guy had sat there, with his drink on the table, calling him 'Jim, lad'. But there'd been something else apart from the glass and the bottle. Jim had the impression that something had fallen to the floor.

He went up to the chair, chewing his lower lip, striving to bring the details of the remembered scene into focus. A book? A map? What had it been? Then, on the other side of the chair, he saw the magazine rack. He sat where Guy had sat and he flicked through the magazines.

In the third one he found it, an article about treasure in the Caribbean. Guy had folded it open at that page. He'd been treating them to his jokes about treasure islands and *Treasure Island* that day. The magazine was an old one, two years, and the article no more than a rehash of stories about Mexican gold and galleons and pirates. Someone, possibly Guy, had drawn a vertical line beside a paragraph that mentioned the *Gloriosa*.

The article said nothing that Jim hadn't previously read. The writer had done a fair journalistic job of reading published accounts and reproducing them as an entertaining piece of writing. Over the page was a map, a diagram really, of the entire Caribbean with dots marking the sites where most of the treasure ships had been lost. The dots were clustered far, far to the north of the Antilles. A few were closer. None, on this crudest of charts, related to the Drew and Rooney wreck.

Jim read the rest of the text. In the penultimate

paragraph he came upon a fact he didn't know. The Spanish had kept details of shipping in the Spanish Main. Records could be examined, in an archive in Seville.

A noise. His hand tightened on the magazine. His head jerked up. The sound came again, a sharp crack. Then again.

Fireworks, he realised. *Not gunfire, a party.*

He hoped the servants were celebrating being left to themselves, or virtually so. They wouldn't count him as he wasn't a demander, a giver of orders, a patroller of social boundaries.

As he hesitated, listening for the next cracker, he saw the silhouettes of islands meld into darkness. A ray of green light fired the horizon and then it was night.

3

He went to Seville. He told Drew and Rooney he was going to New York but he went to Seville. Jane Logan went with him.

'Oh, marvellous,' she said when he invited her. She was full of bright-eyed excitement. 'I know one of the sherry families over there. We *must* go and see them.'

Usually his heart sank when she dragged her friends into his plans. This time he was glad. Jane busy with friends was better than Jane overseeing his activities.

'Why don't you ring them?' he suggested, knowing that was precisely what she was about to do.

He'd told her about Drew and Rooney, saying he'd run into them again while she was away with Guy and the others. The party had swallowed up several days of their lives. According to Lucinda and Charles, it had been too wonderful to tear themselves away.

On his return, Guy had devised a new joke, about 'Jim, lad' having been marooned and the crew of the good ship *Mariposa* arriving to rescue him. Jim chipped in that he'd lashed together a few hunks of driftwood and created the good ship *Caramba* so that, all in all, he'd been content. Jeremy grinned vacantly at all the others laughing at this contest of wit, and said nothing. He wore a new cotton shirt printed with bunches of bananas. Jane murmured it was camouflage.

She was taken aback when Jim mentioned Drew and Rooney to her. Guy's nonsense was fresh in her mind as she commented: 'A likely couple of pirates, methinks.'

'They don't exactly fly the Jolly Roger, Jane. I guess they're OK.'

'Pirates often didn't, you know. They stole ships or used any flag that took their fancy.'

He did know. Not only had it featured in Guy's act but Jim had come upon cases among the books in the so-called library. Drake, for instance, had once used a Portuguese caravel when he robbed for England.

Two of Jim's solitary evenings had been spent browsing. Three authors had listed the Seville archive as one of the sources of their information. Previously, he hadn't bothered to check the snippets in small print in the final pages, they seemed irrelevant. At that stage he'd been in pursuit of drama and intrigue, not prosaic material such as the whereabouts of scientific papers and the titles of long-out-of-print studies of Caribbean life. Yet there it had been all along, the nugget of information that showed him the way ahead.

The evening not spent among the books, he'd been with Drew and Rooney. They were moored in the hurricane harbour, their usual base, hidden from the world. Drew was tinkering with the engine, looking for an air leak into the fuel system. Rooney asked him whether it could be left until later, meaning it was easier to talk without the clatter of tools and outbursts from the engine.

'No, Mike,' Drew said evenly, without looking up. 'If I

don't find it, we'll keep on getting air in the fuel filter and coming to a dead stop.'

Jim suspected he was deliberately misunderstanding the length of delay Rooney proposed. This wasn't the first time he'd caught the pair at odds.

Drew paused from pumping the fuel lines and wiped sweat from his face. He was red, all of him that was exposed to the air: red hair, red limbs, face like an overblown rose. Not the hot climate type, the weather made him prickly.

Rooney ignored him. 'Another drink, Jim?'

Jim lifted his glass to show it was half full and declined with a shake of the head. 'Go on about the disposal, Mike.'

Rooney picked up where he'd left off before the last burst of engine power. 'Right. Well, what I was saying was I ran across a guy up in Florida who was scouting around the wreck hunters. Anybody who was diving, no matter who they worked for, he was sidling up and offering cash for the bits and pieces they brought up.'

'Can you use him?'

'I reckon so. That's all he does, buy up stuff. Anything from silver coins to bronze cannon. Lew – I don't know the rest, he was always Lew as far as I was concerned – well, Lew took care of the risks. If anything was outside the law, then he was the one acting illegally.'

This was the first mention of wrecks being protected by law. Jim asked him about it. Rooney said countries had different rules, so did US states. In Florida there was a government department of marine archaeology to undertake work or else allow commercial salvage companies to do it. The department occasionally let private individuals in, which is how the rich banker he'd worked for had captured his Spanish galleon.

He didn't offer information about the local rules. Jim ignored the omission and asked instead what Lew had persuaded Rooney himself to part with.

'A lamp. I struck lucky, there's always interest in lamps. He gave me a fair sum.'

When he mentioned how much, Jim was unimpressed. Rooney quickly added that it was several years back and anyway you couldn't expect saleroom prices.

Jim fingered one of the Spanish coins lying on the bench between them. The coins and a small vase, plain and twisted out of shape but possibly silver, had been brought up from the *Gloriosa*, if that *was* the name of the wreck and if Rooney and Drew were telling the truth.

'Mike, I think, if I may say this, that . . .'

Jim's circuitous approach was wasted by the engine's roaring. Rooney shot a look of exasperation at Drew who declined to notice. Jim relaxed, shoving the coins around with a forefinger. He was happy with the way the game was going. He had them. All the pressure was on Rooney. Drew was playing Jane's couple of pirates into Jim's hands.

The engine growled and cut out. Rooney encouraged Jim with a nod.

Jim said: 'I was going to tell you I have an alternative to your Lew. Say I contact a dealer I know in New York? You could find yourselves selling direct instead.'

Rooney, who was seldom short of a reply, said nothing. His face worked as he considered it a splendid idea, a dangerous one, a way of cutting out at least one middle man, a matter of putting total trust in Jim Rush, the rich American from St Elena who liked to live with the upper-class English crowd but play around whenever they let him off the leash.

Jim stood up. 'Think it over, Mike.'

He took a step or two to show he was leaving, then added: 'I have to fly to New York on business in a few days' time. If you're interested, I could check it out then.'

He returned to the *Caramba* and lay on a bunk with Radio Caribbean purring. He wasn't listening to it. He was listening for the slap of water against a dinghy, for the touch of a smaller boat on the *Caramba*'s hull, for Rooney to hail him.

'Jim?' Rooney arrived only minutes later than expected. He hauled himself aboard. 'I've been thinking over your New York idea. Sounds great.'

Jim nodded, serious not jubilant. 'If you're sure. But I know it's the way I'd handle it if it were my decision.'

Rooney nodded vigorously.

Jim asked him: 'Drew happy with this?'

Too quickly: 'Oh, yes.'

Another cry from the old fishing boat's engine across the water. They both laughed.

'One thing more,' Jim said. 'I'd like to take something from the *Gloriosa* with me.'

Rooney offered a coin. 'We have several of those.'

Jim demurred. 'Anything more interesting, more individual than that? We have to play a strong hand.'

'Yes, I hadn't thought. I'll bring you something, Jim. Not now, it isn't on board. I'll pick it up tomorrow.'

'Fine. I'll call in here late afternoon. Does that allow you time?'

Rooney said it did. Jim offered him a drink. Rum, there was only rum. Jock, the boat's owner, had left a bottle on board and Jim opened it.

'To New York,' said Rooney, raising his glass.

'To New York,' Jim agreed.

Instead he went to Seville.

But first he rang New York. Daubeney answered the telephone himself. His voice was muffled, as usual he was eating.

'Jim? Watcha want?' He sounded quite pleased to hear him. Not very, just quite.

Jim was used to that. He didn't expect how-are-yous and faked concern. As long as he wasn't bringing trouble, Daubeney couldn't care less.

'How do you feel about gold and silver from a wreck?'

'In *London*?' The last time Jim had contacted him was from London.

'No. London was before.'

'What are we talking here? Bars? Stuff to melt down? Collectors' pieces? I mean, it all depends, Jim.'

'I can't say right now.'

'Ah. Well, you come back to me when you do know.'

'Look, all I'm asking is whether you want to be involved when the time comes.'

'Come on, you know me, Jim, ever willing to help a friend. I'll talk to you, sure I will.'

Jim required more than this. 'A guideline, that's all. How much for bars, how much for trinkets? You can make an intelligent guess, I'm not asking for more than that.'

Daubeney choked on his half-chewn mouthful. 'Jeez. Intelligent guess. What's that supposed to be?'

Jim grew sarcastic too. 'Maybe you'd like me to write you for a professional estimate.'

'Hey, steady boy. Don't write me, Jim, don't ever do that.'

Jim rolled his eyes skyward. 'A joke, I promise. Look . . .'

'No, come on, Jim. When you know what you're talking about give me another call. OK?'

Jim said OK.

That afternoon, dejected, he went to meet Rooney and Drew. The play was going his way but Daubeney had spoiled his fun.

Mike Rooney was on board alone. 'Drew's gone for widgets. You know what these engine types are like, grab any excuse to fiddle.'

'What's wrong this time?'

Rooney realised he'd been foolish to cast doubt on the reliability of the boat. 'Same thing, air in the fuel lines. Like I said, Drew's an engine man.'

Jim got down to business. 'Well, then. What do you have for me?'

'Let's go inside.'

Jim thought such caution exaggerated because the island was officially unpopulated and there were no other boats. He hovered while Rooney lifted a cloth-wrapped package from a cavity beneath a bench.

Rooney tenderly laid it on the table and folded back the wrappings. A cup was revealed, a damaged metal cup with a stem but no handles and encrusted over a large area of the surface. With something akin to reverence, Rooney lifted the cup and presented it to Jim.

'It's the best piece.' He was watching Jim anxiously.

Jim held the cup to the light from the porthole. The thing weighed more than he had expected. It wasn't large, perhaps six inches high, but he was sure it weighed more than a pound. The metal gleamed faintly. He mounted the lower steps of the companionway, wanting better light.

'Gold?' he wondered, his voice breaking on the word.

'Do you see now why that wreck's driving us crazy? We've found her, she's worth every effort and we can't afford to . . .'

Jim jerked away from him and went up on deck, Rooney's voice giving way to the cry of gulls. Jim hefted the cup in his left hand, wondering how much the gold weighed and how much of the overall weight could be attributed to the lumpy accretions. The lumps pressed against his palm. He revolved the cup, with supreme care, studying the matt and scratchy surface. To begin with, when he'd seen it lying on the table, he'd assumed Rooney was showing him the cleaner part but now he discovered there was nothing to choose. It was virtually the same all round.

Jim gasped. The shock of realisation was numbing. He was fixed, gripping the cup, unaware of Rooney prattling beside him or of the thresh of flying fish taking to the air. Nothing existed for him except the gold cup and the lumps that were no longer the random encrustations of sea creatures, but shapes that encircled the cup in a deliberate pattern because they were jewels.

Jane booked them into the new hotel on Cartuja Island in Seville.

'It's the very latest thing, James, built for Expo in 1992. They say it looks like three bins with wonky lids but it's delicious.'

'What kind of bins?'

'Dustbins, English style. It's ultra modern and ultra comfortable. Five stars.'

'Good.' He wondered how many nights of ultra-expensive luxury she'd committed them to, how many he needed.

Jane teased him. 'Look happy, James. And trust me, I know what I'm doing.'

She generally did, he couldn't doubt her. He looked happier.

She said: 'I've stayed in Spanish hotels, you haven't. Unless we opt for top of the range luxury we'll probably encounter reluctance to switch on the heating. If they have any, that is.'

He asked what arrangements she'd made with her friend. Linda, this one was called.

'Linda's coming to the hotel for a couple of days. She'll take me sightseeing while you attend to business. Perfect, don't you think?'

The only improvement would have been sending Jane to stay with Linda well away from Seville. He was confident, though, that he could bluff his way through a couple of evenings in the company of one of Jane's schoolfriends. Unless she was very different from all the others he'd met, she'd be entranced with Jane and leave him alone.

Linda was at the hotel when he and Jane booked in. There was a message asking them to call her room.

Jane immediately lifted the telephone beside the bed. 'Linda?'

A gabble of words with Jane interspersing a few here and there. Jane turned to Jim, holding the telephone pressed against her to prevent Linda overhearing.

'We're invited to a party. She begged invitations for us. Terribly sweet of her, don't you think?'

He said it would be great. To his own ears he sounded less than delighted. Covering up his disinclination, he added. 'Jane, I can't be too late tonight. I have a meeting early tomorrow, you know.'

Her face clouded. Then: 'Linda, we'd love to, really we would, but we may have to be spoilsports and scoot away early.'

A sympathetic squeaking came down the line.

Jane said: 'Jet lag, plus James has an early meeting.'

More squeaking. A trickle of see-you-laters. Jane set the telephone down and laughed. 'She's exactly the same. People never change, do they?'

Jim believed the trouble was they did, whenever you got a friendship right, the other person turned into someone else. Oddly, her remark made him think of Drew and Rooney, how they'd set out on an adventure together, a partnership, and were visibly splitting apart. Rooney pressed for Jim's involvement while Drew held back, either because he was unconvinced Jim was all he appeared to be or because he didn't want to share.

Jane said: 'I remember Linda coming up to me in the school garden with a flurry of words. Heaven knows what it was about, I doubt if I knew at the time. That was our first meeting. She launched herself at me as though we were old friends with heaps of news to catch up on.'

'Which is what you are now.'

She stroked his face, the scent of her filling him. 'Oh, poor darling. Will you feel terribly left out?'

He said he'd try not to mind.

* * *

Next morning he asked himself how in the world he'd survived it. He felt exhausted, his head ached and he was mildly disorientated. Standing in a cool shower, trusting the streaming water to wash away some of the pain, he had a flashback of the party: happy faces loud in laughter; Spanish and English shouted in equal proportions; whirling dancers and a band far too loud for far too long.

If anyone had ever explained to him whose party it was and why he was there, he'd long forgotten. Then there was the awful drive back to the hotel, the taxi juddering through grey and silent streets and over the bridge, Jane asleep on his shoulder and a wide-awake Linda chattering at him.

He examined his appearance in the bathroom mirror, with care and with approval. It was what he had, this slim fair classical beauty, with the regular features, the honest blue eyes and engaging smiles. He had a talent for beauty.

'Heaven knows,' his family used to say, 'how young Jim got to be so pretty.' He'd inherited none of the tough roughness of this family of farming folk who survived the seasons by God and by grit more than guile. 'Heaven knows,' they cried, 'how that young Jim's gonna make out.'

They remarked it in his hearing, adults too thoughtless to curb their tongues until the children were away. So he heard it young, this peculiar flattery that both praised him and set him apart. The other kids heard too and looked him over with the unequivocal appraisal of children.

Brookie, his neighbour and playmate in those days, would shut his fist tight on one of Jim's toys, say his plastic truck, and cram it in his pocket. He could do that sort of thing and he did it, whenever the mood took him, because he was bigger and stronger than Jim. Somehow, though, he never got to keep the trucks and the comics and the other things he stole. Jim always took them back, when he was ready, not by force but by wit.

Jane stirred when he returned to the bedroom after his shower. She mumbled that she was glad she didn't have a meeting to go to and burrowed beneath the bedclothes.

He cursed the necessity of keeping up the pretence. For a couple of minutes he toyed with the idea of claiming the meeting had been delayed, but that wouldn't be credible. Besides, if he changed his plans, he'd have to do his research at a less convenient time. Jane was out of his way for a while and he dared not waste the opportunity.

A taxi took him over the bridge and dropped him within walking distance of the cathedral. The Archive of the Indies was close by. He went purposefully, keeping pace with office workers marching to work on a chilly morning, their shapes distorted by layers of clothes they'd peel off as the day warmed up and replace as it cooled towards evening. His own clothes, chosen for the West Indies, were inadequate. He kept an eye open for shop windows displaying coats.

After a few minutes he ducked into an alleyway and found a café, popular with office workers who chose to buy breakfast *en route* rather than make it at home. Jim revived himself with good strong coffee and ate crunchy *tostadas* spread with a generous allowance of butter. He was in no hurry because the doors of the archive weren't opened until ten thirty and he didn't wish to attract attention by being first through them. Before he arrived, he wanted to be alert, ready for any questions he might face and for all those he wanted to ask.

It felt good to be free of St Elena and its restrictions.

Fleetingly he considered never going back, offering Jane an excuse and staying. But it was indeed fleeting. He would endure and do anything to get the treasure from that wreck. So he was doomed to return and play the game of not noticing how he was sidelined by Guy and those most under his influence.

'Where is he?' Jim had asked one day, quite casually, when Piers' brother, the one wanted for murder, had missed lunch and then dinner. Half a dozen faces fell blank.

'*Who?*' asked a young woman with a cold voice and a nose designed for sneering.

He hadn't bothered to repeat the name or even to reply, because the new trick was apparently to pretend the fellow had never been with them. He wished he could believe they'd do as much for him, although of course it wouldn't be exactly for him, more to protect themselves from association with him.

In the café in Seville, a couple of young women begged to share his table. He looked through one of the newspapers provided for customers and paid the women no more attention. Neither of them was especially dark haired or dashing, they were quite ordinary young women. The city wasn't living up to its holiday poster reputation. If any of its women were striking beauties with haughty carriage and upswept hair, then he'd managed to travel for miles without spotting them. They hadn't been in evidence at the party, either. Jane, with her raven hair and midnight eyes, had won admiring appraisal, and Jane was elegant and cool.

He turned over the pages, understanding an encouraging amount. His Spanish had been picked up in California. He could cope, as he'd coped at the party. Thinking of the previous evening brought to mind Linda telling him about her family's history in the sherry business, a few words to explain why an English family had been rooted for centuries in Andalusia. It amused him, this clinging to spurious identity. The family straddled two cultures and would balance there until kingdom come – so proud to be English, although apart from sending children 'home' to be educated their experience was very unEnglish.

Linda, whom he liked because she was outgoing and friendly like a bouncy puppy, joked that it was similar to coming from an army family. 'Except,' she conceded, 'soldiers do their tour of duty and go home but my people keep soldiering on.'

Jim wished he knew where she was taking Jane sightseeing. It would be awkward if he ran into them outside the cathedral. Then another thought: no, it wouldn't; if a meeting wound up early what was more natural than using spare time to look around a cathedral?

He went out into the crisp morning. The sun sliced across the alleyway, offering patches of warmth. He hurried along, from warm patch to warm patch, thinking about the coat he ought to buy. Soon he arrived at the Archive of the Indies.

A handful of elderly people were going inside, a younger man explaining to them the importance of the collection and the way it was being modernised. They didn't linger in the entrance hall but went directly upstairs, slowly, their guide continuing to talk. The building was ponderous with pink marble, a solemn kind of place. Jim hovered behind the group, listening.

Apparently the building was a former stock exchange, built around a patio. The young man didn't mention when it stopped being a stock exchange and became home to the records of Spain's dealings with the Americas, but he did say the archive was founded in 1758 by Carlos the third. One of the elderly men was having trouble with his Carloses and there was a pause in the narrative while he was persuaded this wasn't the one who built his palace within the Alhambra. That one was the fifth. The third was the one who expelled the Jesuits from Spain and the New World.

Jim caught a few other facts: the archive housed forty-three thousand files, although the young man didn't stipulate what he meant by file; there were eighty-six million pages in these files; and there were eight thousand maps. Jim and the elderly folk, who were breathing heavily on their way to the first floor, were among the fifteen thousand people who used the archive each year.

He approached an official and asked to see material relating to the wreck of the *Gloriosa* off the Antilles. There were a few probing questions, which he parried by claiming to be a writer needing access to the papers, but eventually he was allowed in. He felt small in there, small in stature and insignificant. There was the physical aspect, it was a high room, but also the atmosphere of patient scholarship.

His own researches were always a race, a scrabble to gather facts so that he could fool people into believing he was something or someone he wasn't. To make enquiries for the sake of enquiry was different.

Selected documents were displayed in cases where loose covers protected them from sunlight and glass shielded them from fingers and breath. Most were stored on open shelves in soft card folders tied with blue tape. The folders were labelled with year, territory and additional details such as the source of the information. Often this source was named as the Tribunal, which is to say the Inquisition.

He left this room and went to the reading room, a more modest one, a covered-in gallery of the original patio building. Among the desks and computer terminals, he chose a place to work. Before long he was reading about the *Gloriosa*.

The authors of the books he'd previously read had paraphrased but not invented and then they'd stopped short. Here, though, was the inventory of the galleon's cargo. It was reminiscent of the haul of Giovanni da Verrazano, the original pirate: gold, emeralds, pearls, *objets* encrusted with precious stones . . .

She was only days into her month-long journey to Cadiz when a double disaster struck. The voyage began well, a light wind speeding her away from Trinidad and the grey waters of the equatorial current, that was stained by outrushes from the Amazon and Orinoco. Soon she was in blue water, a strong west-going current driving her on. She left the hump-backed shape of Grenada behind and sailed up the archipelago towards St Vincent.

A ship was sighted, perhaps following. Nervous, her captain altered course. The other ship also did, gaining on her. When the pursuer was near enough for it to be clear she was flying the Spanish flag, the captain of the *Gloriosa* decided to wait. He had delayed for a message at Trinidad but it hadn't been delivered. He thought the ship might be bringing it as she was intent on catching up.

Unfortunately the weather, which had been variable that day, changed for the worse with a rising wind and threatening skies. The pursuer came within hailing distance. By now the *Gloriosa* could read her name: *Rosita*.

The *Rosita* lowered a boat, said she was sending a party aboard with news.

The crew of the *Gloriosa* were desperate to be away. A great front of cloud was dragging a curtain of rain across the sea towards them. They feared they faced a small hurricane, the weather most dreaded by the sailors of tall ships that couldn't respond fast to violent and unpredictable winds. If they were quick, there was a chance of outrunning the storm. But the captain ordered his crew to hold her steady. He knew of a haven they could make for. Then the men from the *Rosita* swarmed aboard, armed, Englishmen in a stolen ship come to seize the treasure.

Chests were hastily tumbled into light boats that battled across to the pirate ship. Rain began to lash and the sky darkened making it impossible to see where the *Rosita* lay. The captain of the *Gloriosa* gave orders to make for the shelter of an island. But he'd left it too late. She was engulfed while going about in her dash for the hurricane harbour.

Two men survived to repeat their story to an inquiry in Seville. They told how they'd been washed from the deck of the galleon, saved their lives by clinging to an upturned boat, and were thrown ashore when it shattered on a reef on the south coast of the island of Santalina. They'd been blown far away from where they'd last glimpsed their ship. Before rescue they endured several weeks on the uninhabited island with ample time to agree upon the details. According to this pair, who were the only witnesses, the ship went down a couple of miles south-west of where Drew and Rooney found the wreck.

Jim made notes of the salient points and of several that appeared not to be. He had a hunch these others could prove significant later. Then he sat back and closed his eyes, twiddling his pen.

The discrepancies between the full story and the truncated versions he'd previously read were attributable to précis, there was nothing seriously contradictory. Yet the more detail he read, the less reliable it all appeared.

Two men, one an officer, had provided every scrap of information anyone had about the tragedy, and they'd been preoccupied at the time with saving their skins, not with charting exact positions or recording the captain's words. Jim imagined the officer standing close by the captain, perhaps thinking it foolhardy to loiter for the other ship to catch up, perhaps arguing that, Spanish flag or no, the pursuer might no longer be in Spanish hands. They were dangerous times.

Jim doodled a diagram of the scene. Two ships from, more or less, the south-west. A small hurricane tearing into them from the north-east. A chain of islands, the tips of a sunken mountain range. He marked the main islands of Grenada and St Vincent and then searched his memory for one called Santalina in between. There were around a hundred of these little Grenadines and he was familiar with the names of only a few. Unless he could pinpoint Santalina, his diagram was useless. But if he *could* place it he'd be able to make his own rough calculation about the *Gloriosa*'s last position because the survivors had claimed they were carried away from her by a wind from the north-east.

People near him began to gather their papers together. The archive closed at 3 p.m. Too many of his questions remained unanswered but this was the best place in the world to answer them. What he'd hoped might be a couple of hours' work altogether would bring him back the next morning and perhaps the one after.

Jim filled in the rest of his chain of islands with a row of swift dots. And then he gave an ironic laugh as he realised how aptly they resembled those dots writers use to create suspense . . .

It was like that moment when he realised the gold cup he was holding was encrusted with gems. He felt the same astonishment, the same overwhelming conviction that it was true, the same inability to move on to another thought. Fixed.

Jane heard his sharp intake of breath and turned over to face him, inquiry on her face. 'Hmm?'

For too long he was incapable of response. Then he mustered a smile, said casually: 'Oh, just something I was thinking.'

The room was cool. She tucked the bedclothes around her neck and gave the grin that was so typical of her. 'I'm listening.'

He shook his head, denying her.

She said: 'You're being mysterious again. You've been mysterious ever since we came here.'

He laughed it off.

She said very softly, not complaining: 'I wish you'd tell me, James. A bit of it, that's all.'

He leaned over and kissed her nose. Then he got out of bed and showered. When he re-emerged from the bathroom she was dozing. He went out of the room.

Sheer excitement gave way to a muddle of doubts. He didn't feel he could tell Jane anything, although it was touching that she was prepared to settle for part and not all of it. There were secrets that could never be told, even to her, *especially* to her. To lose her was to lose his camouflage, his only vestige of security.

Of course, there were a few things that might be said without putting everything at risk. But not yet. In a while it might be good to tell her about the wreck hunt and his involvement with Drew and Rooney. In fact, he'd be forced to if a proper investigation were to be carried out. That would mean spending time away from her, an absence he'd have to explain one way or another. The easiest course then would be to tell the truth.

He took a taxi and asked to be dropped where he'd begun to walk the previous day. It was possible to get closer but he'd long had the habit of preventing taxi drivers from knowing his exact destinations.

The morning was bitter, making him glad of the thick jacket he'd bought the previous afternoon after leaving the archive. He thrust his hands into his pockets and turned into the alleyway where he again ate breakfast in the cosy, busy café.

Over his first cup of coffee he relived the moment of discovery that had taken his breath away. Like many discoveries it was painfully obvious once it had been thought of, and the mystery became why it hadn't been thought of before.

He had the table to himself. He opened his notebook at yesterday's doodle and struck a line through the *Gloriosa*. He no longer cared what had become of her and where she lay. The truth that had been so hard to come by was that the *Gloriosa* was an empty husk when she capsized. By then her treasure had been transferred to the *Rosita*. He was going to switch his search to the pirate ship.

His great good luck was that the pirate ship had originally been Spanish and her fate, or what was known of it, was somewhere in the same archive. With barely suppressed excitement, Jim chased after her.

He chased her through computer records and through documents from ribboned folders. There was much less on record about her. Unlike the *Gloriosa* she hadn't gained an illustrious name by carrying home the plunder of the New World. National pride hadn't been sadly wounded when she was lost.

Several of the documents were in poor condition, foxed and stained, but the computer enhanced the original images and made them readable. In one of these Jim learned how the *Rosita* had fallen into the hands of the English enemy in a classic piece of sea fighting off Hispaniola. By intent or instinct, the English captain had followed the orders drawn up by Thomas Audley for Henry VIII's sailors:

If they chase the enemy, let them that chase shoot no ordnance till he be ready to board him, for that will let his ship's way . . .

In case you board, enter not till you see all the smoke gone, and then shoot off all your pieces, your port pieces, the pieces of hailshot and cross-bar shot to beat his cage-deck; and if you see his deck well rid, then enter with your best men, but first win his top in any wise if it be possible.

It was recorded, in Spanish of equally beautiful rhythms, how the *Rosita* sank a few months later while making for harbour in the Antilles during a hurricane. There were survivors, Englishmen whose accounts eventually found their way into the Spanish record. The day of the disaster was the day the *Gloriosa* sank. The position was closer to land. It was also close enough to the site of Drew and Rooney's wreck for Jim to revive all his hopes that he hadn't been entirely misled by them, that they had indeed found a wreck rich in New World treasure.

Afterwards he sat in another café and amended his diagram, plotting the *Rosita* where Drew's and Rooney's wreck lay. He was no wiser as to which of the suspense dots went by the name of Santalina but the island had ceased to be important once he'd given up the *Gloriosa* in favour of tracking down pirates. With time to spare he'd have checked from pure curiosity but the *Rosita* kept him occupied right up until the moment the archive closed. He considered having another session there, double checking to test his theories, but decided against it. Better to spend the next day with Jane and then fly back to the West Indies.

She and Linda had toured all the city sights she cared to see and so when Jim asked what she'd like to do on her third day she suggesting leaving Seville and travelling south. Her idea was that it would be warmer and they could journey east through Andalusia as far as Malaga and fly from there.

He fell in with this. They went by car with Linda for the first stage, staying a night on her parents' ranch. Then they hired a car for the rest of the trip. Driving off, alone at last with Jane, Jim felt free. He didn't know the country, for him it was new and unmarked. No one knew him except the people he'd spoken to in the previous few days. The chance of running into anyone from his past was minimal.

He loved the space of Andalusia. Driving its empty roads he studied the crouched white towns, the empty miles of sierra, and knew it to be a land that offered breathing space. Perhaps it was too open, like those great swatches of America. A human being could be inhibited, reduced, by so vast an emptiness on which he could leave no impression. Abandoned farmhouses, their coats of limewash weathered away, sank back into the landscape. Brown stone returned to the brown earth from whence it came. Nothing that a man did to this land could impinge on it. He loved it and understood that it was an unnerving place to live.

When they were on the coast they visited the neat white port of Sanlúcar de Barrameda where manzanilla is made and the names on the bodegas are English. Her friend, Linda, had cousins there. One of them showed them the spot from which Magellan and Columbus had set sail.

Then Jane drove to Cadiz, with its memories of Drake and the Armada, and more of Columbus. She wondered aloud how St Elena had been tossed back and forth between the great powers during the centuries of struggle in the Caribbean. But Jim was picturing the great galleons coming home to Cadiz with lowering sails and their holds crammed with the extravagance of Mexico.

She drove east. They frittered sunny days along the Mediterranean, Jane disparaging the modern resorts on the Costa del Sol but knowing them well enough to sift out the older and more acceptable hotels. She was an excellent guide but Jim's thoughts were too frequently taken up with wreck hunting and those two adventurers who believed he was in New York. When he closed his eyes at night it wasn't the softly lapping Mediterranean he saw in his mind's eye, nor white villages dotting a huge landscape, but a small metal cup, faintly gleaming, its surface patterned with precious stones.

4

They'd been away from St Elena a matter of days and yet everything had changed. Guy was morose, Lucinda and Charles had flown home to London, Jeremy was talkative and Claude, the house servant, had news that the *Caramba* was reported stolen. But there was worse: when he and Jane landed at the international airport Jim saw Martin Peters.

Peters was burdened with an important looking camera bag and appeared to be meeting an incoming flight. Jim spotted him first. He touched Jane's arm.

'Jane, Martin Peters is over there.'

She frowned. 'Oh, no.'

Jim said: 'He's seen us. I'll have to say hi to him.'

'Well, I won't.' She slipped away, glad to be warned in time to avoid renewing acquaintance.

Peters called out. 'Jim!' His bushy hair quivered as he hurried forward.

'Hi, Martin. I thought you'd gone to London.' This was a perfect chance to find out how soon he was leaving. Jim didn't want him around, getting in the way. From the beginning Peters had been getting in his way.

'Change of plans, Jim. One of the papers asked me to stay on a while.'

111

'For anything special?'

Peters chuckled, wickedly. 'All my pictures are special, Jim.'

Jim tried again. 'Is Princess Diana the target or is there someone else?'

Peters rubbed the side of his nose and winked. Jim had never actually seen anybody perform this gesture before. It looked silly enough when comedians did it on television but utterly ridiculous when Martin Peters aped them.

Peters dropped his voice, his soft confiding Hampshire voice that belied the intensity in his eyes. 'Diana's expecting an important visitor. The picture desk got a tip in London.' He raised a forbidding hand although Jim wasn't attempting to break in. 'Don't ask me who, I've said more than I should have.'

Jim nodded gravely. He didn't know whether to assume the visitor would be the Queen or a lover.

He asked: 'Got your other camera back yet, Martin?'

The switch of topic surprised Peters. He stumbled over an explanation for not having gone up to the plantation house to fetch the one he'd claimed he abandoned there the evening they were shot at. Jim was uncertain how much to believe. Everything Peters said in connection with the plantation house was dubious. It was possible the camera might not have been left there, and also possible that Peters' excuse for not fetching it was false.

An athletic young man with greasy brown hair and a mahogany tan was bearing down on them. Peters waved a greeting. Another journalist, Jim supposed. Perhaps this one was going to snoop on the British royals too or perhaps his assignment was the arms trade story Peters had been

excited about. Jim didn't care what they got up to as long as
the pair of them stayed out of his way.

He paused long enough to be introduced to the young
man. Witherspoon, he was called. He was an American
with a voice that was unmistakably Californian. The name
seemed inappropriate, too floppy for such a well-muscled
hulk. Denny Witherspoon should have been blessed with
sturdier names.

Jim caught up with Jane and they went out into the
glowing heat. He said: 'I'm sorry I was so long but I wanted
to check Martin really was leaving.'

'And is he?'

'Not yet. His paper's asked him to stay.'

'Well, at least we can keep him off St Elena.' Decisive
words, a warning tone.

The changed atmosphere on St Elena, a change that hit
like a cold wind when they reached the island an hour later,
astonished Jim. He'd steeled himself for more boisterous
tomfoolery and yo, ho, ho-ing. Instead there was a
grudging greeting followed by silence. Jim raised a
questioning eyebrow at Jane and left her to discover where
everybody was and why Guy had metamorphosed into
crabby old age.

In their bedroom he took advantage of her absence to
look at the gold cup. He lifted a bag from his cupboard,
reassured as soon as he felt its weight. Unzipping it on the
bed, he held it open far enough for him to fumble with the
cloth wrappings and touch the cool gold surface. Then he
rapidly returned the bag to the drawer. Jane came into the
room within seconds.

'Jim, Guy's totally depressed because we all went away
and left him and the reinforcements have been delayed.'

'*All* went?'

'All except for Jeremy. He's around somewhere. But Charles was called to London and Lucinda went too.'

Bewildered, Jim admitted a gloomy Guy was a development he was unprepared for.

Jane immediately flew to Guy's defence. 'I know you think he's terribly silly but Guy can be quite sensitive.'

'Really?' He didn't mean to challenge her but the remark was preposterous. Whatever Guy was sensitive to, it wasn't other people's feelings.

Jane pursed her lips and left an admonishing pause before saying they must both be awfully kind to Guy.

Supper was served on the terrace. Lamps cast mournful shadows. Four people were simply not enough. The house demanded more, preferably many more. The terrace seemed deserted. Jim had always known it was a house designed for communal living, that smaller numbers would rattle around uncomfortably. Now it was being proved.

Jeremy was doing his utmost to fill the breach. For a man who usually said little and got that little wrong, he was extraordinarily voluble. Jeremy it was who broke the news about the *Caramba*.

'You'll never guess,' he said, while they were helping themselves to the great bowl of shellfish, 'but when I was chatting to Claude today...'

Jim stopped, fork halfway to mouth. *Chatting to the servants!* How things had changed.

'...he said he'd heard the *Caramba*'s reported stolen.'

There was murmured surprise from Jane and Guy. Jeremy addressed the rest of his story to Jim: 'The owner told the police he wants it back and fast.'

Jim and Jane, the supposed hirers of the yacht, exchanged

mystified looks. Jeremy was delighted with the effect the story was having on them.

Guy liked it too but excluded Jane from culpability when he made his sour little joke. 'Better turn her in, Jim, lad.'

Jim gave a mischievous smile. 'Better talk to Claude first, I think. Let's hear exactly what it's all about.'

Normally one was allowed a dig of this sort at Jeremy because he was notorious for misinterpreting or confusing facts. But Guy didn't follow up with one of his pieces of barbed merriment. All he said was: 'If you really think so,' which was what he usually said when he disagreed. Jane said nothing.

Jeremy thought hard for a moment before telling Jim: 'I *think* he said he's home tonight.'

Jim walked along a shady forest path to Claude's house after supper. He was reluctant to disturb him as it was his day off duty and he'd already had a lonesome Jeremy looming over him as he tended his patch of garden. On the other hand, Jim thought it best to appear concerned about allegations that the boat had been taken from her berth illegally. To play it down would be peculiar.

Claude lived on the south of the island, in one of the old-fashioned gabled houses built of silvery wood and made fancy with fretwork. Jalousies hung over the windows. He was sitting outside, on his veranda. If he was bothered by a second intrusion that day, he didn't show it. In fact, Jim guessed he was enjoying stirring them up.

One of his cousins had called in the previous day and told him about the boat. Claude told Jim: 'He didn't say the name straight off, only said a man reported to the police his boat's gone. Then out it came, *Caramba*. And I thought, well, a strange thing is going on here.'

Jim said he'd tell the police he'd chartered the boat.

Claude said: 'And that's one other puzzling thing, Mr Rush. The owner told the police a man called him on the telephone to ask about trying out the boat because he was thinking of buying her. An Englishman, he said. Definitely English. He didn't say he'd hired her to an American.'

Jim agreed that was odd. He was annoyed with himself. Tricking the owner had been a prank but as the police were now involved that piece of recklessness might lead to enquiries that stretched far beyond his involvement with the yacht, as far perhaps as London and the hunt for the man who killed the railway official or the one who disguised himself as a millionaire orchid collector.

Claude laughed. 'That owner's putting in a big insurance claim for her, for sure.'

'Then I'm going to spoil it by taking her back.'

'You know, Mr Rush, the police don't expect to find her. They think the man sold her and wants the insurance payout too. Happens all the time in these waters. Piracy, they call it. Owner piracy.'

Claude's sly amusement gave Jim an idea. 'Claude, did you tell your cousin the boat's here?'

He folded his arms and shook his head slowly. 'No, Mr Rush. I don't tell anybody anything that goes on in this place. I guess that's what my job's all about.'

'Not even your cousin?'

'Not even him, not even though he *is* the police.'

Jim headed back along the inland path leading to the main house. Trees crowded him, sucked his energy, denied him light and breathing space. They were no longer the luxuriant protection of his outward journey. Instead they were a manifestation of the unpleasant way things were closing in on him. He cursed his foolishness in taking the boat, and just for a game, a game he'd played merely to test whether he could win.

There were ways out of his predicament but none perfect. If he paid a hiring fee, he'd satisfy Drew and Rooney who, being friends of the owner, presumably knew of the reported theft. He'd led them to believe he hired the boat. But to satisfy the owner he'd have to explain why his trial run had been extended; and although he was adept at plausible invention, Drew and Rooney knew the truth. She hadn't gone on a long voyage, or broken down or been delayed by bad weather or accident. He'd kept her, that was all.

Jim felt a panicky urge to break free. He'd fled New York for London and escaped from London to the paradise islands. However often and however far he ran, it was never enough. Restlessness, boredom, ambition got him into scrapes. He understood that but not at the moments when he was giving in to temptations that, sooner or later, led to disaster. He was cursed with optimism.

A slender path led away to his left. He ran down it, moving fast through the fading light, pushing past prehistoric ferns and hideous bulbous succulents. He hoped to burst out on to the cliff path, but could see nothing but trees, creepers and thick, thick, vegetation. Plants crowded him, leaning in on him, fat and warty plants, or spiky creations with flapping tendrils, or slippery smooth things. They were grotesque props for a horror film. And over them and through them wove the strangling vine.

He was suffocating, sweating, upset by his extreme

reaction to what was, so far, a minor setback. If the boat was a prelude to disaster, then the moment of truth was a long way off. He could accomplish much in that time, stave off catastrophe. He worried because it was unlike him to be nervy at the faintest hint of trouble. He was a taker of chances, a thriver on risks. Trouble was a challenge he took on and defeated every day of his life.

The path petered out in a clearing. This was where they dealt with the island's rubbish. St Elena seemed too smart for rubbish to have any place in the scheme of things. If he'd thought about it, he wouldn't have known what they did but here was the answer: bins with tight-clamped lids and a pit where fires were made. Blackened soil, scorched earth, a charred tree stump, it was a depressing place.

He fought his way through trees on the far side of the clearing, forcing a path where there was only a vestige. Creepers slapped at his face, roots conspired to trip him, and the cloying green dampness filled his head, his lungs, smothered him. But he didn't dream of retreat. He struggled on as though the solution to all his difficulties lay in this one, of breaking through jungle to air and light and safety.

Threads were snatched from his clothes. Good shoes were scuffed. His breathing grew jagged and painful, his hands bled as he grappled with impeding branches. But he refused to turn back. Once he stopped and rested his weight against a broad trunk, looking up high, higher, to a break of pale blue swaying above the treetops. Sweat was trickling down his body. He shivered and was afraid.

He was afraid he would die and afraid he would not. Sweat dripped from his hair and from his eyebrows. He wiped at his face with his shirt sleeve and the sleeve was

118

drenched. He shut his eyes. Jungle enveloped him, he was in its web. He heard its sounds. Spiders? Snakes? Which creatures inhabited the forest? What warnings had he been given? Were those warnings genuine or Guy's jokes, his island hazards? His brain burned.

Then he heard a different sound, a familiar much desired one. He heard the song of the sea, to his right. *To the right?* The left, surely. Possibly directly ahead but not to the right. How could it be to the right? Arguing, he battled towards it and within a minute or two the dense green was giving way to the colour of water.

Dazed, he looked down on pretty wooden gables, the servants' quarters. It took a moment for him to realise he'd circled. A breeze whipped his soaking shirt against his skin and dried his face and bleeding hands. There was enough light left for him to reach the main house at the other extremity of the island but it was an effort to do so. His limbs felt heavy. He trembled and was cold.

Jim was ill for two more days, angry that it was so. On the second the fever abated leaving him listless and weary. Jane had been solicitous but as medicine was to hand no one else was disturbed. Guy was too rapt in his own concerns to fuss about one of his guests being ill with a complaint that was familiar and of no consequence. Jeremy offered to keep out of the way and did, determined not to be infected.

On day one, which Jim later remembered only in a dim and patchy way, Jane begged him not to fret about the *Caramba* because she was going to explain to the police on his behalf. He tried to dissuade her but the words jammed. She put his anxiety down to delirium and told him to trust her, that everything was absolutely all right. Guy, she said, had quizzed Claude and everyone understood about the muddle. When Jim next opened his eyes the room was empty.

Next day, if in fact it *was* the next day, Jane was telling him she'd contacted the police officer interested in the fate of the boat. All was well and Jim needn't worry.

Jim worried.

He worried he was allowing matters to slip out of his grasp. Events were achieving a momentum he didn't like. He fell asleep worrying at it. When he awoke Jane was at his bedside and most of a day had drifted by. He was weak and anxious. He wanted to ask her precisely what she'd said to the policeman and what the man had replied. But he had the wit to realise how absurd it would be because who would care ordinarily?

On the third day, by which time he was virtually recovered, he sat alone on the terrace. For once its spacious solitude was comfortable. He wasn't up to sociability, and the bedroom, although a good size, had come to box him in like a prison cell.

A servant, not Claude, brought him a light snack and he sat there a long time eating not very much and wondering where energy went when it was gone and how he'd ever replace it. Then into his view between a pair of sentinel palms came a policeman.

Jim brushed aside the apology for intrusion and offered one of the cane chairs. The man sat heavily, pushed back his hat and stared at the house behind Jim. 'Nice,' he said.

'About the boat . . .' Jim had no wish to prolong the pleasantries. He wanted to be polite and apparently helpful but more than that he wanted the man gone.

'Yes, sir.' With reluctance the man stopped admiring the

house and looked at Jim. 'The young lady telephoned me. She said you hired that yacht and there's no question of her going missing.'

'She's moored at the dock down there right now.' He tilted his head in the direction, not knowing whether the police launch had moored alongside her or in one of the other bays.

'I know she is, sir, I saw her as I came by. Now the owner, he says she's gone. I talked to him again after the lady's phone call.' A smiling shake of the head pitied the owner's stupidity.

'I see.' If it was a straightforward matter of his word against the owner's, he was going to be believed. He was the one at the big house on the private island and therefore above suspicion.

The policeman fanned his face with his hat. He was overweight and had climbed a steep path. 'We have a few cases of this kind from time to time. I said to him, "We're wise to it, you know." But he wasn't ready to admit anything. Later he might but not yet.'

'Insurance fraud? You think that's it?'

'Sure to be. When there's a theft, they're supposed to report it to the police. When there's a make-believe theft, well fine, they'd better be careful to report that one too because if they don't the first thing the insurance people say is, "Hey, how come this man never told the law?" You see how it goes, Mr Rush?'

Jim looked disapproving. 'I'll return that boat tomorrow.'

'That's going to please him.' A smile underlined the irony.

'Maybe not but it's going to keep everybody else happy. No need for you to chase up here again, no hassle for me.' His air of finality had the policeman rising to his feet.

'I hope you get your cash back, Mr Rush, whatever's due to you for cutting the hiring short. Too bad if you got ripped off.'

Jim promised him: 'That won't happen.'

Guy flung himself down into the chair the policeman had vacated. 'Who was that *extraordinary* man?'

The answer was obvious unless Guy had truly forgotten what a police uniform looked like.

Jim said: 'As a matter of fact he's Claude's cousin.'

He said it because it wasn't the answer Guy was expecting. Guy wanted him to be apologetic about attracting the police to the island.

'Cousin? Well, they all call each other that, don't they? Doesn't mean a thing.'

Jim said that in this instance there probably was a close relationship. In spite of his extra weight the policeman had a look of Claude about him.

Guy assumed his most world-weary manner. 'One might as well have stayed in London if one's to have policemen running everywhere.'

He regarded Jim with distaste. His animosity had never been far beneath the surface, and since the jokey Guy had been swapped for the dour one, it was undisguised. Jim met his eye, unflinching. Then Guy dragged himself to his feet and went away.

As Guy had gone towards the house, Jim walked off in the opposite direction. He didn't particularly fancy going to the beach because he lacked energy for the climb back up but Jane was sunning herself there. He paused for a little to watch a humming-bird darting for nectar in a dazzling pink blossom. Colours were intense: feathers, flowerheads, foliage, sky, sea. Such brilliance was immoderate. Nature was putting excessive effort into everything she did. It demoralised him, that and the heat.

He looked down into the bay, the one where Guy forced them to play bounce. He remembered especially the day it ended in unusually prolonged argument, the day he'd swum out after the red ball and seen Drew and Rooney's boat. That was also the day Guy had embarked on his *Treasure Island* jokes.

Puzzled at the time, Jim knew now what had caused the argument that ruined the game: *he* had. By fumbling and dropping the ball instead of tossing it cleanly ashore he'd provided Guy with the opportunity to invoke an obscure rule. Lucinda, backed by Charles, had disputed the existence of the rule. Jeremy had thought it existed but didn't apply under those circumstances. Jane had supported Guy.

Later she'd relayed the argument to Jim because there was a sequel he was at a loss to understand. The point was Guy had triumphed and Lucinda was declared out, but Charles had appealed to a higher authority by telephoning Simeon, who by then had moved on from the Seychelles to Sydney. Simeon, who was credited with a greater understanding of the subtleties of bounce than anyone alive, declared the decision unfair and Guy at fault.

Guy had been only mildly discomfited by this rebuke from afar. It came when he was jovially yo, ho, ho-ing and chattering about pieces of eight. Since his lapse into unamusing spitefulness, he'd twice referred to it, putting the blame for the fiasco squarely on Jim because he was the person whose incompetence at throwing a ball had sparked off the whole affair. Jim had begun to wonder whether Guy was entirely sane.

Down below, Jane walked over the headland with Jeremy who, competing with gaudy Nature, had chosen to wear magenta and lime shorts. They had their heads bent together, giving the impression they were talking confidentially. She appeared to be speaking, then Jeremy, then Jane again.

Jim called out before they could spot him by chance and wonder whether he was spying. He realised it was like this all the time. He needed to be careful, defensive, not allow anyone the chance to fault his behaviour.

He met them on the path between the beach and the house. After asking how Jim was feeling, Jeremy scuttled away. It was unclear whether he thought he was tactfully leaving them alone or dodging germs.

Jim asked Jane to go with him next day when he returned the *Caramba*. She said yes, then guessed he wished to sail back in the *Mariposa* but Guy would forbid it.

'Don't worry, I'll speak to him, James.'

Guy resisted her at first, then softened. Immediately, to Jim's horror, Jeremy suggested he and Guy sail the *Mariposa* on the outward journey and they all return aboard her. Guy snatched at the idea. Beguiled out of his meanness by Jane, he was being presented with a way of ruining Jim's day all the same. That was how Jim saw it.

Fuming, Jim strode about the garden wishing all kinds of ill luck on Jeremy for his stupidity and on Guy for his malice. He worked off his anger on the murderous vine, ripping its tendrils from the shrub suffocating outside the library window. Jane sought him out. He put on a passable performance of a man looking forward to a day rearranged as her friends had rearranged it.

She wasn't fooled. 'Never mind, James. Tomorrow will be wonderful.'

He mustered a disbelieving smile. Eager to protect him, to patch up differences, to do her utmost to make life all right, she insisted: 'Honestly it will.' Then: 'Why don't you come up to the house now?'

'Because I've been stuck indoors for days. I need air, all this.' He gestured at sky, sea, garden, openness. She knew he was avoiding Guy.

'Well, don't leave it too long.' She kissed him quickly and was gone.

About an hour later he went inside. Jane was sitting on the side of their bed. In her hands was the gold cup.

She gave a nervous start as he came in. 'Oh! I was looking . . .' Explanation trailed away.

'In my bag.' The accusation was out, too fast for him to conceal his reaction. He hated people messing with his possessions, hated sharing bathrooms and cupboards, bedrooms too. His private space was sacrosanct to him, surely she appreciated that. And yet how could she when he said nothing of it, when he gritted his teeth and kept to himself the fact that he preferred aloneness, that often her very presence was maddening?

Jane's eyes twinkled. 'Actually *my* bag.'

'Oh. Yes.'

She'd loaned it to him. He owned only one and had needed a second.

She said: 'I've lost a note, a slip of paper with a friend's new address. I thought I might have left it in one of the pockets the last time I used the bag.'

He reached out for the cup. He wasn't interested in what excuse or explanation she was offering, the appalling truth was that she'd done this. Opened his drawer, delved into the bag allotted for his use, and unwrapped his secret.

Jane rose and moved to the window, not giving up the cup. 'What is this, James?'

His answer was a shrug although she wasn't looking his way. Like Guy with his question about the policeman, she was claiming not to know what was plain to see.

She didn't wait for him to speak. 'Where did you get it?'

Jim went to stand close to her, fighting down the compulsion to pluck the cup from her hands. In his head a voice was screaming: *It's mine. Mine, and it's going to change my life. I shall be rich, I shan't need your ridiculous friends, I shan't need anyone. I shall buy my freedom and do what I like.*

All he said, quite casually, was: 'It doesn't belong to me. I'm returning it to the owners tomorrow.'

'Yes, but . . .' She turned a shade towards him. Her elegant long fingers played over the gold surface. 'It's from a wreck, isn't it? Oh James, how exciting.'

He practically saw the next thought forming, watched her take the intuitive leap that had her blurting: 'Mike Rooney's found a wreck! I'm right, aren't I?'

Jim conceded with a nod but mocked her conviction. '*You* told me he was surveying for oil deposits, Jane.'

Rueful, she said: 'I know I did. That's what he said last year when we met him. But virtually everyone else has known for ages he's a wreck hunter. You remember that party I went to with the others? Well, a man there was talking about it.'

She broke off and studied him intently. 'James, did this really come from the wreck Rooney's found?'

He put an alternative question. 'Did your man at the party have doubts about Rooney and Drew?'

'Heaps. They've been trawling for investors, offering a share of the proceeds. No one was willing to play.'

Her voice dropped. 'James, are you deeply involved with this? Financially, I mean.'

'No. Why did no one want to play?'

'Because it was too much of a gamble. There was only Rooney's word he had a wreck and later there was a rumour that he'd found one but it was worthless. They say it's an old schooner, one of those high-sided schooners they used to build on Bequia for whaling. He's said to be using it to fleece investors who think they're going to raise treasure. Pieces like this.'

She held the cup up between them. Her eyes begged him: 'Tell me.'

Jim considered her, considered the risk. Then he said: 'What Rooney and Drew have is no schooner. It's more than possible this came from it and that there's more.'

Jane gave a little gasp. Her cheeks grew pink. When she spoke her voice was a conspiratorial whisper. 'Let's find out.'

She was smiling the smile he loved. He clasped his hands around hers. They stood there in silence, holding the cup between them.

He didn't tell her any more but she believed he did. He was adept at that, at letting people think he gave as well as took. By the time they found out, he'd moved on or situations had changed and different things mattered.

Jane was brimming with questions he dodged without

seeming to. He made her rewrap the cup and put it back where she'd found it. Next day, he said. It must be handed over to Rooney.

It interested him that Jane and the man she'd met at the party and, apparently, everyone else interested in the subject, referred to it as Rooney's hunt and Rooney's wreck. Mike Rooney was the talker but he was ineffective without Drew. Jim wished he could discount Drew as easily as others did because he found it easier to handle Rooney. But Drew was there, always there like the shadow on the far side of the moon.

The morning was everything he feared and worse. Only Jane made it bearable, creating diversions when he needed them and keeping Guy from needling him.

The *Caramba* was delivered to the barnacled jetty whence she came. The woman with the yellow and brown scarf twisted high on her head came out of her shack to watch. The man was working on his tatty launch again, fixing it with filler, so many places that it was becoming mottled. Nothing had changed in that quiet place, nothing ever did.

Jeremy recommended lunch at what he said was an especially fine restaurant, overlooking the port of an island Jim hadn't visited before. He'd avoided it, imagining gulches of hotels among sugar beaches or, like Martinique, a fragment of the Côte d'Azur that had floated out to sea. The empty coastline proved he was wrong, tourism wasn't dominant. Perhaps treacherous tides prevented that, as drowned holidaymakers did the industry no good. The harbour was excellent, though, the town bigger and better than most.

As they moored voices called them, half a dozen young men and women waved. Jim didn't recognise any of them but Jeremy said: 'Isn't that . . . ?'

And Jane said: 'Yes, it's Sarah.'

And Jeremy said: 'And isn't that . . . ?'

And Jane said: 'Yes, that's Roland.'

And so on.

And Guy said: 'How *incredible* to see them here.'

All the time they were hurrying towards them. Jim hung back but Jane waited for him and explained these were people they'd got to know at the party. New friends, she called them.

Jim dawdled as she sped on again. They'd be reminiscing, swapping stories, refreshing impressions of each other. As there was no place for him there, he preferred to stay on the outskirts.

'Hi there, Jim.'

A man stepped out of a shop doorway right beside him, an athletic Californian with greasy brown hair. For a split second Jim thought he'd been lying in wait, then realised the timing was coincidence. The shop sold equipment for aqua sports and in his hand Denny Witherspoon swung a pair of flippers.

Jim said hi and wasn't the weather great, and he looked around for Martin Peters. The previous time he'd seen Witherspoon, Peters was welcoming him at the airport.

'Is Martin with you?'

'No, he's busy being a journalist today and I have to get some equipment together.' He waggled the flippers.

Until this Jim had supposed him also to be a journalist. 'I had the idea you worked with him.'

'I'm a diver. He has a job for me but not yet. I guess I don't mind hanging around if one of his papers is picking up the tab. You have time for a beer?'

There was a bar within yards of where they stood. Witherspoon meant that one.

'Give me a couple of minutes.'

'Sure. See you over there, Jim.'

Witherspoon ambled to the bar while Jim caught up with Jane and her ever-growing band of friends. He told her he'd met someone he needed to speak to and would catch up with her at the restaurant.

'No, James, if it's to do with . . .' She was trying to say 'the wreck' without using a word that might give it away if she were overheard. They were standing on the edge of the group, there was a danger of being overheard if the laughter and talk fell away suddenly as simultaneous voices often do.

'Jane, it might be. I don't know yet. I have an idea, maybe it won't work out but . . .'

She looked crestfallen. 'I'd be in the way.'

'I honestly don't know.'

She understood him to mean he wasn't prepared to have her spoil it. She ran the tip of her tongue around her teeth then smiled up at him.

'Come to the restaurant if you can, James. Otherwise we'll meet at the boat later.'

He stroked her cheek. He wanted to tell her she was marvellous but he was conscious that several of her friends were watching, and that he should go immediately if he weren't to be caught up in introductions and excuses.

'Jane, what will you tell them?'

'That you met someone. They won't need more.'

He kissed her lightly and walked away so fast he was almost running.

Denny Witherspoon had two beers on the bar in front of him. They carried them over to a table in the shade and sat protected from the sun and the eyes of passers-by.

'Diving?' Jim went straight to the subject that interested him.

'Sure. It's what I love to do. You ever tried it, Jim?'

'A little. Surfing I love but diving not so much.'

Over a slowly sipped beer he learned all he needed to know about Denny Witherspoon and decided to make him an offer. Witherspoon was a type he recognised, an open, free and easy youngster who'd scraped through college and now meant to have the time of his life doing what *he* wanted. Chafing routines were left behind, he was opting for physical work and a modicum of excitement. It was a young man's life and he was going to live it to the full. The rest could wait.

When Jim asked him how he felt about doing a diving job for him while he was waiting for Martin Peters, Witherspoon said he'd enjoy that very much.

'Seems a shame to hang about doing nothing, Jim, a waste of a boat and all the gear.'

Jim encouraged him to believe Peters had told him everything about the arms trade story. Tricked, Witherspoon explained the rest. He said he was hired, by an American paper that Peters sold pictures to, to dive down and photograph dumped crates.

'We'll have information about the place and the time those crates go over the side of the ship. Then we get out there and I photograph them. The guys that come to collect, they come on the scene later so there's no

131

connection between them and the ship. They use sonar to locate the crates, then raise them and bring them ashore. Neat.'

'Neat.' Jim drained his glass and offered Witherspoon another. He was wondering whether the whole scenario wasn't too neat for Drew and Rooney. It was very hard to believe what Peters said about them, not that he doubted Peters' own faith in the story. Peters had heard it initially from an American journalist and had subsequently offered photographs of the drop to a rival magazine. Martin Peters believed and had convinced the magazine staff, but that didn't make it true.

When they left the bar Jim and Witherspoon went down to the boat that Witherspoon had hired. She was an average unobtrusive motor cruiser, nothing special or outstanding. Ideal, in fact, for Peters' purpose. Ideal for Jim Rush too.

'Tell me where and when,' Witherspoon said, spreading a chart on the table in the cabin.

Jim's eye went straight to the site of the *Gloriosa*, as supposed by Drew, Rooney and several published accounts. He put a finger on the place.

'OK,' said Witherspoon and replaced the fingertip with a faint pencil mark. 'And the timing?'

'Now?'

'Sure. Let's do it.'

Jim's heart lifted as the boat reached open water. After a terrible morning his luck had changed. Fate was taking a hand.

'Jim, time to ditch Guy and his jolly crew.'

'Certainly, Fate.'

'Here's a diver for you. Now you get him down on that wreck fast, Jim.'

'Right now, Fate.'

Denny Witherspoon held the throttle wide open and the boat surged over the water. She wasn't the speediest boat in the islands but, in a whimsical way, Jim fancied she seemed keen. He laughed aloud, for the sheer pleasure of racing across the brilliant water, for his great good luck in hiring Denny Witherspoon, for the hope that before he was much older he'd have his haul of treasure.

Witherspoon grinned back at him, then also burst into laughter. 'Can you think of one thing, one single thing, you'd rather be doing right now?'

'Not a thing.' True. For once it was absolutely true.

'Me neither.'

Witherspoon had pulled on a white cotton cap to anchor his hair. He tugged the brim down at a sly angle and urged the boat on.

They snaked between islands, passed cruise boats of snorkelling tourists, waved back at waving arms on a rusting island ferry, and shuddered through rough-water channels to cut distance and save time. By now Jim knew most of the routes because of Drew and Rooney's habit of varying their journey to protect the site of their wreck. He navigated while Witherspoon steered.

He took sight lines to determine when they were, more or less, above the wreck: the shape of a distant island mountain peak directly ahead and the craggy southern headland of an islet at forty-five degrees north-east. Witherspoon went over the side.

Jim lay back on the cabin roof and stared into blue infinity. The day enveloped him like warm velvet. He closed his eyes and enjoyed the dazzling colours swimming beneath his eyelids. Heat. Christopher Columbus believed heat meant gold. That's where he'd gone wrong, where the alchemists had slipped up. Gold and silver and precious stones, so they thought, were made by the action of the sun upon the earth. And Columbus, sailing from island to island, clung to the belief. He wrote his tragedy in the log of the *Santa Maria* as she lay off Cuba: 'On account of this heat there must be very important deposits of gold there.'

The waiting seemed interminable. Jim was patient, then anxious, then resigned, then convinced Witherspoon had come to grief in the embrace of an octopus. Eventually up came Witherspoon, to say yes he'd found her and to correct their position.

'She's a beauty, Jim. Good as anything I saw in Florida.'

He was glowing. There was none of that craftiness about the eyes that Rooney and Drew had when they talked about the wreck. Denny Witherspoon was a straight-forward guy doing a job he loved, and it showed.

Jim asked him: 'Is there any way you can identify her?'

That was the nub of it. She might be archaeologically wonderful but worth, to Jim, nothing whatsoever. Witherspoon had already mentioned archaeology. He'd last been employed on a properly run investigation of a wreck and knew it was equally as important as on land sites that finds were recorded before they were disturbed. He spoke of making a chart and marking the position of cannon, buckets and the rest of the paraphernalia they found, of allowing for the tilt when the ship went down and the shock to the hull when she hit the floor. His seriousness, though, hadn't prevented him bringing up a couple of pieces on that first dive: a dented metal plate he said was silver and a bronze pin.

Witherspoon said: 'I want to go down with the camera, Jim. Do we have time for that?'

'As long as you need.'

They didn't break off until the pull of the tides changed, signalling evening. Witherspoon flopped on the deck, exhilarated and exhausted.

'Jim, this has been one incredible day.'

He'd flippered his way around a smashed Spanish galleon. He'd photographed tumbled coral-encased timbers and virtually intact metal fittings. He'd seen men's bones and bronze cannon. He'd ignored the bones and photographed the exposed sections of several cannon, some toppled and one apparently in its original position although its wooden chocks were concealed by coral. He overflowed with information and enthusiasm.

Jim seldom interrupted except to clarify a point. He asked him about the cannon, especially the cannon. This was the only question the diver had trouble answering. Otherwise he was efficient, knowledgeable and keen. When Jim hired him he'd hired a bargain. He was taking a chance on the man's discretion but there was no reason for Witherspoon to gossip about what he'd seen. If word got around and other wreck hunters moved in, then among the people who'd lose by it would be Denny Witherspoon. He was already talking about the amount of work he'd like to do on the wreck: photographing it; recording the exact spots where items were found; logging finds as they were brought up; and assessing what work they could manage themselves and at what stage they'd need expert help. No, Denny Witherspoon wasn't going to jeopardise all that.

Jim pulled the rings on a couple of cans of beer from

Witherspoon's galley store. They were cruising away from the site now, had moved on immediately Witherspoon was back on board as there was no sense in lingering there like a marker buoy when they didn't need to. No boats had come near them all afternoon although a number had passed in the distance and were bound to have noticed them.

The sun was sliding down towards the horizon. Jim increased the boat's speed and headed for an island away to starboard, intending to make the journey as confusing as the outward one. Spray licked at his skin. Frigate birds came low over the water.

Witherspoon was ready to develop the film. He promised Polaroid slides in a few moments. His camera was a standard 35 mm fitted with an electronic flash and waterproof housing. The equipment was newer and more expensive than the stuff Jim had seen lying around on Drew and Rooney's boat.

'All I have to do,' Witherspoon explained, 'is drop the film in here.' He put it in a plastic box. 'I don't even have to time it, it's all automatic. A few minutes, that's all. Then you can see your cannon.'

'Technical wizardry.'

They stood and listened to the whirring within the box. Witherspoon was chirpily optimistic, Jim cautious. He'd once had a job in a photographer's shop in a dusty American town where all the films that came in were of weddings and cacti. It had taught him anyone could have a camera but hardly anyone had the eye of a photographer.

Jim spent the waiting time thinking about Rooney and Drew. Fate had kept them out of the way while he'd shown the wreck to another diver but they were certain to catch up with him soon. After all, he had their gold cup and they were waiting to hear whether his dealer contact in New York was prepared to sell the bounty they raised. And then there was the matter of the *Caramba* and what kind of story their friend, Jock, had told them. When he next met Drew and Rooney he'd have to pick his way carefully.

Of course, the wreck was no more theirs than it was his or any other individual's. Different governments had different attitudes to wrecks in their waters, but he didn't know what the local one might be or whether Rooney had bothered to find out. Nor did it matter as long as Denny Witherspoon's penchant for maritime archaeology was curbed. It would never do to have him sending in reports and seeking permissions. He'd have to be humoured but not unnecessarily indulged.

The whirring finished. Witherspoon opened the box. He uncoiled a strip of transparencies and held them up to the light.

'*Fast* wizardry,' he said as he invited Jim to look.

They were good, they were as clear as could be hoped for. There were cannon. Jim asked especially to see the shots of the cannon. Witherspoon snipped those from the roll and clipped them into plastic mounts. Looked at in the slide viewer, they were very good indeed. A cannon protruded from a mound of rubble. It was unmistakably a cannon and the shape of the insignia on it was plain. Spanish. He studied a second cannon. This one had been photographed from a more oblique angle because Witherspoon wanted to record its position. The insignia was the same one but vague. Jim popped another slide into the viewer and saw figures. He flicked from one to the other of the four cannon slides, back and forth. Insignia and figures leaped out at him.

So she was Spanish and she might be sixteenth-century. A sixteenth-century date on the cannon didn't prove her age, because cannon were switched from one ship to another. All it meant was that the possibility she was old enough to be the *Gloriosa* or the *Rosita* wasn't ruled out. If the cannon had been later, say eighteenth-century, there'd have been no hope as they couldn't have sunk with a ship two hundred years before they left the foundry.

Witherspoon was turning the plate over in his hands. 'Silver, I'm sure of it. If there's more of this . . .'

Jim interrupted. 'What's that pattern?'

The diver peered at the plate, angling it so that the marks caught the light. 'Letters. They don't make a word.' He rubbed at them with a thumb.

Taking the plate from him Jim agreed. No, they didn't make a word, not in English and not in Spanish. There were five letters, difficult to decipher because of the old-fashioned lettering and the way they were worn down. He tried to fit the word *Rosita* to them, knowing it was silly because ships weren't kitted out with silverware and didn't have their names on everything, and besides . . . A different thought stopped him. It cast him back to the archive in Seville. He tried out the letters as the initials of a Spanish name he knew. They fitted. They belonged to a man who would have used his own plate on board and marked it. They were the initials of an unfortunate captain whose vessel had been seized by English pirates, the captain of the *Rosita*.

He bit his lip to suppress his excitement. But Witherspoon wasn't looking at his face anyway, he was chattering about the plate and the cannon and the difficulties of identifying wrecks.

'If we can find her bell, Jim, we'll know for sure which wreck she is. That's foolproof, nobody can argue with that.'

But Jim had in his hand all the proof he needed. He hardly heard what Witherspoon was saying to him. He was off on one of those little journeys of the mind.

5

Drew heard the engine and came out on deck to wait for him. He stood there with the attitude of a cowboy in an old-fashioned western, looking for a fight.

Jim hardly had time to pay off the fisherman who'd brought him up to the hurricane harbour before Drew went on the attack. 'We thought we'd seen the last of you.'

There was movement behind him and Mike Rooney came up from the cabin. He looked enormously relieved. 'Jim, great to see you. How was the trip?'

'Fine but good to be back.'

Drew loomed over Jim, a great red creature exuding anger. 'Where's our cup? You went off with our cup.'

Jim raised a placating hand. 'I have it safe.'

The eyes screwed up until they were points of light, hard like mica. 'Safe with your fancy New York friends, you mean.'

Jim refused to rise. 'No, safe on St Elena. You'll have it back but not today.'

Drew snorted. Rooney said: 'Drew,' in a warning tone. Evidently they'd been arguing about the whereabouts of the cup and Jim Rush and whether they'd ever see either of them again.

Jim addressed his reply to Rooney. 'As you see, I don't have my own transport today. I spent a night with a friend and scrounged a lift this morning from a fisherman going this way.'

Drew snarled something sarcastic about it not being like the St Elena crowd to be roughing it. Rooney spoke over him, an anodyne remark about making coffee.

Jim responded to Drew anyway. It was no part of his plan to fall short of St Elena standards. Anything he'd achieved had been achieved because they believed he was a fully paid-up member of that rich men's club.

He said: 'I can't pretend I'd like to make a habit of hitching rides around the islands but plans went awry and this was the best I could do. I wanted to be here early, to be sure of catching you. The fisherman offered.'

It was too long, too involved, too apologetic. He wished he'd ignored Drew instead. That's what Guy or Jeremy would have done, except they'd never have put themselves in a defensive position.

The true story was that the *Mariposa* had sailed for home long before he returned from his outing with Denny Witherspoon. He'd spent the night on a boat beached in a secluded cove.

Rooney asked Drew to boil water for coffee. He had to insist before his partner withdrew to the cabin. Rooney apologised to Jim by rolling his eyes skywards. Jim accepted with a brushing-aside movement of his hand.

Jim said: 'Mike, I have encouraging news but I'll hold it until Drew's with us.' He spoke loudly enough for Drew to hear.

He went to the bows and peered down where the anchor

chain shimmered away through limpid blue. Rooney came to stand beside him. Jim said, very low: 'He didn't know you gave me the cup, did he?'

It was a guess based on Drew's fury. He wanted to wrongfoot Rooney before they opened the dealing. Today was the day they'd deal.

Rooney said: 'I can talk him round but it takes time. I didn't want to waste time. You had your deadline to get to New York . . .'

Jim nodded gravely. He was pleased Drew and Rooney were at odds again. Busy worrying about each other, they'd pay less attention to him than they ought.

When they were settled with their mugs of metallic coffee, and had been through that business of who took what sugar and how much milk, Jim told them about New York. The dealer was very interested, he said, and impressed with the quality of the gold cup. He looked from Rooney to Drew and back, gauging their expressions before he went on.

'What he says is he needs fuller information before he's prepared to talk figures. Your cup, for instance. It would be worth much more as part of a famous hoard. If the wreck yields sufficient pieces of that quality, it's certain to be a famous one. On the other hand, maybe that's the only real prize and the rest is scraps and coins.'

He gave them several minutes of this nebulous information, snippets remembered from his reading. While they absorbed it he studied their reactions. Rooney was the keener of the pair as he always had been. Drew rubbed a hand on his cheek, fiddled with an ear, fidgeted. Rooney was stock still, leaning forward, snatching up every crumb of encouragement. Jim injected enthusiasm into his voice.

He knew very well this was what Rooney was praying for, Jim's own enthusiasm.

In a while Rooney put the crucial question. Was Jim ready to put cash into searching the wreck?

Jim gave him an idle, lopsided, teasing smile. 'Oh sure,' he said.

He watched Rooney's left hand, the one that had been resting loosely on his thigh, form a fist, an involuntary salute to success. Rooney turned sideways to say to Drew: 'We're in business.'

Drew contrived a smile, a few words of agreement. Then: 'How are we going to split this?'

And so the wrangling began, with Drew immovable and Rooney shifting considerable distance to meet Jim's demands. They didn't settle anything. Jim preferred to break off and let them fight over it, with Rooney fearing he'd pull out if they weren't more compliant and Drew arguing parrot fashion that they'd done all the work so far and as Jim's involvement was to be less then so should his rewards. Drew mentioned more than once he'd paid the major share of the cost of the boat.

Jim invented a reason to be back on St Elena that morning and asked them to ferry him to the next island where he could take a boat the rest of the way. Rooney offered to go to St Elena but Jim persuaded him against it, saying that if he arrived with them explanations would be due, and the less said about their activities the safer.

As they weighed anchor, he asked how often they'd been out to the wreck in the past few days. There was a momentary awkwardness. Then Rooney said: 'We've been here for nearly a week now. Drew keeps tinkering with the engine.'

Drew was testy. 'It needs fixing. Mike thinks it's a hobby, he doesn't know about engines.'

'Nor me,' said Jim happily. 'I'm definitely a sail man.'

And he pictured the *Rosita*, her sails full set, flying ahead of the wind, one of the most beautiful vessels ever designed, a romantic dream that men still dreamed of.

Jim returned to St Elena. He loathed it, the place was a honeyed trap. Long gone were the days when it had been a haven, a respite from a harsh world. But however unkind Guy was, however tiresome the endless friends, he needed them. That was what irked, he needed them.

The *Mariposa* was in the harbour. He clambered over the headland into the bay below the house. Jane and Jeremy were sprawled on beach mats. It was Jeremy's day for blood-red shorts with green and white fish swimming across them. He was sprinkling sun oil on her back. Her bikini bra was undone.

Jim felt a surge of distaste, a deep-rooted puritan objection to their intimacy. He blamed himself. He neglected her, left her alone too much and didn't provide closeness when they were together. She hadn't appeared to mind, she'd seemed that way too. For the first time he wondered how fond Jeremy was of Jane, whether they'd pair off if he went away. He realised he'd never find out because once he parted company with her he'd hear no news of any of them again. When he left it would be a clean break.

This time he chose not to call out to them. They weren't talking confidentially, they were quiet except for the occasional question from Jeremy and murmured replies from Jane.

Suddenly Jeremy saw him. He dropped the bottle of oil

in agitation, then recovered with a greeting worthy of Guy. 'Ahoy there, Jim, lad.'

Jane twisted her head round, smiling her pleasure at his arrival. She made it all right. She always managed that. She said and did the appropriate things and smoothed away difficult situations when they'd barely arisen. He often noticed her doing it, not in a calculated way. It was simply Jane's instinct to make things easy. He didn't wonder that she was popular, that she courted and kept those hordes of friends. If Jeremy were a little in love with her he wouldn't be surprised, for who was not?

Jim sat with them on the beach for a while, Jane moving up a few inches for him to share her beach mat. He asked her what she'd do with herself if she could stay in the islands for ever and ever.

'Work on my suntan and watch the sun come up and the sun go down,' she said. Then she stretched languorously and kissed him.

He told her she ought to practise her sailing. 'You're better than you think. You lack only confidence.'

There was a hiatus. Then Jane said, in her lazy manner: 'Too athletic, you know. I'd much rather be crew than captain.'

Jeremy looked at Jim, doubt on his face. Then Jane said: 'James, why don't we sail together this afternoon? Guy's booked Jeremy to help him with something or other – well, yes, actually I do know but it's to be a secret so I have to pretend I don't.'

Jim smoothed her silken hair. 'That sounds as though I'm the only one on the island it's a secret from.'

She laughed. 'Yes, you are. Come to think of it, you are.'

Jeremy said: 'Oughtn't we to tell him, then? It seems a bit unfair, Jim lad being the only one.'

Jane pulled frowns and faces to indicate serious tussling with the problem. 'I'd like to tell but you know what Guy's like.'

Jim said: 'Oh, I'd hate to spoil one of his games.'

Jeremy asked how he'd guessed it was a game.

A servant came down from the house to say lunch was ready. They left the beach things where they were. Another servant would tidy up after them, would probably go to the trouble of finding the cap Jeremy had lost from the sun-oil bottle.

Hurrying ahead, Jane left Jim to keep pace with Jeremy who was telling him it was rotten bad luck he'd missed the lunch at the restaurant. Apparently the meal had come up to expectations and confirmed Jeremy's opinion of it as one of the best eating places in the islands.

Jim tried to get him to elaborate on the meal but Jeremy was keener on finding out where Jim had disappeared to. There wasn't, though, any word of regret that the crew of the *Mariposa* had marooned him. Jim made vague remarks about having bumped into a man he used to know and one thing having led to another.

Jeremy said: 'But surely Jane said you were working?' He managed to make the word pejorative.

With one of his sunnier smiles Jim reassured him. 'Oh, I don't think work features very much around here.'

'Gosh, no. Hardly.'

Jim was reflecting that Jeremy could have stepped straight out of the covers of an English boys' novel about boarding-school pranks. Frightfully easy to imagine the old fellow involved in midnight capers in the dorm. But perhaps not, it was just a cultivated vagueness, just an old-fashioned trick of speech, nothing more serious.

And then Jeremy said, with a curious switch to the tentative: 'Look, don't mind my asking this, Jim lad, but you do know about Janie and the boat, don't you? I mean it sounded a mite as though you didn't, and I thought . . .'

Jim's face confirmed he had no idea what Jeremy meant.

Jeremy did a bit of throat clearing. 'Well, the thing is, if Jane hasn't told you herself, and, I mean, if no one else has either, then perhaps it would be wrong of me to . . .'

'Jeremy, please. I haven't a clue what this is about.'

'That's what I thought. I'm sure you wouldn't be pushing her into all this sailing if you did.'

'Pushing her into . . . ?'

'She used to sail but gave it up because there was an accident. She got the most awful fright.'

Jim remembered her reluctance to take the *Mariposa* single handed in any but the smoothest waters. He asked Jeremy whether he knew exactly what had happened.

'Oh yes. She was sailing off the north Norfolk coast with a cousin. They capsized in a squall and he was washed away.'

'God, I had no idea.'

Having decided it was his duty to tell all, Jeremy told some more. He produced details, possibly inaccurate ones as he didn't claim to have been present at the tragedy or at the aftermath.

While he spoke, Jim was rerunning memories: Jane declining to go out when he sailed with another of her cousins off the Norfolk coast; Jane refusing to sail the *Mariposa* alone; Jane looking palely brave whenever a wind whipped up where there'd been none, and he'd sprung to the sails and been exhilarated by his chance to show mastery of the elements. Not only that, he'd exaggerated danger so he might demonstrate his expertise in controlling it. While he'd been showing off for her admiration, she'd been afraid.

They came to a halt part way up the path. Jeremy said: 'I hope you don't mind me telling you. I mean I hope that if you tell her I did that she won't mind either.'

Jim touched his arm. 'I'm glad you did.' And he couldn't stop himself adding: 'I wonder why no one else did.'

'She doesn't like a fuss, you know.'

'A *fuss*?' By now he was feeling unreasonably exasperated with Jane for allowing him to be unkind to her, and cross with himself for not having registered her unease and avoided situations that distressed her.

They went on up to lunch. Jim's head was full of the story of the boating tragedy. It was difficult to concentrate on the discussion about whether to join the new friends on a jaunt to watch cricket in Barbados. Jeremy admitted he'd prefer to go over for the racing and was reminded he hadn't enjoyed the last meeting. Then Guy made them drop Barbados sports in favour of a topic of his choosing. But Guy was being so cryptic that even Jeremy, who was supposed to be in on the secret, found him impossible to decipher.

Jane broke in and told Guy: 'James and I are sailing this afternoon. We'll keep out of your way until supper.'

Guy looked petulant. 'Supper?'

'A late supper, Guy. You have heaps to do, you can't possibly be ready before then.'

A servant brought more plates of food. After the interruption the conversation moved on and there was no further challenge to Jane's proposal, although resentment flickered across Guy's face when Jane led Jim away from the table once the meal was over. Guy and Jeremy remained behind plotting, which involved making sketches on napkins of fine sea island cotton.

In their bedroom, Jane pressed a finger to her lips to warn him walls had ears, and then went through a rapid mime to enquire whether they'd take the gold cup with them and return it to its owners. He said not, he didn't want them to know she was aware of its existence.

She was comically disappointed so he cheered her up by showing her the photographs of the wreck. All the slides had been mounted and he'd bought a small viewer in the port where he'd been marooned.

Jane gasped. 'Oh, that's fantastic. She really is a galleon, isn't she? And that bit, that's a cannon, surely?'

He nodded. 'She's good.'

'Did you take these?'

'No.' He told her about Denny Witherspoon, and that he was a secret too.

She reminded him with a sly look that she was adept at taking care of his secrets.

'I have a diver,' Jim said. 'He's called Denny Witherspoon. He's done this type of work before, up in Florida, and he takes pictures.'

He tossed the slides on to their cabin table in front of Drew and Rooney.

Drew flared: 'You've had some guy diving on our wreck?'

Rooney lowered his eyes from Jim's. His hand went for the slides.

Jim said, not raising his voice at all: 'It's free out there, Drew. Not your wreck, or mine or anyone else's.'

'We found her. Dammit, we searched all around for that wreck.' He turned to Rooney. 'Mike.'

Rooney was holding one slide after the other, not waiting for the viewer that Jim was offering. He gave Jim the shadow of a wink. 'It's good to see some action, Drew.'

'*Action?*'

'Yes, progress. Instead of sitting here with half the engine out and the tide coming and going and us being no nearer getting our hands on that gold.'

Jim stopped them wrangling by asking Rooney: 'What do you think of them?'

Rooney revealed a suspicion. 'Easier to read than the screen. Is that why you did this? Or to show someone else?'

'I can't read the screen the way you do. Also I wanted to test Denny Witherspoon before taking him on. He's OK, right?'

Drew had picked up the viewer and was slotting slides in and out of it, rapidly. He admitted they were fine.

Jim said: 'I want you both to meet Denny out there tomorrow.'

Drew shook his head. 'There may be a problem about tomorrow.'

'A pity. I've already set it up with Denny.'

Rooney said he was sure they could make it tomorrow. 'Where did he come from? I don't know the name.'

'No, he just got in. It was a lucky chance, running into him.'

Drew came up with another question. 'What's the deal with him?'

Jim explained he was paying the diver himself. 'For the

moment anyway. We may want to vary that later, but I had to make a quick decision before he was snapped up by someone else. The way he talks, he's not a guy who's ever short of work.'

Mike Rooney asked who he'd previously worked for. Jim recalled some of the names. Rooney said: 'Good outfits.' He didn't sound overjoyed about that.

'OK,' Jim said. 'I know what you're thinking, he's going to want to go by the book.'

'Archaeology.' Drew held his head, feigning pain.

Rooney shifted uncomfortably. 'Jim, I'm not going to say he isn't correct, strictly speaking correct, but we're going to lose that wreck if he starts reporting this and that.'

Jim shook his head, mocking Rooney's nervousness. 'Not his job, Mike. Let him take his photographs and write up his records and help us carry our treasure to the surface. But he doesn't send in any reports, *we* do.'

Rooney gave a whooping laugh of realisation.

Jim asked tongue in cheek: 'Do you want to take on that onerous task, Mike Rooney, or shall I?'

After the hilarity about the fate of any records Denny Witherspoon compiled, Jim spun the slides towards him and spread them out. Only a few showed details, the rest giving a general impression of small sections of the wreck and likely areas for investigation.

'Show me where you discovered the gold cup.'

He stepped back to allow either of them space to move round the table and select a photograph. There was a long and telling pause.

Jim timed it until he heard the faint intake of Rooney's breath and then he spoke first. He spoke with an icy intensity they hadn't discovered in him before.

'I don't believe it came from that wreck. Where did you get it?'

They kept up the pretence for a sentence or two but it was a feeble performance. They gabbled at once or they left embarrassing gaps. They disagreed about where and when and how the cup had been recovered. Jim was reminded of the day Rooney said they were surveying a telephone cable and Drew said it was a gas pipe. They were hopeless.

He gathered up the slides and viewer and put them back in his bag. They were watching his hands, watching him preparing to walk out of their lives and take with him their chance of money, not necessarily sunken treasure but the cash a rich man might pour into their venture. It disgusted him that they were so bad at it. If they were going to set up a scam they should be able to do it better than this.

Rooney said unsteadily: 'Jim, the cup.'

He pretended to misunderstand. 'My guess is it's the spoils of your adventures in Florida.'

Drew positioned himself between Jim and the exit. He was big and florid and breathing heavily. He blocked the stairway. 'You've got our cup, Jim.'

Jim nodded. 'Expenses? Insurance?'

Drew dropped a hand on Jim's shoulder, fingers grinding into bone. Rooney was nothing like quick enough. He shouted at Drew not to be an idiot but it was too late, Drew had hold of Jim and was pressing against his throat.

Jim kept cool and let Rooney handle it. There was no room for fancy footwork or sweeping movement and whatever he did himself Drew would continue to block the exit. So he let Rooney cope. Rooney smashed his fist down on Drew's arm, slackening the hold.

'Christ, Drew,' he said. '*Christ*. He's got the cup. What are you trying to do? Make sure we never see it again? What the hell's got into you?'

Rooney apologised to Jim in his usual way, with gestures and much pulling of faces to remark on Drew's stupidity. Drew swore and crashed up the steps to the deck.

Rooney slumped on to the seat with a groan. 'Christ.' And after a minute's silent misery: 'What are you going to do?'

Jim cocked his head in the direction of Drew. 'About that clown? Call the police?'

Laughter helped. When Rooney sobered he said: 'Jim, it's been a bad business but . . .'

'You want your gold cup back. I got the message.'

'I was going to say that's still the wreck of a Spanish galleon out there. Gold cup or no gold cup, she's worth the game.'

Jim looked hard at him for thirty seconds and made it feel longer. Then he slowly put his bag on the table and sat down opposite Rooney.

Denny Witherspoon brought up a number of modest artifacts from the galleon, some so encrusted that Jim was sceptical about his identification but others in remarkably clean condition.

'They could have been dumped there yesterday.'

Witherspoon enjoyed telling him how various materials survived in those waters. Coral loved wrecks and covered the spars, growing at a rate in excess of three inches a year in some of the warmest waters of the Caribbean. But some things, such as bronze cannon, ballast stones and anchors, remained uncovered and untarnished. So forth.

Then he said: 'There's something that might be a box, Jim, right down in the hold.'

Inwardly Jim shuddered at the notion of anyone penetrating the wreck as far as that. 'What's it made of?' Much of what had once been wood was now covered in inches of coral.

But Witherspoon said: 'I'd say wood reinforced with metal, but that's a guess based on a metal-bound chest they raised in Florida. Judging by the bit I can see, this thing has the same kind of dimensions. But I can't actually see too much, most of it's embedded in sand. It obviously hasn't been lying like that for hundreds of years, must have been partially uncovered when the wreck shifted.'

'Is it possible to dig it out?'

'Not impossible, but the one wooden panel I can see has a fair bit of teredo. It's going to be fragile. And supposing we *can* dig it out, then if we raise that beauty it has to have tender loving care, otherwise all we'll have is dust.'

'Plus the contents.'

'Sure, if there are any.'

Jim asked whether it was possible to open the box.

'Hell, no,' said Witherspoon. 'I told you, it's only that end that's exposed. If you start pulling it about you're going to do damage.'

They popped that day's film into the plastic box and listened to whirring wizardry. Within minutes they had slides of a dubious smudge he said showed the top part of the end of the chest. He was apologetic that the shots were poor, although it was a tribute to his skill and persistence that he'd got them at all. With a leap of faith, Jim accepted he was looking at a misty box-like shape peeping from a confusion of sloping sections of interior fittings that had collapsed, such as cabin panelling, bulkhead battens or stanchions.

Witherspoon said the shock wave when she hit the bottom caused much of that damage, but he pointed out signs of more recent disturbance. However it had come about, the present situation was that there was a more or less negotiable passageway leading to the chest.

Misleading, as photographs often are, the slides gave no hint of the difficulty of access to that area of the wreck. Witherspoon had stressed the problems of squeezing through cavities and feeling his way around. Jim didn't think it significant Rooney and Drew had failed to get in there.

Later, on St Elena, he was looking through the slides again himself when Jane came in to shower and change before supper.

'More?'

He enjoyed her excitement as she clattered them in and out of the slide viewer but she made nothing of the one that was supposed to show the putative chest and he had to point it out. Then she said: 'Wonderful!'

'It may be nothing.'

'Nonsense, James. That's straight out of *Treasure Island*. All we want is Long John Silver to come yo, ho, ho-ing on to the scene and it will be perfect.'

She pretended to search the other shots for a glimpse of Long John Silver. 'No, not even Guy yo, ho, ho-ing.'

He narrowly avoided saying thank God for that.

Then she asked: 'What can *I* do? Repel boarders while you dive down and raise the treasure chest, you and the intrepid Witherspoon?'

'The intrepid Witherspoon tells me it's riddled with worm and has to be dug out, preferably by blasting away the surrounding material with water jets. We don't have the equipment.'

'Oh, that's a shame.' She swung her legs off the bed and stretched, then strolled towards the bathroom loosening the ties on the wrap she wore over her swimming costume.

That evening Guy continued to be engrossed in his mysterious plans although it was openly acknowledged that the only person not in on the secret was Jim. Tempted to point out the folly of a game with only one player, he desisted because he'd been mocked too frequently for missing the point of Guy's games. As usual he felt isolated in the midst of their camaraderie.

Then, when supper was nearly at an end, he learned there were actually going to be plenty of players. Half a dozen new friends, who'd been at the party and later the restaurant, were coming to stay for a week and were bringing their friends with them. No wonder Guy had cheered up. He was about to become captain of the biggest jolly band he'd ever skippered.

In the morning Jim and Denny Witherspoon went out to the wreck again. The weather was duller and more blowy than they'd become used to, not ideal for them. The diver went down a couple of times and returned with a fork he hoped was silver, a small bronze lamp that had proved heavy for its size, and a porcelain bowl. They weren't discovered near what he now confidently called the chest. He resisted disturbing that, he said.

Jim was tiring of this high-mindedness. If they didn't get what they could out of the wreck, they might as well save their energy. The trouble was that Witherspoon was being paid wages and not a share of the haul. He could afford to entertain lofty ideas about archaeology and historical perspectives. Jim chafed but said nothing to upset him. Witherspoon was the best thing he had. He'd found a possible chest and was squirrelling around down there for other bits and pieces. When they took a break Jim warned him off mentioning the chest to Drew or Rooney.

'The point is, Denny, they might be too keen to get inside it.'

'Oh. Right. Impatient, I guess.'

'They've been at this a while. It's safer to say nothing about the chest for now. We'll show them the rest but not the pictures of the chest. OK?'

Witherspoon agreed, then asked what would happen when Rooney or Drew dived down with him as planned.

Jim said: 'You don't go near the chest, that's all. Don't go through that gap you told me about. Concentrate on the area where you found the fork and the bowl.'

Denny Witherspoon said that was wise because where there'd been one fork and one bowl there'd probably be more of the same. He repeated this when Rooney and Drew came out to the site and he was showing off the results of the morning's work.

Whatever Rooney's misgivings, he appeared to welcome the newcomer to the team. Drew observed Witherspoon and suspended judgment.

Witherspoon was keen to get back to work. 'Who's coming down with me?'

Mike Rooney went. A terrible silence settled over the

boat once Jim and Drew were left there together. Witherspoon's cruiser was swinging on its anchor a few yards away, otherwise there was a feeling that everything had come to a halt.

All they brought up that time was an amorphous lump that had caught Rooney's eye but turned out on inspection to be no more important than a cluster of coral and shells. He would have tossed it over the side except that Witherspoon said you never knew, when an expert put that beneath one of those fancy machines it might prove to have a ring or a coin right in the centre.

Rooney laughed that off as unjustified optimism. 'This one's pure paperweight through and through, Denny.' But he kept it anyway.

Rooney had done badly in his deal with Jim Rush. He hadn't been handed a blank cheque to pay for divers and equipment, which is what he'd initially pressed for. Nor had he been promised tranches of money as they became necessary, which is what he'd later angled for. Jim was paying for things, such as Denny Witherspoon's wages, but Jim was holding the purse strings. The revised deal gave Jim half of the proceeds, the rest to be shared between Drew and Rooney as they saw fit.

Drew didn't learn the details of these new arrangements until several days after Rooney and Witherspoon began to dive on the wreck together. Mike Rooney had misled him, and for reasons Jim well understood. If Rooney hadn't given in to Jim's demands then he had no deal of any sort, no money. Rooney, Jim believed, had capitulated too quickly again, an indication that he still intended to cheat him.

It was a game, a battle of wits, a contest in which the prize could be enormous financial gain or could be only the satisfaction of beating the other player. Mike Rooney was a player. He was seriously handicapped by Drew. Drew was the mechanic, the man who made the nuts and bolts work. His dream of paradise was a house on the Costa del Sol, not risking life and limb on a Caribbean treasure hunt.

Rooney was gambling on more than sunken treasure, and on fleecing an investor in dreams. He was also gambling on Drew. How long could he keep him interested? How well could he stifle his objections? How could he convince him it mattered not a jot what unfavourable deals were struck with Jim Rush, because Jim Rush wasn't going to collect?

Jim could practically hear Rooney arguing with Drew, talking him round, could calculate most of what he'd said. He wondered how long it would be before Rooney failed. And what would happen then? Would Drew leave with the boat and its invaluable gear? Or would Rooney take it on and expect Jim to buy Drew out?

Jim thought ahead, looking for the likely twists and turns in the game and preparing for them. He always relished this part of an adventure.

A pattern was emerging. Jim and Denny Witherspoon would go out very early to the wreck and Witherspoon would explore it before Drew and Rooney arrived. Witherspoon used this time to dig out the chest by hand, slow work as he was painstaking about not causing damage. As soon as they were all together they'd have a coffee break. Jim had upgraded the galley of the old fishing boat from jars of instant to tins of Colombian ground. Usually it was Drew who made it, although with a smirk that made it plain he refused to admit Jim had instituted a change for the better. After coffee, Rooney and Witherspoon would dive together. Sometimes Witherspoon took Jim back to St Elena, sometimes Rooney and Drew set him down where he could pick up a boat the rest of the way.

The finds made while Jim and Witherspoon were alone were handed over to the others and kept on the fishing boat. As Jim could hardly step ashore at St Elena in the evenings burdened with them, he had no choice about letting Rooney and Drew store them. He held back a couple of pieces, a chain Jane might like and the silver plate bearing the initials of the luckless captain of the *Rosita*. The chest remained undisturbed, with Rooney and Drew unaware of its existence, Witherspoon believing expert advice was being sought about ways of handling it, and Jim fearing he knew what he must do but afraid to do it.

One afternoon, when rags of cloud were blowing up from the east, Rooney and Witherspoon broke off early and went in search of extra tackle to raise the cannon. Drew was to take Jim ashore and they were all to meet later in the Green Parrot bar at the harbour where Witherspoon usually moored.

This was the day Jim returned the gold cup. Drew had kept on about it. If he hadn't done so Jim would have given it back sooner. He'd used up a number of excuses but that day he'd decided the time had come to return it. Drew had looked it over closely, perhaps fearing Jim had prised out one of the stones. Then he'd wrapped it up and stowed it in the locker it had come from weeks earlier. He did it with the air of a man who wished he could secure the locker too but it wasn't that kind.

As the boat carrying the others receded into the distance,

Drew, instead of starting up the engine, flicked on the scanner. The outlines of the wreck took shape on the screen.

'Tempted to go down, Drew?' Jim asked.

Drew said: 'Why are you doing this?' His eyes were on the screen. There were pale shapes and dark shapes, tilted things and fallen things. They both knew the images by heart.

Jim waited for Drew to make himself clearer. A light wind whipped at his shirt. He picked up his jacket and put it on.

Drew said: 'That's what I want to know, Jim. Why are you doing this?'

'What do you want me to say, Drew? The thrill of the chase?'

'That's not the *Gloriosa* down there. I warned you, months back. Mike, he wants to believe it is, so for Mike it's become the *Gloriosa*. But that doesn't make it true. You know it isn't true.'

Despite Drew's cold accusing tone, Jim kept his own voice light as he asked him to explain.

Drew said 'Even Mike's going to have to accept it one day, something's going to come up that makes it plain even to him. She isn't big enough, but he won't see it. We've got her dimensions and whatever's lying down below us doesn't fit.'

'Denny took photographs . . .'

'Yes, a date that puts the cannon in the right century. The pictures weren't all that great either, maybe it *isn't* the right century.'

Impatient, Jim said they'd know about that soon enough once one of the cannon was raised. Drew asked what he proposed to do when the day came that it was proved it wasn't the ship they wanted it to be.

'Are you going to pull out or carry on as though it's all the same?'

Jim started to say they'd all have to discuss that but Drew cut him off by saying they should also discuss Jim's New York dealer friend and whether he existed.

He swung away from the console, thrusting his fiercely red face at Jim. 'You didn't go to New York. Denny Witherspoon saw you at the airport, he knows what flight you came in on.'

Before Jim could refute it, Drew was moving towards him, making him back out of the wheelhouse. Drew was saying: 'You went on holiday with that girlfriend of yours but you spun us a story about taking our cup to New York, and how your friend was a dealer who was going to sell what we salvaged.'

He kept moving towards Jim, shouting. Jim retreated, knowing there was barely room for retreat but not seeing how he could defend himself either. Drew was heavier than him and strong. He remembered the grip of the hand on his shoulder, the force against his windpipe. If Drew got a hold this time, there was no Mike Rooney to call him off.

The deck was littered with wetsuits and ropes. He stumbled. Then Drew had him, throwing him down, kneeling on him, punching his head. Jim butted, summoned the strength of a man in fear for his life and broke free. He fled to the cabin. It was a stupid move, dashing into a cramped cul-de-sac that was immediately blocked by Drew's bulk. Jim ripped open a drawer, desperate for a weapon, a kitchen knife, scissors, anything. His hand closed on a gun. He raised it, not knowing whether it was loaded or empty. He saw the red blur of Drew coming for him, saw the tremor of his own arm with the gun whipping foolishly at the end of it. And then he knew the gun was loaded because he saw Drew check.

Jim pulled the trigger.

The sound was tremendous. It bounced around the cabin and reverberated on and on in his skull. Afterwards there was a peculiar silence, an aloneness.

Seconds later he was on deck, not knowing how he'd arrived there because Drew's body had collapsed against the companionway. In panic he'd clambered over it without being aware.

He looked around. A cruise liner threaded the horizon. A small aeroplane was island-hopping from one snippet of paradise to another. A flock of birds arced over a purple reef. Peace.

Jim wanted Drew up on deck so he could clean the cabin. He didn't know where the shot hit him, whether blood had spurted and spattered, how much there was to do. He squeezed past the body and into the cabin. The red stain was on Drew's shirt front. Jim aligned the body ready to haul it up the stairs. Then he had to get past it again. He squatted at the top of the flight and worked his hands under Drew's armpits. Overbalancing, he hung perilously and let the body slump. Drew was far too heavy but he could think of no other method. The stairway was too narrow for any manoeuvres. Jim crouched there, renewed his grip and pulled.

He humped the body up what he guessed was the height of one step and attempted to rest it there but it would not. The steps were too steep, too ladder-like, for the feet to perch. Also, Drew was on his back and his feet pointed the wrong way, into the cabin instead of towards the steps. The body dragged Jim forward. He let it sag.

For a minute or two he sat thinking it over, devoid of inspiration. The space was too small and the body too big. An idea came to him but he thrust it away. It appalled him, he couldn't do it. When no other idea came he tried once more to drag Drew up by his armpits. Again he failed. Then he attempted the appalling thing.

He stripped off his clothes, put on one of the wetsuits, and climbed over the body. Standing at the bottom of the steps and facing Drew he wrapped his arms around the body, lifted it and mounted one step. He did this again and again. Drew's blood smeared the wetsuit. It stank in Jim's nostrils with the sickening sweetness of warm fresh blood. Jim's stomach churned. He clamped his mouth shut and forced himself on because what he was doing was what had to be done.

The face that was red as an overblown rose lolled above him. The angry ginger hair flopped like the mop of a rag doll. Drew oozed blood and sweat and urine and faeces. Waves of it rose as the body was shoved and hoisted. Clothes soiled at the moment of death were rubbed against the stairway and against Jim's wetsuit.

He felt the stickiness of blood against his cheek and a dampness, that might have been either his own sweat or more of Drew's blood, in his hair. He was desperate to break off, to gulp clean air and give his muscles respite. But he resisted for fear he'd never steel himself to do this thing again. There was no other way. He shut his eyes against the horror and he heaved the body up the next step.

Jim opened them when a cool breeze slapped at his face. He was almost there. With a final flourish of energy he forced Drew up a few more inches and let him crash back on to the deck, slack face staring at a cloud-flecked sky and legs dangling down the stairwell. Jim crawled over him and dragged him clear of the stairs.

Fetching a rug from the cabin, he covered the body. He couldn't bear the sight of it. Then he sprang over the side and washed himself, rubbing all over the wetsuit, all over his face and hair, scrubbing and tearing at himself and imagining he stained the sea with the violence of sunset.

When he felt as clean as he might, which wasn't totally clean because he believed he'd never feel truly clean again, he scrambled back on board and took a bucket and a rag and swabbed down the cabin where there were suspicious marks, several that he had made when he went for the rug; and he washed over the stairs and the hand rails and swilled the deck where his own bloodied feet had left a trail. Satisfied there were no more marks, he raised another bucket of water and washed it all again.

After that Jim sat on deck and examined the gun. He'd expected to find the bullet when he'd washed the deck because he'd fired up at Drew, but either it had flown out to sea or it was in the body. He broke off to turn the body over and look for an exit wound but the clothes were now so stained and damaged he couldn't be sure what he was looking at. Sickened he replaced the tartan shroud and returned to the gun.

It was a Walther, a model issued to some European police forces. There were two more bullets in the magazine. He considered emptying it but decided against it, although he made sure it was no longer cocked as it had been when he'd grabbed it from the drawer.

Jim wiped the gun and put it in his bag. Then he looked at

his clothes. His jeans and his shoes were definitely stained with blood, so were his jacket and shirt. After washing blood out of the garments and spreading them to dry, he scrubbed at the shoes and excised traces of red from the seams and welt. What blood remained was invisible to the naked eye.

Since the killing he'd been compulsively busy. Now he stopped and took stock. There were no aircraft puttering across the sky, no boats near. He couldn't guarantee no one had watched him through binoculars or a telescope from one of the islands, but if somebody had, what might they have seen? A young man scrabbling about low down on the deck of an old fishing boat, humping something heavy and diving overboard to cool off. The shooting had taken place out of sight. Perhaps a persistent snooper had seen Drew chase him into the cabin and was wondering why the big man hadn't reappeared. But that was less damning than having seen him shoot Drew.

He hadn't needed to shoot. He knew he'd pulled the trigger after the threat to his own safety was over. It had ended at the instant Drew saw the gun. Drew had stopped his attack because he'd known it was loaded. Shooting him had been gratuitous, deliberate and avoidable. The realisation surprised Jim but he didn't try to twist the facts to form a more comfortable reality. He disliked violence, thought it a crude means of achieving an end or pursuing an argument. He despised violent people. Yet he'd pulled the trigger.

Jim anchored his drying clothes to prevent a gusting wind carrying them into the sea. Then he went into the cabin, into the further section where Drew and Rooney slept. He searched through Drew's possessions.

Drew, he learned, was the man's first name. Although he was only ever referred to by that monosyllable, officially he was Andrew Bennet. Had been Andrew Bennet. There was one address in a town in the Thames Valley, an hour's drive from London, and another in Spain. Jim sat on the bunk and read papers and a colour brochure touting villas overlooking an Andalusian beach. The Costa del Sol. Jim wondered how close to the villas he and Jane had driven on their sunshine trail along the coast road. Quite possibly very close because it resembled a number of places they'd seen and he, mainly for the sake of agreeing with her, had scorned.

He was delaying. There was something else he ought to do but was afraid to do. Putting it out of his mind, he continued to poke around among Drew's things. He couldn't have said what he was looking for exactly, except that he felt compelled to learn about the fierce, difficult and obstructive man who'd stood once too often between him and the treasure of the galleon.

Jim collected the gold cup from its locker and put it in his bag. Then he bullied himself to go down to the wreck.

He loathed every second, only sheer necessity kept him at it. After strapping on the equipment he'd frequently helped Denny Witherspoon don, he plunged down to the seabed. From the diver's photographs and descriptions he knew where to head and what to anticipate on the way. The water was clear. He saw creatures sidle away from him more scared than he was but there were none of the octopuses that horrified him most or the sharks he feared might have tasted blood. Once he'd swum in under the wreck he had to keep going because if he cried off he'd lose a unique chance. In future he'd be accompanied by Witherspoon or Rooney.

At the narrow gap between fallen timbers transformed into slabs of coral, he wriggled his way inside. With Witherspoon's description of the layout in his head, he struggled down a passageway as inviting as the entrance to a megalithic passage tomb. His lamp illuminated ghastly shapes, most of them innocuous when he reached them although he noticed the bones of a human skeleton. At last he came to the chest.

Jim was terrified. Trapped in a ship that was already a grave, he thought he'd go mad if he couldn't have space and fresh air *immediately*. But there in front of him was the chest, the mystery at the centre of the mysteries, the justification for his days in Spain, his game with Rooney and his murder of Drew.

Witherspoon had talked about wood bound with metal but that was experience or guesswork talking. It looked different from the photographs because one of the diver's daily tasks was to dig around it, free it. Now it appeared more promising, an end of it was about two thirds exposed, protruding from a mound. All at once Jim understood what Witherspoon meant. There *were* bands of a different colour, a pattern that suggested the strong kind of chest valuables used to be transported in. The men who packed it had meant to carry it on a month's journey across the oceans but here it was, hundreds of feet below the surface of the sea.

The thought of all that depth of water brought on another attack of panic. *Out*. He must get out. But first . . . He secured the lamp to his belt and unclipped the hammer.

His first blow loosened the surface where he struck the

wooden panel between the metal bands. Witherspoon had warned there was worm, teredo he called it, and that the wood might turn to dust when it reached the air but he seemed to have been unduly pessimistic about its fragility. Jim struck repeatedly, his blows ineffective.

Then it happened. Water clouded. It swirled darkly towards him, stirred by his movements. Particles were breaking free, the centuries-old fabric disintegrating. The cloud enveloped him. His lamp seemed to dim. He swam forward for another assault but before he could strike there was a rumbling sound. No, not a sound, it was more like a tremor. And then he was lost in a dark soup. He turned around to face what he prayed was the right direction and began a blundering exit, crashing into shapes that had formed the passage to the tomb on his way in but were now sentinels to frustrate his escape.

His brain was screaming. The blindness was nightmarish, the worst experience he'd ever endured. Every nerve begged to be released, either by transportation to the surface or by death. He didn't care which.

He went on, a staggering progress that could hardly be called swimming. When gradually his lamp began to show the way, he was too shocked to trust it and continued to grope and bump into obstructions, and not notice when coral grated his skin and sea creatures glided smoothly from him.

At long last light. He was in the light and knew it. He came out from beneath the wreck and kicked himself to the surface and bobbed there, debilitated, relieved, ashamed of his fear, and glad after all to be alive.

In a few minutes he heaved himself on board the boat and fell on deck, physically and emotionally shattered. He spared only a glance for Drew's body stretched out a few feet away beneath its tartan rug. All he could think was that he'd dared the intolerable thing and had survived, and it need never be done again.

He was already rehearsing how to respond on the day Denny Witherspoon flippered his way to the surface with the shocking announcement that the chest had suffered damage. Jim decided to say that under these new circumstances they must rifle the contents. That's what his orders would be and Witherspoon would have no high-minded argument to counter them.

When his palpitating heart had calmed and the dying sun was setting the horizon afire, Jim rose and collected his clothes. They were dry. He was about to change out of the wetsuit but spotted just in time it would be a mistake. He had yet to dispose of Drew's body, another messy job.

He switched on the engine, the deep throbbing engine on which Drew had lavished his attention, and he set out on a loop around an uninhabited islet, no more than a scrabble of seawrack and rock veiled in dusk. When he was a good way off he toppled Drew's body over the side. The current, always pronounced there, was reinforced by a harrying wind. The body would be carried out into the ocean, far away from land – or else the sharks would come for it. A mile later, having used it to clean questionable marks off the deck, he threw the rug away too. Then he pulled the knob to cut the flow of fuel and stopped the engine before jumping over the side. After another cleansing dip he changed into his ordinary clothes.

Jim expected to be in the harbour well before Witherspoon and Rooney. He was. He moored near the far end of the quay, the boat conveniently obscured by others.

For fifteen minutes he stayed on board, breathing the spicy scents of the island and keeping watch in case Witherspoon's cruiser was coming into harbour. His luck continued to hold. There was no sign of it.

Jim walked down to the quayside bar, the Green Parrot, to wait as arranged. As he went in, he looked all around and then asked the barman where Drew was.

'He said he'd wait for me here.'

'Haven't seen him today, not at all.'

'The guy with red hair. Big guy.'

'Sure, I know Drew but he hasn't been in today.'

Jim seemed at a loss. He shrugged. 'Well, I guess it's a lonesome drink for me until he shows up.'

The barman poured rum and lime. Jim stayed for a few words, about the fishing and the warning of a change in the weather, and then carried his glass over to a table where he could look out for anyone going down the quay. In this way he kept up the pretence of seeking Drew but didn't mention him again.

The harbour, with the lights of the boats and the houses on the hill above it, had a festive air. A fisherman was singing to himself as he pottered about on the quayside. From a window came the persuasive rhythm of soca, probably a radio but you were free to pretend it was live. Points of light that scattered the water became glittering script as an anchor was dropped or a dinghy was paddled or a bird skimmed the surface. Rigging tinkled like benediction bells. It was a perfect evening except that Drew was dead and Jim Rush wasn't at all sure he was going to get away with it.

6

Mike Rooney and Denny Witherspoon walked into the Green Parrot weary but pleased. Rooney stuck a thumb in the air as he greeted Jim.

'Got it! We could raise the *Titanic* with this gear.'

Jim gave him his ironic smile. 'That's next year's project, Mike.'

Witherspoon went direct to the bar and ordered drinks and food for himself and Rooney. He looked over his shoulder. 'How about you and Drew, Jim?'

Jim indicated his half-full glass. 'I'm fine, thanks, Denny. I ate a while back. Don't know about Drew, I'm waiting on him.'

Rooney pulled out a chair next to Jim. 'Where's he gone, then?'

Jim said he didn't know, that Drew had left the boat as soon as they arrived. 'He was in a hurry to go someplace or do something. He left me tying up. We said we'd meet in here but he didn't show. And the guy behind the bar hasn't seen him either.'

'How long ago did you get in?'

'Two and a half hours, going on that way.'

Rooney's frown deepened. 'Didn't he say where he was going?'

Jim shook his head. 'No, and I didn't feel invited to ask questions.'

Rooney pulled a face, a comment that this was typical of Drew's uncivil behaviour.

Witherspoon carried over the drinks. 'Food will be right along, Mike. Chicken. OK? They don't have a great selection here.'

He sat opposite Jim. 'Did you have the chicken? Was it edible?'

Rooney was asking Jim: 'You've checked the other bars?'

'That was all I could do. That and keep a watch for him walking back to the boat.'

Witherspoon caught on. 'Hey, are you saying we've lost Drew? I thought he must be in the men's room or on the phone or something.'

Jim told him what he'd told Rooney. He kept it very simple: Drew had left the boat before he did and had made for an unstated destination; they were to rendezvous at the Green Parrot but Drew hadn't shown up; Jim had looked for him in several other bars; end of story.

Witherspoon took a Sherlockian turn. 'Jim, did you guys have a bust-up? He can be real tetchy, don't I know it.'

Jim said there'd been no bust-up. The lighting in the bar was weak, he relied on it to hide the puffiness where Drew had hit him in the face.

Witherspoon said: 'Mike, has Drew done this kind of thing before?'

The Californian's intensity made Rooney sarcastic. 'Been late for an appointment? Who hasn't?'

Quelled, Witherspoon took comfort in his beer and left

conversation to the others. When the chicken arrived he helped himself to his share and pushed the serving dish across to Rooney, with the briefest word. He was listening hard and thinking over what they were saying. Jim thought it unreasonably bad luck that Denny Witherspoon was displaying the curiosity of the mystery fan. He'd already inquired about motive and precedent. What next?

As soon as Rooney had eaten he went to the boat. He made rather a clumsy point of going alone. Left with Jim, Witherspoon came to life again.

'He's real mad with Drew.' His eyes were following Rooney's back.

'He wanted to tell him about the lifting gear.'

Witherspoon frowned. It took him a moment to grasp what Jim was talking about. 'No, it's not that. My guess is he has a damned good idea where Drew's gone and why he's gone there.'

Jim was teasing. 'And what's your guess about his guess?'

'I just listen, OK? And when I listen to Mike I hear a man who's been fighting Drew every inch about the way to get at that wreck and now he sees Drew walking out on him.'

Jim wanted him to expand. It was a useful topic to explore as it kept attention on the difficult Rooney–Drew relationship instead of the period when Jim and Drew were alone together. But, having started, Witherspoon had more to say before he allowed questions.

'Jim, I can't believe Drew expected to be back here to meet you. He didn't run into a friend and get caught up, not the way you say he must have. Drew had something on his mind, he was acting out of character before he came ashore.'

'He was?'

'You said he let you bring the boat in. When has he let you touch her before? When does he let Rooney handle her? You know how he feels about that engine. OK, maybe he's a little crazy when it comes to engines but if he said you were to bring her in, then to my mind that shows Drew acting out of character.'

'That's a good point, you know, Denny.'

Jim thought it might be all to the good if Witherspoon were to spread this idea. A missing Drew who'd behaved oddly before his disappearance was a more credible one than a man who was his usual self up to the moment he vanished. Jim was glad he'd decided to play it this way rather than claim Drew had steered them into harbour. People might have noticed Jim at the wheel. Even if they couldn't identify him they'd know the boat had been brought in by a man of shorter, slighter build than the memorable Drew.

By now Jim had been in the Green Parrot a very long time, with just the short break when he'd toured the other bars. He got up and told Witherspoon he wanted to stretch his legs.

The night had become deep velvet. A golden chain of lamps hung above the quay. Through that velvet night Mike Rooney was going to come, anxious, at least one of his fears confirmed. Jim began to stroll towards the boat, a figure lost and found and lost and found as he moved from one link in the chain of light to the next. Before long he recognised Rooney's stride in the shape hurrying towards him, hurrying intermittently as the night hid him in its dark places between the lamps. The evening was cooling. Rooney had put on a cotton jacket. A metal badge glinted on the pocket.

Jim loitered until Rooney came up to him. 'Don't tell me, Mike, you found him tucked up asleep in his bunk.'

'He has some stupid ideas, but this . . .' He checked his flow of exasperation and ended with a groan.

Jim said: 'Look, Mike, if you can think of anywhere he might have gone why don't you get over there yourself?'

He was testing Denny Witherspoon's theory. When Rooney didn't reply he pushed on. 'Isn't there a place the pair of you go to on this island?'

Rooney admitted there was. 'We have a place we store things but if he's gone there, he's gone without his key. I found it on the boat. But you're right, Jim, I must get over there and see what he's up to.'

Jim went back into the bar and interrupted the man who he knew was the driver of a taxi parked around the corner. Before Rooney could object arrangements were made. He had no chance of brushing Jim off. Then Jim was with him in the taxi and Denny Witherspoon was heading for another quiet night on his cruiser in the harbour.

Rooney said: 'You don't have to do this, Jim.'

'Well, I feel responsible. I'm the one who arranged the meeting that didn't work out.'

'Yes, but . . .'

'Forget it, Mike.'

The taxi was climbing through humid darkness above the town. Soon they'd be wrapped round by trees but for the first mile they looked down on the harbour, its water rippling like shot silk. Then the car took a hairpin bend and the trees closed in. In a few minutes the driver pulled over to the side of the road. They got out and walked up to the old plantation house.

Rooney led the way, down the path through the trees and overgrown bushes, over the paving and around the side of the house. His flashlight picked out the angle where Jim had one night waited for an assailant who turned out to be Martin Peters. Rooney tried the knob of a back door. It didn't open.

'Wherever he is, Jim, he's not here.'

'Might he have locked it from the inside?'

'Without his key?'

'Bolted it, maybe?'

Rooney inserted his own key in the lock and the door creaked open. There was a square room, a lobby really, and beyond that a passage with closed doors on both sides and at the end. Jim asked how much of the house Rooney and Drew used.

'A room, that's all. We need somewhere to keep things. You can't keep everything on a boat.'

'A strange place to choose, though.'

Jim was following him along the passage, through the door at the end, and into a hallway from which a flight of stairs rose. There was no light apart from Rooney's flashlight. Shadows lurched as its beam bounced around. For a second Jim was back on the wreck, in that tomb-like passage. A wave of adrenalin set his nerves jangling.

Rooney was fumbling keys, finding another one. He unlocked a door on the right and then they were in a room crowded with boxes and bundles.

'I see what you mean, Mike. You'd never stow this lot on board a boat.' Jim was hoping to draw an explanation of what was in them.

'We met the guy who looks after this house, or what remains of it, and he said we could rent a room. Nobody comes up here. The place has a bad name. Apparently the slaves upped and massacred the plantation owners. Or maybe they weren't slaves any longer, I don't remember. Anyway, the guy said the house is haunted and that keeps people away.'

He set the flashlight down on a couple of stacked boxes and delved into another one where the beam fell. After a moment he asked: 'Was Drew carrying anything when he left the boat?'

'I didn't notice. I was messing with ropes at the time.'

He knew what Rooney was seeking and that it was crucial Rooney believed Drew had carried a package when he left the cruiser. But he dared not make the simple statement the situation required. All along he'd been adamant he hadn't actually watched Drew leave, that they'd called goodbyes while Jim finished mooring.

Rooney sat down on one of the boxes and rested his hands on his thighs. He looked squarely at Jim. Jim was standing back slightly from the shaft of light. His face felt sore and he was trying to avoid Rooney noticing.

'The gold cup,' Rooney said, 'It's not on the boat and it's not here with the rest of our stuff.'

Jim looked as though he'd suddenly realised what Rooney was driving at. 'Oh, I see. You think Drew took it with him?'

Bitterly Rooney said: 'Well, he didn't leave it around for you or me, did he?'

'Perhaps it *is* here. He might have put it in a different place.'

Rooney opened the flaps of a box. 'Look, Jim. We keep

it here, except for that time when you had it. It goes in there, with the rest.'

Jim saw a couple of metal bowls, a cluster of coins, a heap of loose ones, and misshapen bars he surmised were silver. To the side of them was a space into which the gold cup and its wrappings would have slotted neatly.

Laughing, he startled Rooney. 'The smugglers' hoard!' In his own ear, he sounded like Guy about to embark on a series of *Treasure Island* jokes. He curbed the temptation and asked whether all this had come from Florida or whether it had been acquired locally. Rooney said the gold cup was the only piece from his Florida days.

Although he was convinced it would end in failure, Rooney followed Jim's suggestion and carried out a search of the rest of the room. Jim hovered unable either to help or to go away because there was only one lamp. Then Rooney came upon a torch and gave him that, saying they might as well take it back to the boat. Jim flicked it on and went out of the room.

Upstairs he entered the room Martin Peters had mentioned. An upright wooden chair stood near a window. From the window he could see the harbour, a toy harbour far below. Jim played the beam around the room. On a shelf he found the camera, a compact one slender enough to slip into his pocket. He mooched around the other rooms before rejoining Rooney.

'Any luck, Mike?'

'No more than I expected. Come on, let's get out of here.' He finished securing the box containing the relics.

Jim waited outside the room. He'd seen nothing that supported Martin Peters' story about arms dealing. The contents of the room looked precisely what Rooney said they were, the overflow of personal possessions that couldn't be crammed on to a boat.

They locked up and went down the path. The taxi had gone. Jim said it was ridiculous because the driver hadn't been paid.

'Ghosts,' said Rooney. 'What did I tell you? They're scared of this place.'

They walked down the road, the long winding way they'd driven. Rooney said there were paths and shortcuts but he wasn't confident of finding them, especially not at night. Then he reverted to the nervous attacks brought on by proximity to the old plantation house. Apparently this wasn't the first time he'd been stranded there.

Jim asked what the ghosts were alleged to do and Rooney said it was hard to say because there were variations on the stories. The commonest version was that faces pressed against the windowpanes.

'Sometimes they say they see flames licking the rooms. But that's it: they see something from a distance, almost always from the roadway. Of course that's because they're too damned scared to get any closer.'

Over the next mile he described specific incidents. As ghost stories went, they were feeble. Rooney couldn't even claim personal experience of strangeness although he and Drew had used the house for months.

Jim didn't waste his breath asking whether Drew had encountered ghosts. Drew had been too hard-headed for such fancies.

But Rooney said: 'Drew had something odd happen to him, though. He came up on his own one evening, got a lift part of the way and walked the rest. He was trying to find a spanner, I think it was. Anyway it was a tool he couldn't find anywhere else and decided he must have stored it up there.'

They were below the line of trees now. Lights of hotels and a few streets were shining but most of the coastline was dark. The sea was insistent, battered by a strengthening wind. They paused to listen, then Rooney continued his story.

'Well, he hunted around and then gave it up. The spanner wasn't there. Out he went, locked up, walked down to the road, by a side path not the main one, and suddenly something made him look over his shoulder.'

Jim obliged by asking what Drew had seen.

Rooney said: 'Light in one of the rooms. A flickering light. You know, like flames.'

'The ghostly light?'

'God knows. Drew said he wasn't going to be taken in by that rubbish. Do you know what he did? He shot it.'

'*Shot* it?'

'Yes. He dodged across to the front path to give himself a direct line of fire and *bang*. He shot it.'

'When did this happen?' Jim knew the answer, to the hour and to the minute.

Rooney supplied the answer he expected. 'And out went the light. No more ghosts.'

Jim said that well, well, he'd never heard of anyone scoring a hit on a ghost.

'Jim, the most weird part of this story is that when we went back to the house the next day there was no broken glass. Drew said he'd fired straight through that centre window upstairs and killed the light. But the glass was unbroken. I saw that for myself.'

'Weird indeed,' Jim murmured. He waited until they'd

walked a little further, apparently musing on the strange tale, and then asked whether it was normal for Drew to carry a gun.

'You have to understand, Jim, Drew's been in situations where the man who didn't have one was a fool. Or dead.'

'But here?'

'Look, I'm not saying I agree with him.'

Jim answered with a grunt that commented it wasn't unusual for Rooney and Drew to hold opposing views. They were nearing the town. They walked the last leg to the harbour in silence broken only by a buffeting wind.

Denny Witherspoon was an early riser. Skeins of dawn mist were floating above the valleys when he stirred. He was surprised to find Jim Rush asleep on his deck but tiptoed around him and made himself a mug of instant coffee while he thought about the mysteries of the previous evening. He did rather enjoy a detective story. In a way, that's what excited him about working on the wrecks. It was unpredictable and you had to piece together all the fragments of information you gathered and try them this way and that until eventually you understood. Perhaps you were slightly wrong because you rarely had all the facts, but with intelligence and experience you could build up a fairly accurate picture of what had happened and what you'd found.

Jim opened an eye. He was used to seeing Jane Logan in the mornings; Witherspoon came as a shock.

'Coffee, Jim?' He accepted a yawn for a yes and went to tip more powder into a mug. There was a spoon somewhere, *had been* a spoon somewhere, but he hadn't seen it for days.

Jim sat up and looked around. He touched his face. Tender.

'You're an unexpected guest,' said Witherspoon as he poured water on the powder. He jiggled it about, it was a nuisance mislaying the spoon.

'Mike offered me Drew's bunk but that would have been awkward if Drew turned up. I told him I'd arranged to camp on you.'

Witherspoon gave a solemn wink and said he remembered the conversation well. Then he asked about what he called the Drew hunt. Jim told him a brief story about going with Mike Rooney to a storeroom but finding no evidence Drew had been there.

Jim said: 'We ought to check with Mike and see whether Drew's back. No point in us hanging around here if he is.'

'Nor if he's not,' said Witherspoon. 'Either way we ought to get out to that wreck.'

Witherspoon's eagerness to get on with the job was encouraging. He didn't have his mind wholly on Drew and it made it easy for Jim to send him over to see Rooney while Jim freshened himself up. Witherspoon dragged a comb through his greasy hair and pulled on his white cotton cap. Somehow the cap always appeared clean and the hair always dirty.

Denny Witherspoon was taller than him. Jim peered up into the small rectangle of mirror on the wall and saw, with a surge of distaste, the pinkness and the welt on his left cheek. He hated being marked in this way, he always had.

Young, say three, he'd amused them by howling after a tumble by the barn. It wasn't the pain, which was nothing, that shocked him but the ugly rawness that spoiled his soft, pale skin, his smoothness where the shadow of veins flowed. The skin was torn to grubby rags, blood came speckling through. Too young for vanity, he'd objected to being spoiled.

He tilted Witherspoon's mirror and fingered the red weal. His face felt worse than it looked, which seemed a miracle when he remembered the way Drew had flung him about, slapped him around. His eyes were tired, though. Somewhere there'd been a storm during the night. The island had escaped, except for flurries of wind that set the boats rocking despite the protective stone arm of the harbour, and woke Jim from fitful sleep.

As Jim finished washing, Witherspoon returned to say there was no news of Drew. Jim was prepared for argument with Rooney about whether to wait for Drew or go without him, and he was taken aback when Rooney came to say they couldn't afford to be messed around by Drew any longer.

'He's not the only one who can steer that boat. What do you say, Jim?'

Jim said yes they should go. He travelled out with Witherspoon and Rooney took the old fishing boat. The sea was choppy, the ride no pleasure. Altogether it proved a difficult and unrewarding day.

Rooney was alternately angry and worried. He said he was going to dive but changed his mind. Instead he made calculations regarding the cannon and the lifting gear. Jim heard him with half an ear. He was keyed up waiting for Denny Witherspoon to emerge from the depths with news that the chest had a hole punched in it. Jim was ready to remind him with glares and glances that Rooney didn't know of its existence.

Suddenly Witherspoon surfaced. When he could speak, he blurted all the things Jim prayed he'd have the wit not to say.

'Jim, the chest . . . Something's happened down there. It's gone. Caved in or something, it's just . . .'

'Denny . . .'

'I mean I can't see it. The water's thick, I can't see. But it's all changed, the chest isn't there.'

'Denny.' Jim tried again but it was useless, Witherspoon gabbled on.

Rooney was staring from one to the other of them. 'What chest?'

Jim said: 'We weren't sure, Mike. It might have been nothing.'

Witherspoon cut in. 'It's nothing now. A mound of nothing. God knows what happened down there.'

Rooney said, with the cold patience of anger: 'So you two found a chest down there and neither of you told me? Whose idea was that, to keep it to yourselves?'

Witherspoon looked to Jim for explanation. Jim repeated: 'Mike, we weren't sure that's what it was.'

'Denny sounds pretty sure. You found a chest and you didn't tell me.'

Witherspoon looked to Jim again but Jim did no more than give the slightest shrug showing that he refused to be riled. Rooney, though, continued to attack.

'It's my wreck down there, Jim. I found her. I ought to have been told about that chest straight off.'

Trying to wind up the argument, Jim said that perhaps it

would have been better that way. 'But it hardly matters now. The contraption seems to have collapsed.'

Rooney snapped back that it wasn't the chest itself that interested him but what was in it. He shot his questions at the diver. 'Can't you tell, Denny? Aren't there things lying there?'

Witherspoon said the water was cloudy with particles, every movement he made stirred them and it was no good attempting photographs until they settled. 'But I think the wood of the chest has crumbled and whatever it was supporting has fallen forward.'

Rooney groaned. 'Are you telling me the contents of that thing are now buried by the remains of the chest plus a pile of rubble?'

'I'm telling you they might be. Mike, it's too soon to be definite but I guess that's right.'

Rooney swore and turned his fury on Jim. 'If you'd told me about that chest, Jim, I'd have been into it right away. We'd have had whatever it contained. Now all we're getting is a lot of excuses.'

Jim sounded calmer than he felt. If Witherspoon's fears were right, he'd made it extremely dangerous to go anywhere near the pile that hid the contents of the chest.

He said: 'Mike, it was never standing there like a box waiting to have the lid lifted. Part of it was sticking out of a mound, that's all. Denny's been trying to dig it out. He was sure it was fragile and would need specialist help if it was to be salvaged. Well, he was right.'

Rooney flared. 'Denny was sure? Denny seems to be running this show.'

Jim raised a placating hand. 'Mike, the thing's collapsed. It's happened.'

'And what else have you discovered down there? What other little secrets do you have, Denny?'

Meekly Witherspoon said: 'Nothing.'

Rooney kept at him. 'How long before it will be clear enough for us to investigate what's left of the chest?'

A shake of the head.

Jim said: 'Mike, we thought the wreck was stable and we now know she's not. I have to say that for me this changes everything. I won't ask Denny to dive on her again.'

Rooney's chin went up. 'All right, I'll go down.'

'No, Mike.'

'Do you realise how long it took Drew and me, sweeping up and down with the scanner, before we found anything worth diving on? It's different for you, Jim, but she's my wreck.'

'Your life too. How's it going to be down there when the rest caves in?'

Witherspoon told them that although the part that was turned to coral was safe, they'd better assume the more recently exposed area, where the chest lay, might collapse. But Rooney wasn't concentrating on him. He was watching the waves smacking against the side of the diver's cruiser.

'Denny,' he said after a moment, 'what do you think caused the chest to give way?'

'No idea. I've been really careful and there haven't been any signs this might happen. Every time I've gone down, it's looked the same as I left it. But I'll tell you, I'm really glad I wasn't down there when she went.'

'If you didn't smash it, Denny, then something or someone did. Have you seen any other boats hanging around here?'

His question encompassed Jim as well. Jim and the diver said no, they'd seen no one.

'Well,' said Rooney, 'even if you didn't, that's my best guess. The *Gloriosa*'s been found by other wreck hunters.'

Jim let this idea take a grip. 'It certainly looks that way, Mike. It's the likeliest explanation.'

And he didn't object when Rooney went so far as to hint at Drew's involvement.

Witherspoon was saying: '*I* haven't said a word about this wreck, not to anyone.'

He hadn't been accused but could sense the moment wasn't far off. There'd always been that split: Rooney and Drew as one faction and he and Jim as the other.

But Rooney wasn't thinking about him just then. What he said was: 'Only four people are supposed to know about it. Now the chest has been smashed to smithereens and Drew's disappeared.' He looked knowingly at Jim. 'He didn't go empty handed either.'

Rooney was referring to the gold cup. As Witherspoon didn't know about it, he assumed he meant Drew had cleared out with the hoard of objects he and Rooney had been bringing up. There were silver forks and spoons, a bowl of indeterminate metal, and trinkets that would remain mysterious until they were cleaned.

'Hell,' said Witherspoon. 'So Drew's gone off with our stuff? *All* of it?'

Jim set the matter straight. 'No, a piece that came from a different source.'

He'd slipped in ahead of Rooney, fearing mention of Florida would lead the detective in Witherspoon to deduce chicanery.

'More valuable than our finds here, then?' said

Witherspoon. It was barely a question. 'If he took that one and ignored the rest, it must be a good one. Or does he have a better claim to it than to the stuff here?'

Rooney's eyes narrowed. The diver was showing him aspects of this affair that hadn't occurred to him. 'He has no claim at all to it. It's something I came by before Drew and I got together.'

'In Florida?' Witherspoon's question was fast as gunshot.

Jim jumped in, to change the tack because it would be unhelpful to have Witherspoon realise his own impeccable standards weren't matched by Rooney's. He said the first thing he thought of, that he'd like to see for himself that the *Gloriosa* hoard was intact.

They went into the cabin and Rooney opened the cavity where the items were kept. He'd checked them himself the previous evening, when he'd noticed the gold cup was missing as well as Drew, but he didn't challenge Jim's right to see for himself. Jim toyed with some of the items, talked about their likely origin and how much they might be worth. Then he let Rooney drop the lid on them.

They were both thinking the same thing. Rooney said it. 'I'm not sure it's safe to keep it here. But you've seen the other place, Jim, it's not ideal either.'

Witherspoon chipped in that nowhere was truly safe, not when you were talking about gold and silver. 'The temptation's too high.'

Jim made a joke of it. 'OK, Denny. We'll keep it well away from you.'

He and Witherspoon laughed but Rooney was scowling. He said: 'I don't know, it's incredible somehow. If Drew got hooked up with some other people and showed them our wreck . . .'

Jim pointed out Drew needn't have done that, they probably found it themselves, after all it had been lying there for centuries. 'There's nothing to say you were the first to find her or the last.'

'All right. Well, if Drew got hooked up with these other people and decided he'd rather work with them than with us, well, what I don't understand is when he did it. I mean, I've been living on this boat with the guy for months. If he'd been going off on his own, I'd have known. Do you see what I mean?'

Jim remembered a time Rooney *had* been alone, the day Drew had gone in search of engine parts. Widgets, Rooney had called them. Before he threw in a remark about it, Witherspoon spoke.

'Yes, and what about yesterday, Mike? We were on that wreck early yesterday afternoon and everything was normal. Whatever went on down there happened after you and I had travelled south.'

Quickly Jim said: 'And after Drew and I left the scene. There were no other boats around. I don't remember any.'

The cabin was crowded. Rooney led the way on to the deck. Denny Witherspoon followed, Jim came last. As he mounted the stairs something caught his eye. He didn't falter, he carried on up into the fresh air.

Witherspoon was asking him: 'Jim, what time did you and Drew leave here?'

Jim could practically see him adding up on his fingers and the truth was that things didn't add up, not at all. Fortunately Jim had an excuse to be extremely vague.

'I can't say precisely. There wasn't any hurry, we had

hours to kill. Drew said he wanted to have another go at finding the leak in the fuel system. So he pumped away at the fuel lines with a hand pump and I lazed. Time just drifted by.'

Impatient with what he saw as a diversion, Rooney said the crux of it wasn't what Drew and Jim had done out there. 'It's what Drew did when he went ashore. He met somebody and he went somewhere with him. That's obvious.'

'But . . .' Witherspoon didn't get any further.

Rooney leaped in. 'Either he came back out here and helped somebody smash up our chest or he knows who did.'

The Californian gave the slightest shrug and withdrew into taciturnity.

Jim spoke to Rooney. 'We're wasting our time here. If we're not diving I ought to get back to St Elena.'

Rooney was ahead of him. 'Don't offer to take the loot, Jim. This mightn't be Fort Knox but at least I know where it is. If Drew comes back for the rest, then OK, I'm making a mistake. But until then I'd rather keep that hoard together right where it is.'

'Fine.'

They arranged to meet next day at the Green Parrot bar. Jim would have preferred to keep away from that harbour but was given no choice. Rooney had said he was going to moor down there until he found Drew. What would be the point, he asked, of taking his boat up to the hurricane harbour on another island when Drew had no means of reaching it? Jim noticed that part of the time Rooney was looking forward to Drew's return and the rest of it was assuming Drew had walked out on him for good.

Denny Witherspoon took Jim up to St Elena. The only

food he had on board was a bunch of bananas. He snapped off a couple and tossed one to Jim.

'Jim, Mike's determined to blame Drew for everything. Did you notice that?'

Jim laughed. 'Mike's as confused as we are. Drew goes, the chest goes, the gold cup goes . . .'

Witherspoon pounced on that. 'Gold cup? Is that what he got in Florida?' A pause, then: 'A lot of guys keep souvenirs of the wrecks. You can't stop that, you can only hope they don't keep the cream of it.'

'Assuming they know which that is.'

For a time neither of them spoke, except to say a word about the sky filling with the puffball cloudlets of the trade winds. Coral reefs came and went. A holiday cruise ship threaded the horizon. Witherspoon began to speak again, recapitulating his thoughts on the puzzle of Drew's disappearance.

'The guy acted strangely in letting you bring in the boat, especially as he was nursing the engine yesterday. He left in a hurry but it was already dark. If he'd gone out to the wreck they'd have been working through the night. I'm not saying it's impossible but it's not good, and last night was rough out there.'

'What are you driving at, Denny?'

'Wish I knew. All I *do* know is Mike's theories don't hang right. He's pinning a lot on Drew.'

Jim chanted the points he'd made earlier. 'Drew's gone, the chest's gone, the gold cup's gone.'

'Hold on, Jim. We don't know anything that links Drew to the collapse of the chest and we have only Mike's word Drew's taken his cup. When you get down to it, all you and I know is Drew's missing.'

'Hey, I love this analytical brain of yours, Denny. What did you major in? Police work?'

For reply Witherspoon flung his banana peel at Jim who deflected it into the sea. It swirled briefly, a flash of yellow against turquoise and then it was gone.

There was a Clarissa in the room. She wore a towel and she was curled on Jim's bed with a hairdrier in her hand. She flipped the switch and its purring died.

'Hello, James. I'm Clarissa.'

'Did room service send you?' The last thing he was prepared for was cheery banter with a strange young woman in a towel.

'Jane said it would be all right.'

'Then it's fine.'

With a negligent gesture he tossed his bag into a cupboard. There was a gem-encrusted gold cup in it, there was Martin Peters' camera, and there was a gun in it. He pretended it weighed nothing. The tousled blonde in the towel would never be able to report he'd come in burdened.

She put a hand to the towel where it tucked between her breasts and she swivelled, swinging her legs round and dropping her feet to the floor. He glimpsed a dark shadow of pubic hair.

Jim went into the bathroom. Clarissa's swimming costume dripped from the hook in the shower. Her wet hairs clung to the porcelain and congregated around the plughole. He felt a wave of disgust and saw in the mirror over the washbasin that she saw it too.

'James, let me take that out of your way.'

She reached past him and removed the swimsuit. He

closed the door behind her, lifted down the shower head and swilled away her hairs. When the water stopped running he heard the hairdrier buzzing.

Jim stood in the shower a long time and washed away the salt and grime of two days without such comfort. He enjoyed the sting of water almost too hot to bear, its soothing effect on aching muscles and tired brain. By making it hot enough he cleared his mind of everything except the sensation of standing under that water.

After a while he reached for the rich luxury of a white velvety bath towel. The first one he lifted from the fresh pile that appeared daily was a hand towel so he tossed it aside. The second one was a hand towel too. There were no bath towels. Clarissa had helped herself to those.

As he rubbed himself over with the little towels he thought what hell it must be to live with someone else permanently, to marry them, to assign them rights to share your sheets and your towels and your everything else. He loathed the awful proximity that meant doors need never be knocked on, requests never made, that everything was taken for granted because it had indeed been granted.

When he came out of the bathroom, carrying one of the small towels strategically in front of him, the room was empty. Clarissa had left the hairdrier on Jane's bedside table and a heap of thick white bath towels on the floor. Jim stepped over them and opened his wardrobe. The clothes hung undisturbed, spaced evenly along the rail. He lifted out a pale cotton jacket and trousers but decided on something perkier: black linen trousers with a vivid mauve silk shirt. He didn't especially care for the shirt but Jane had bought it for him in Jermyn Street, one of her impulsive gifts that made him feel he was her new pet being petted.

He combed his hair and then pushed the comb into a pocket while he examined the marks on his face. The hot shower had made them look angry. On the left side the weal was very obvious, on the other a red puffiness looked as tender as it felt. He took a face cloth, soaked it in cold water and pressed it against the sore places. After that there was nothing more to do but join the others. The game was about to begin.

Guy's game was about to begin too. He was sitting, one leg tucked beneath him, on a bench on the terrace by the pool. He wore a stuffed toy parrot on the left shoulder of a long blue jacket and he tapped the tiles with a crutch to emphasis what he was saying.

Where in God's name did he get a crutch? Jim wondered. He slipped into the shadows at the back of the terrace but it was no use.

'Ahoy there, Jim, lad,' cried Guy, leaning forward so that his parrot wobbled.

Several voices chimed: 'Pieces of eight! Pieces of eight!'

Heads swivelled towards Jim. He gave them a movie star kind of wave, emanating phoney shyness, and when they laughed he turned it into a full movie star entrance with bowing and smiling and touching hands and signing imaginary autographs. His audience were delighted, including those who'd seen him do it before. The new faces saw he liked a game, he was one of them.

Jim squatted down beside Clarissa. He'd been on his way to Jane but realised she and Jeremy were so close they were practically sharing a chair. No, they *were* sharing a chair. Either way, no room for him.

'Clarissa, you stole the bath towels.'

His accusation didn't bring apology. 'Jane said it would be all right.'

He recognised the flowered cotton dress she was wearing. Jane's.

'What did you do? Trip into the pool?'

'Dodo threw me in.'

'But . . .'

'Shhh. I want to listen to Guy.' She leaned away from him, cupped her chin in her hand.

Jim sat back on his heels and listened to Guy.

Guy said: '. . . and you can cast off now, my hearties, and don't let me catch any of you sloping off or, shiver my timbers, you'll walk the plank, and you may lay to it.'

Jim had the awful presentiment this game was going to last for days, maybe a week. He tried to ask Clarissa but Guy was rising to a full hop and Clarissa was joining in the chant they all gave whenever the parrot wobbled.

'Pieces of eight! Pieces of eight!'

Jim saw Jane standing, away from Jeremy, and went across to her. 'Jane, I'm sorry I've . . .'

She dismissed his apology with a fleeting frown. 'Clarissa said you'd come back. What happened?'

'Oh, well, I went to . . .'

'No, your face.'

His hand flew to his cheek. 'I'm not the sailor I thought I was. I got caught when the wind changed. You know how it happens, OK one minute and all hell the next.'

Her features tightened. 'That's dangerous.'

'Not this time, I was just careless.'

He shouldn't have been doing this to her. He hadn't forgotten. She'd come through a boating tragedy and made herself brave again. He appreciated that and yet he did it, because it was a handy excuse for a bruised face to pretend you'd been smacked by a mainsail boom. Because, too, it engaged Jane's sympathy and distracted her. She didn't demand to know where he'd been, who he'd been with and why he'd stayed away almost two days without explanation.

'Come on,' she said. 'We must collect our maps.' She led him to a cluster of people around a table piled with envelopes.

Guy's game was immensely elaborate. Everybody was given a *Treasure Island* map but everybody was given a different one. Each map was marked with a cross which might or might not be the site where Guy had buried the prize. In fact, the prize might be hidden anywhere and people were free to search for it anywhere.

Players could work singly or in pairs but with only one map, so if a couple chose to operate as a team they first had to choose which of their maps to keep and which to discard. Jim had heard only part of this rigmarole of rules and procedures and was piecing together the rest from the antics of the people around him. There was a lot of argument among pairs unable to decide which of their two maps was likelier to be the prizewinner.

Couples who'd resolved the question, and players working alone, fell silent as they set about interpreting the first of Guy's riddles that would lead them down the treasure trail. There was an enormous number of riddles: everybody had six but as the maps varied so did the riddles.

It can't possibly work, Jim thought. *Different maps and different clues. How can that lead to one treasure?*

He asked Jane: 'Where do they look?'

'We,' she emphasised the we, he wasn't to be allowed to escape this dreadful pastime, 'go anywhere. There's nothing to say the treasure's even on this island.'

Jim didn't take a map. He wanted to see whether Jane intended them to work separately or not. She opened an envelope and gave him the map.

'Don't bother with another one, James. We'll only face intolerable decisions.'

'Wrong. I must take one. Otherwise Guy will fuss because I didn't. But I won't open it.'

'Mmm. Smart.'

He put the unopened one in his trouser pocket and forgot it. Jane's map was quite entertaining. She said Guy had explained that the outlines were of fictitious islands because he didn't want to make the game too easy.

She slotted her arm through Jim's and led him away through the trees. 'We don't have to do a thing until morning. Guy assumes we'll all go rushing off by torchlight but I think our map requires long and thoughtful consideration first, don't you?'

They walked and talked for a while, not about Guy or his map although it was hard to forget the game when whoops of laughter proved he'd been obeyed by a number of his merry band. When supper time came around, there was a buffet laid out on the terrace instead of the usual meal. Guy didn't expect his pirates to want to waste any precious time wining and dining.

Jim and Jane ate alone. She wanted to know about the wreck and about Drew and Rooney and Witherspoon. Had they, she wondered, devised a method of reclaiming the chest? He said not. He told her about the things they'd recovered, and mentioned the chain that was almost certainly gold and the silver plate with the initials, although he didn't explain the significance of those. Then he decided to say Drew had disappeared. It was expedient, a way of stopping her probing his arrangements with the wreck hunters. Her questions had been getting more detailed, dangerous.

'Pirates,' she said, with her teasing laugh. 'Didn't I tell you Drew and Rooney were a couple of pirates? They're not people one should trust an inch. You're sure the gold chain and the rest of the pickings didn't wander off with Drew?'

'Absolutely sure. I thought you quite liked them. Mike Rooney, anyway.'

'They amuse me. Or Mike does. Drew's always a bit dour for my taste. He frowns at me as though I'm getting between him and some urgent business he has in hand. Of course he hasn't any. He's just bumming around waiting for money to float his way. And I doubt he'd care whose it was, either.'

Then she looked serious for a moment. 'James, you're not letting them talk you into financing their escapades, are you?'

'Of course not. I've told you.'

'That was before. It might have changed.'

'Well, it hasn't.'

'Not a penny?' She looked extremely sceptical.

'Nothing that isn't covered.'

A young man in a stripy T-shirt and jeans burst through the trees and fled into the house. A few seconds later a young woman in a yellow halter-neck sundress flew after him, squealing for him to wait for her.

She appealed to Jane and Jim for sympathy but without

breaking step. 'Oh, it's too bad of Dylan. I'm the one who worked out the riddle. Dylan! Wait for me.'

Inside the house Dylan's feet pounded over wooden floors, his girl's clattered after him, then there were flurries of objection, hers and his, and then thudding, heaving, thumping noises. Jane shuddered but she was laughing.

'Can Guy possibly have intended this?' She answered herself with deep irony. 'Quite probably.'

'Someone call?' Guy appeared from another direction. As soon as he knew he was in sight, he was up on one leg and a crutch and poised for a yo, ho, ho.

Jim got in first. 'Suppose there's a tie. What then, Guy?'

Guy thought this a very stupid question, a challenge to his ability as game-maker extraordinary. He snorted and said: 'There can't be one. Simple as that. All thought of.'

'But if?'

Guy slammed the crutch down resoundingly but didn't answer. Instead he asked Jane why she and her partner were sitting around instead of battling their way towards the buried treasure.

She said: 'We're taking the intellectual approach, Guy. Thinking it through before we start.'

Jim couldn't resist asking whether there was anything in the rules against that. Guy continued to ignore him. From the house came more sounds of investigative destruction. Guy looked slyly pleased and hopped behind a palm tree, breaking into a trot once he was out of sight of the terrace.

'I suggest we take the intellectual approach for the rest of the night,' said Jim. He folded up the map that lay on the table between them, took Jane's hand and led her to their room.

He wanted her and he wanted her as an excuse to keep a distance from the others. Jane would make love with him and would make everything all right. Guy couldn't harm him while she was with him. Dylan and his squealing girlfriend couldn't rip their room apart while they were there to defend it.

They lay on the soft bed beneath a lazy fan and made love. Jane was her usual languorous self, teasing him with her smiles and the delicate touch of her fingertips. He willed himself to appear as he usually was, not angered by the dreadful intrusions of Clarissa, not unnerved by the killing of Drew, not alert for the blundering arrival of Dylan and his girl. In the end it was all right, just all right.

Afterwards, Jane sat up, leaning an elbow on the pillows, and looked down at him, running the tip of her tongue around her teeth as she did when choosing words. Whatever they were, he knew they'd be gently ironic, a joke they'd share, a joke against the rest of the world.

The telephone beside her rang. She spun away from him. 'Oh,' she said into the receiver and in a tone that was distinctly displeased. 'One moment.'

She muffled the receiver by pressing it against her breast. 'For you. Someone who won't give his name is asking for Jim Rush.'

'Ask them to put him through.'

Jane spoke to the servant who'd taken the call. Jim lay back, declining to show concern or special interest. He held out a hand for the receiver. He got Mike Rooney.

Without preliminaries Rooney said: 'You're going to say you can't talk, so OK, listen.'

'Go ahead.'

Rooney said Drew hadn't turned up, that he'd spent all day asking around the island for him and nobody had seen him.

'Jim, he was supposed to collect a part for the engine but he didn't get there, and the shop is about one hundred yards from the quay.'

All at once Jim understood where this was leading, why Rooney was agitated. He'd made a huge mistake and it hadn't taken Mike Rooney very long to spot it.

Jim forced himself to yawn and sound less than riveted by Rooney and his tale. 'Sorry, Mike, it's been a lively evening here.'

On cue a group of players chased by the window, shouting so loud that Rooney heard them down the line. 'What the hell's going on there?' he asked.

'Pirates.'

'What?'

'Nothing.'

'Look, Jim, this business with Drew. It's not as simple as we thought it was.'

'Can't this wait until tomorrow? I can get down to see you then, if you like.'

'I know you can't talk now. Yes, come tomorrow. But what I want to tell you is it looks very doubtful Drew meant to cut and run. His stuff's all here, on the boat. I mean, why would he leave his cash and his credit cards and all his clothes and gear, and . . .'

'Everything.'

'That's it, everything's here. Denny says . . .'

Jim had been waiting for this too. Denny Witherspoon. The eager Californian with the Sherlockian mind had been helping Rooney piece things together. Well, it couldn't be helped. The damage was done. Only one thing could make it worse. Jim prayed it wouldn't happen but if it was going to nothing would stop it. It was a matter of wind and tide.

Mike Rooney was rambling on. Jim felt Jane stir beside him. She was pulling a face at the burbling receiver, stretching a hand to snatch it. Jim twisted away from her, held it out of reach. Mischievous, she depressed the button on the grey plastic box and cut him off.

The fat policeman was waiting for him on the quay by the Green Parrot next morning.

'They said you were coming down this way, Mr Rush.' He pushed his cap back to a jaunty angle but didn't explain who 'they' were.

'You waited for me?'

'Not long. You were right by the headland, it wasn't so very long.'

'Well, then?'

'That *Caramba*, Mr Rush. Seems she slipped her moorings again.'

Jim showed bewilderment in the shake of his head. 'I delivered her as promised. I haven't seen her since.'

He was doubtful how he'd fare at the hands of the police now he was away from the protective aura of St Elena. Some of the islands were careless about human rights. Even Guy's disapproval was preferable to hours or days in a police cell while the truth was confirmed.

But the policeman smiled, looking passably like his cousin Claude when he did so. 'No problem, Mr Rush. I had to ask you, though. Routine, you might say.'

'Of course.' Jim returned the smile and took a step back. 'Well, if there's nothing I can help you with . . .'

'Not a thing, Mr Rush.' The man sketched a lazy salute and strolled away. He had the same fluid movements as his cousin but, being overweight, his stride became an arrogant swagger.

Jim went on rapidly. Mike Rooney was on his deck watching out for him.

'The *Caramba*'s gone again.' Jim swung himself up.

'I know. That policeman came along asking everyone if they'd seen her. He asked about you, too. I told him you were on your way here.'

'Where does your friend Jock claim she is this time?'

'No idea. I haven't seen him either.'

Jim jumped down into the cabin. It wasn't normal for him to go in there when he was on board, he spent most time on deck or in the wheelhouse, but he wanted Rooney to show him Drew's possessions.

They were scattered around, Rooney hadn't put them away after his own explorations. Jim picked up a handful of papers, mostly certificates and bank books, from a pile lying on a bench. 'Is this Drew's?'

Rooney said it was. Jim riffled through it, not reading but in an absentminded way. 'All kinds.'

'Plus all that.' Rooney indicated another heap and Jim flicked through those papers too. If Rooney had been briefed to help him he couldn't have done better. He showed Jim one thing after the other, and Jim took the opportunity to finger them all.

When they'd finished, Rooney said: 'See what I mean? It's all here. Everything. How can a guy walk out and leave everything?'

Jim bit his lower lip and looked thoughtful. His own puzzlement appeared as complete as Rooney's. He looked around the cabin, apparently seeking inspiration about the mysterious motives of Drew who'd wandered out of their lives without his passport or any other papers, without even his wristwatch or a change of underpants.

'You don't think . . .' Jim began.

'Think what?'

'No, it's nothing.' He made a dismissive gesture, knowing how it would encourage Rooney to press him.

'No, go on. What is it?'

Jim said, reluctantly: 'It's a stupid idea, just something that came to me. But I wondered whether Drew mightn't have gone off in Jock's boat.'

'The *Caramba*?' Rooney was startled.

'OK, I said it was a stupid idea. Forget it.'

'No, no. You might have something there, Jim.'

Jim turned to leave the cabin for the fresher air on deck. He was pleased with the ease with which Rooney was latching on to the theory.

Rooney said, before Jim had started up the companionway: 'She wasn't moored here, though.'

Jim shrugged. 'It was only an idea.'

'Hey, but what if Drew met Jock when he came ashore? And Jock asked him to go with him to the *Caramba* and then spirit her away?'

Jim was very pleased indeed with the way Rooney was developing the idea. He felt like a hypnotist with an especially receptive client. A hint from him and Rooney was articulating the scenario that was in Jim's mind. Elaborating on it, too.

'OK,' Rooney was saying, 'Jock wants to do his insurance company. I imagine you worked that out?'

'Owner piracy. Someone told me.'

'Well, the way Jock looks at it, he had a bad deal out of them over something else and he reckons they owe him.'

'Does Jock have another boat?' If not, the theory wouldn't work.

'Yes, he scoots about in a glassfibre dinghy with the noisiest outboard you ever heard.'

'So it's feasible he was here without the *Caramba* when Drew went ashore?'

'Yes.' Rooney looked rueful. 'I don't know why I didn't think of this. If Jock wanted someone to help him out, Drew was perfect. They talked about it once, about how that went on and how easy it would be to do it.'

Jim started up the companionway. It seemed impossible Drew was dead, that he'd killed him and lugged his body up these steps. With more than half his mind he believed Drew was sneaking the *Caramba* away through the islands to a secret place where she'd lie until the insurance money was paid. He even pictured Drew as the one who repainted her hull and lettered a new name on her bows.

And then he saw it.

For the second time his eye fell on it, as it was bound to do now each time he mounted the steps. It looked bigger than when he'd noticed it before.

Behind him he heard Mike Rooney mounting the lowest step. Any second, he thought, Rooney would cry out. And then all the theories and fabrications would dissolve because the truth would be known.

No cry. Jim's legs weakened as he crossed the deck. He sat on the seat and looked around. Gulls were squabbling over fishy scraps on the quay. Two men were shouting a long-distance conversation. A radio was happy with steel-band music. He heard none of it. He was listening for

Rooney, for the man's exclamation of shock, for his feet pounding up the steps or his voice calling Jim to go below. The only sounds he was willing to hear were Rooney's.

Rooney called. 'Hey, Jim.'

The beat of Jim's blood shuddered. A cat raided the fishy scraps and gulls took to the air in raucous whirls. Jim looked over his shoulder with what he hoped was an expression of inquiry and nothing more fearful. Rooney was on deck, something in his hand.

'Catch.' He lobbed a can of beer.

Jim caught it and pulled the ring. The can wasn't cold. He'd have preferred it colder but had long accepted the British didn't drink it that way. Besides, the cool box on the boat was inefficient. Grateful, he drank.

Rooney sat across the deck, his feet planted where Drew's body had lain beneath its tartan shroud. He said, picking up the earlier conversation: 'He'd do it for a cut. He told Jock that. Split the insurance money with him and he'd help.'

'He actually said that?' Jim was sceptical whether Rooney was remembering or enhancing.

'Yes, he said it. Of course, it was theoretical. They were joking, at least Drew was. Well, I thought he was.' He swished his beer around in the can. 'It looks pretty obvious what happened, he ran into Jock who said: "You're on but we have to do it right away." So Drew cut and ran.'

Denny Witherspoon came along the quay and joined them. 'Still no Drew?' He put the question to Rooney who said no.

'That's too bad.' Then Witherspoon said: 'I've gotten busy all of a sudden. Martin Peters needs me now. I have to go off with him for a few days. Maybe I'll be back by the weekend but I don't know for sure.'

A flicker of annoyance crossed Rooney's face. Jim said: 'We always knew Denny was only filling in with us until Martin was ready.'

Rooney asked Witherspoon: 'Does this mean you leave the area after this trip?'

'Depends.' Witherspoon looked at Jim, at the prospect of employment.

Jim said: 'Can we discuss that when you get back, Denny?'

Rooney amplified. 'We have to settle what to do about the wreck, now it's been damaged. And Drew could be back by then.'

'Sure, no hurry.' Witherspoon looked ready to leave, then asked: 'Any more guesses about Drew's whereabouts?'

Rooney pitched in with the story about the *Caramba*. There was nothing Jim could do to stop the flow without raising questions about his motives. He sat there studying Witherspoon's sleuthing brain sending messages of incredulity to his face.

When Rooney finished, quite convinced by his own tale, Witherspoon pursed his lips and said that as a matter of fact he'd be very surprised if that were the truth of it. Rooney, who'd been faulted by him more than once, bridled.

'All right, Denny, what's wrong with it?' His mockery was a thin disguise for curiosity. He genuinely wanted to know why the youngster was unwilling to swallow his story.

Witherspoon said: 'It doesn't change anything. The guy

still vanished without one single thing he wasn't wearing at the time. And still nobody saw him around the harbour or in the town.'

Rooney defended his hypothesis. 'Denny, if he stepped off this boat and Jock was tied up a few yards away in his runabout, Drew could have jumped aboard it and headed out to sea with him.'

But Witherspoon was shaking his head vigorously. 'No, no, Mike. If Drew had a chance meeting with Jock right here in the harbour, he'd have been more likely to leave you a message and collect a few things, clothes and so on. How long would it have taken him? You could measure it in seconds.'

Rooney stroked his chin, absorbing the logic of the objection. He was putting up another defence when Witherspoon broke in.

'Mike, this is one theory you can check out. Ask Jock. Why don't you?'

'I don't know where he is. He moves around.'

'But the police do. He reported the *Caramba* missing, you just told me. I bet they know where he's hanging out.'

Rooney raised an eyebrow at Jim who nodded. Witherspoon rose to leave, saying he mustn't keep Martin Peters waiting. As he stood, he spotted the policeman in the distance and told Rooney. Rooney reacted by dashing along the quayside.

'Wow!' said Witherspoon. 'He has some speed when he wants it.'

Jim was wry. 'Reckon we've lost him too?'

Witherspoon found this very funny. 'Then the wreck's all ours, Jim, yours and mine. And first off, we divide up the stuff stashed away in there.' He jerked a thumb towards the cabin.

Then he stopped laughing and said: 'That's also an interesting point. If Drew slipped away with Jock to conceal the *Caramba*, why take a gold cup with him? You see what I mean, Jim? Mike's full of stories about Drew and where he's gone, but not one of them makes sense. Not real sense, not when you get down to it.'

Then he rapidly descended the companionway. With foreboding, Jim followed.

'A mess,' Witherspoon said. 'It wasn't like this before. Mike's turned the place over.'

'He was checking Drew's things.'

'Or looking for something he wanted.'

Witherspoon mused for a moment, then wheeled towards the steps. 'I really have to go now.'

Jim watched him. The first step. The second step. Up and up, without noticing. How could Denny Witherspoon not notice? How could Mike Rooney run in and out of his cabin a dozen times a day and not notice? It was there, directly in front of them. And as Jim mounted the steps behind Witherspoon he saw it again, bigger and more obvious than before. It was growing, soon it would be the size of a fist. His mind reeled with the unreality of it all, with the preposterous notion that the thing was growing and the ridiculous suspicion Rooney and Witherspoon were bewitched.

Jim and the diver walked along the quayside together and parted by the *Mariposa*'s dinghy. The yacht was anchored out in the harbour because the fishing boats were in and there hadn't been a convenient space when Jim arrived. Witherspoon offered to let Rooney know Jim had sailed for St Elena. No trouble, he said, he'd be passing Rooney and the policeman. They were talking near the Green Parrot bar.

As Jim left the harbour he looked back for the final time in their direction. How skilful was Mike Rooney, he wondered, at eliciting the whereabouts of Jock without revealing his suspicions about the concealment of the *Caramba*? But the two figures were no longer there. Then, just as he felt the yacht lift to meet the open sea, Jim glimpsed them on the quay. They were striding side by side, on their way to Rooney's boat. Rooney was gesticulating, doing the talking. The policeman pushed his cap back and swaggered in the sun.

7

He went out to the wreck with Mike Rooney. He'd
been on St Elena playing games for five days when
Rooney rang and persuaded him. It didn't take much
persuasion.

'I don't like leaving her, that's all,' Rooney said.

'You can't stand guard, Mike.'

If all Rooney wanted to do was check no one else was
diving on the galleon, he could have done so alone. *But if
anything's happened, he'd have said so straight away*, Jim
thought as he hung up. He told Jane he was slipping away
for a while.

'The wreck?' Her eyes shone. It amused her greatly that
while Guy had a dozen friends digging up the island in
search of fake buried treasure, her James had the real
thing.

He pressed a finger to her lips although there was no
need to caution her about discretion. Jane cherished his
secret.

Rooney came up to St Elena to fetch Jim and by great
misfortune was accosted by Guy and several of his friends.
Guy was up on his crutch, the stuffed parrot wobbling on
his shoulder. The friends responded to the tremor with
cries of: 'Pieces of eight! Pieces of eight!' Mike Rooney

looked stunned. He'd blundered on to the set of a pantomime he hadn't been warned about.

'Avast ye!' shouted Guy, striking the air with his crutch.

Rooney gaped, unable to think of a suitable reply. Ahoy came to mind but he balked at joining in the tomfoolery. This was less a matter of dignity than worry that the others knew the script and he didn't. Suppose walking the plank were involved? He looked around frantically, praying for Jim Rush to rescue him.

Jim was late, delayed in fond farewells to Jane. From halfway along the path he had an excellent view of the outlandish scene, a piece of real-life open-air theatre.

As the days had gone by, loud with the clang of spades on earth and with the yelps of riddle-solvers, the friends had gradually acquired stripy jerseys and rolled up their jeans. Several were now running to knotted handkerchiefs on their heads. A handful of these pirates clustered about Rooney, who looked appropriately intimidated even before Guy's flailing with the crutch.

Jim ran down the path. Guy was challenging Rooney's right to be on the island. Rooney found his voice and an altercation took place, although all that could be heard clearly was the chorusing of 'Pieces of eight! Pieces of eight!'

Jim bounded into Rooney's boat. As Rooney scrambled after him, Jim was already casting off.

'*Christ*,' said Rooney, his favourite acknowledgment of amazement. 'They're all mad. What do they think they're doing?'

'Oh, just a game.' He got out of the way to let Rooney start the engine. A couple of pirates were hauling on the boat, holding her at the dock. One was heaving himself up, swinging a leg over to board.

Rooney depressed the throttle. The boat leapt backwards and the pirate yelled and fell face down in the water. Rooney swung the boat round and raced towards the open sea. Jim looked back at the mêlée: soggy figures dragging their companion on to the dock, Guy and his Captain Flint beside themselves with rage, and the chorus jumping up and down and chorusing. He was delighted to leave them all behind.

Once they were out of the bay, Rooney slowed to a calmer pace. He looked like a man who'd awoken from an appalling dream and was trying to reassure himself that it *was* only a dream.

'Jim, what in hell's going on back there?'

'I told you, a game.'

'But they aren't kids.'

'Right.'

'Is everybody on that island crazy?'

'Everybody except me.'

'Well, remind me never to call for you again, OK?'

After they'd travelled some way Rooney asked: 'What would they have done to me if you hadn't come along?'

Jim adopted his Southern drawl. 'Somethin' real mean.'

'I believe it, I really do.' Rooney shuddered. 'Crazy,' he murmured. 'That guy with the parrot . . .'

Jim laughed. 'His name *is* Guy. His cousin owns the place but all the people there now are Guy's friends. And as Guy likes to play games, everybody has to play games.'

'Except you. I can't see you as a pirate.'

'Oh, I play. It's just that I play at playing.'

'Looks like a bloody dangerous game.'

'Theirs or mine?' He was laughing still, knowing there was no way Rooney could know about the games Jim Rush played, the truly dangerous games.

On the telephone Rooney had sounded anxious about the wreck but now they were on their way he was in no special hurry. He set the course, settled for a medium pace and went into the cabin to fetch beer. Jim stayed on deck, feeling free for the first time in days. He was with the man whose partner he'd murdered, he was being taken to the scene of the crime, and yet he felt more at ease than he'd done for days.

St Elena, he decided, was killing him. It was stifling him. It never allowed him to be himself and neither did it allow him to be whoever the other game-players pretended they were. There were games within games, rules about rules. The only rule that mattered was the one ensuring he could never win.

Rooney re-emerged, oblivious of the thing he ought to see every time he mounted the steps from the cabin. He tossed Jim a can of beer and they sat across from each other and drank. Jim didn't notice it was warm. He was too happy to be bobbing along in the freedom of the seas and the great skies to care about details like lukewarm beer. On the nearest island a woman was spreading gaudy washing on rocks by a blue shack. Sugar cane bent to the breeze. Distant islands were invisible, signalled only by the cumulus gathering above them. Jim thought he'd never tire of loving it.

'Jim, you haven't asked about Drew.'

The remark took him by surprise. It was true he hadn't mentioned Drew, not realising the omission would seem odd.

'I assume there's no news or you'd have told me.'

Tilting the can, he took a long draught. Rooney was watching him, he could feel it. He wondered whether he was imagining the suspicion in Rooney's dark eyes.

Rooney said: 'I checked out that *Caramba* idea but it was no good. Jock hasn't seen Drew for months. He levelled with me about hiding the boat but he was adamant he hadn't seen Drew. I believe him.'

Jim was remembering the policeman walking to the boat with Rooney. He wanted very much to know what they'd talked about. He tried in a roundabout way.

'Denny had a bright idea then, Mike. That fat policeman told you where Jock was?'

There was a pause while he drank. Jim remained silent, encouraging him to say more. Eventually Rooney did. 'He got me to tell him about Drew. I didn't mean to get into all that but once I started asking about Jock *he* had a few questions. Why did I want him? Was it in connection with the *Caramba*? That sort of thing.'

Jim prompted. 'I saw you walking along the quay together.'

'He came aboard and took a look at Drew's things. Then he asked if I wanted to report him missing. I said well what difference does it make, the guy *is* missing.'

Jim had a premonition of Drew's florid face on posters all over the islands. 'Did you give him a photograph?'

'Of Drew? He didn't ask for one. Anyway, I wouldn't know where to find one.'

'In his passport?'

'All I could think was he isn't someone who poses for holiday snaps and he's been cut off from his family so long they wouldn't have anything recent.'

Rooney tipped the beer can right up and drained it, then wiped his lips with the back of his hand. 'The thing is, Jim, I've been going round and round it and I don't understand it any more now than I did that first evening. Every time I get a handle on it, something else comes to mind – Denny Witherspoon says something, or Jock says something, or that policeman says something – and I realise it's no good.'

Jim asked, with an effort at casualness, what the policeman had said.

'He said usually if somebody goes and leaves everything behind, it's because they didn't have a choice about going. Something like that, just a throwaway remark. But it set me thinking, Jim. All along I've been cursing Drew and supposing he'd done this and that, none of it good, but what if I'd got it the wrong way round? Something might have been done to *him*.'

Jim looked doubtful. 'Drew isn't easy to push around, Mike.'

He'd dented this theory as easily as Witherspoon had dented earlier ones. Rooney agreed, Drew wasn't a man to be pushed where he didn't choose to go.

'Anyway,' Jim said, 'who'd want to push him around'

And then Rooney reminded him Drew had led the kind of life where one felt safer with a gun in one's pocket.

'He didn't want it any more. He sold up in England, the lot. That's why he bought this boat. Oh, and a place in Spain. He said it was important to put your money in bricks and mortar, some of it anyway. Didn't matter where it was but bricks and mortar was the safest place to put money.'

Drew's logic amused him. 'Do you know, he never saw that house? Not once. He was going out there when I talked him into this instead. It was all furnished, ready to step into, so he said, but he came here. I expected him to be hankering for a holiday there. I mean, this place is great but you can still fancy a holiday, can't you? Not Drew. He wasn't bothered. He'd look at the brochures some nights, and he'd think about his little house but he didn't ever go there.'

'Mike, you don't think . . .'

'Without his passport or any of his gear? No, I don't.'

When Jim offered nothing else he said, frowning: 'It's been too long for him to be keeping his head down if everything's all right.'

'These people he left England to avoid, do you know who they are?'

'Me? No. That was Drew's scene, not mine. I never tangled with anything like that.'

'Was he afraid of them catching up with him here?'

'I told you, Jim. He carried a gun.'

And next, thought Jim, *you're going to tell me the gun's gone as well as Drew*.

Mike Rooney leaned forward, confidentially, although there were miles of empty sea between them and eaves-droppers. 'I didn't tell that fat policeman this because I could see it leading to more questions, but it's missing, Jim. That's the only thing of his that Drew took with him, that bloody gun.'

'Your gold cup and his gun?'

'Not the way you pack to go to Spain, is it?'

Jim answered with a slow shake of the head.

They dropped anchor and Mike Rooney switched on the scanner. Familiar light and dark shapes filled the screen.

Rooney left the wheelhouse. A couple of wetsuits lay on deck. He unbuckled his belt, began to strip off.

'Are you coming down too?'

Jim said not. 'Unless there's anything special you want me to see.' Not even then, he was terrified at the very thought of it.

Rooney was putting on a wetsuit, a dark peel over his olive skin. He stopped for a second, peered at the leg, and then brushed at it with his hand before continuing.

Jim imagined Rooney's hand reddened with Drew's blood, or a twist of Drew's ginger hair in his fingers. Even though he could see Rooney carrying on dressing, unconcerned, the mental picture wouldn't fade. He was convinced it was *the* wetsuit, the one he'd worn to grapple with the body. There were several on board, one bigger one Drew had used but the others average. Although they weren't identical, Jim couldn't remember which logos and trims distinguished the one he'd worn. And because he couldn't, he convinced himself Rooney was wearing the bloodstained one.

He watched him lower himself into the water. Jim sought specks of red in the foam, a pink bubbling rising to the surface. There was no evidence for Rooney to find but, all the same, he expected him to find it.

Rooney was down a long time. Jim had anticipated a brief exploration with the diver reporting what he'd found and then going down a second time with a specific task in mind. That had become the routine. Rooney was changing it.

Jim was at a loss. He needed some guaranteed uninterrupted time on his own in the cabin, and now he didn't know whether he'd get it. Evidence of Drew's fate was in there, the time Rooney was diving was his only chance to destroy it.

He ran down the companionway, his eyes going instantly to the mark. It no longer seemed big and growing, and he felt confident he could disguise it. As he reached out a hand to touch it, he heard Rooney attracting his attention.

Jim helped him over the side. 'You were a long time, Mike. Everything OK?'

Rooney said yes but made it sound as positive as no. He said he'd poked around, trying to find whatever remained of the chest. He hadn't found that but he'd discovered something else.

'Jim, whatever went on down there shifted stuff around. There's a bell. Denny didn't mention *that*, did he?'

Jim caught a tinge of sarcasm and realised Rooney was still smarting at once having had news of the chest withheld from him. Jim excused Witherspoon by saying visibility had been very poor the last time he went down.

'It's excellent today, Jim. There's a slab of something covered in shells and sticking out from under it is the bell.'

'Great. As soon as we fix up the lifting gear we'll see if we can . . .' Rooney's face prevented him going on.

'He was right.'

'Denny?'

'No, Drew.' He sighed, sounding thoroughly depressed. Jim waited for him. Rooney slumped with his head hanging down. He said: 'Right from the start he said it and I wouldn't believe him.'

'Right about what, Mike?' He felt excluded from the conversation, Rooney was talking to himself.

Then Rooney shared the truth he hated to face. 'Drew

said that wreck wasn't the *Gloriosa* and he was right. *Christ*. The time we've spent on her, the money . . . And for what? For the wrong damned ship.'

He stamped about the deck, cursing himself for not listening to Drew, for over-ruling him when all along Drew had been right.

Jim tried several times before he could put questions Rooney was ready to answer.

Rooney said: ' That bell says *Rosita*. Drew tried to tell me the insignia and dates on the cannon weren't proof she was the *Gloriosa* but I couldn't see it. *Wouldn't* see it. She was the right period and in the right place, and so I wouldn't even think about it.'

'What,' Jim asked, 'is the *Rosita*?'

'God knows. Any old ship that fell apart in a storm.'

'No, hold on, Mike. You said to me once that even if she's not the *Gloriosa*, she's still a Spanish galleon and she's worth the game.'

Rooney shrugged. 'I said it, Jim, but I believed it *was* the *Gloriosa*.'

'Mike, in the cabin behind you there's a bundle of pieces from that wreck.' He was pushing Rooney to size up the situation and reach decisions that would stick. He'd seen how Rooney could be swayed this way and that, and it was crucial it didn't happen this time.

Rooney hooted a dismissive laugh. 'Yes, OK, Jim, we've had a few pickings from her. But I've seen those Spanish treasure ships, I've been down on them in Florida. And I've come up with pieces that have financed the entire expedition.'

'OK, we haven't had anything as grand but we're only just beginning.'

'You think that gold cup Drew's run off with is pretty good. Well, that's nothing. No one was going to quibble about a thing like that going missing. The real treasure was in another league. Ingots of gold. Doubloons. But not only valuable materials, there were beautiful things. Gold necklaces and pendants. Porcelain so fine you could see your hand through it . . .'

Jim tried to speak but he cut him off. 'You remember what Denny was gabbling about the other day? The *San José* they've found off the Colombian coast? *That's* real treasure.'

'Mike, nobody's going to match that, it's the richest underwater treasure hoard in the world. And they haven't got it yet, all they've done is locate the wreck. You can't compare . . .'

'No, you can't, can you? We had one possible chest that's disintegrated before we got into it. The *San José* was loaded with four hundred and ten trunks of gold and silver things, gold ingots and doubloons, from Peru. It took them six months to load her and they valued it at way over half a million pesetas, back in 1708.'

'OK, I know. I heard Denny's lecture too.'

Witherspoon had read them acres from a newspaper article about the search. It said the Spanish had sold bulls of indulgence to amass that amount but that historians believed the real value of the cargo was twice the official figure because of the high level of smuggling. Within a few miles of leaving the Bay of Cartagena she was sunk by an English pirate. After scanning fifty thousand square miles of seabed, some American wreck hunters found her, three hundred metres down. The images on their screen fitted her description and the piece of wood they raised proved to be the same type used by her Basque boat-builders. But so far they didn't have the treasure.

Rooney came to a halt by the wheelhouse. He went in and scowled at the screen, then reached out a finger to flick off the scanner.

Jim followed him to the doorway, stood with a hand resting on the jamb, his arm a barrier to keep Rooney in there until he'd finished with him. He spoke evenly.

'Mike, we have to decide whether we're going on with this.' He was almost certain what Rooney's reply would be, the man was at the lowest ebb of disappointment. That talk about the *San José* hoard hadn't helped. There was a world of difference between a minisub search carried out with the help of a government, and the cowboy outfit that was all Rooney could aspire to.

Rooney sagged on to the chair by the wheel. 'No point in it, Jim. None at all. I can't ask you to carry on, on the offchance of a few more silver forks. It's time to cut our losses, both of us.'

'We could talk about this tomorrow. A day makes no difference.'

But Rooney was firm. 'I've decided, Jim. I'm finished with this one.'

'If you're sure.'

'Yes.'

Jim let his arm fall and walked slowly across the deck. He looked down into the smoothly flowing waters. Behind him Mike Rooney came out of the wheelhouse and begin to strip off the wetsuit.

Jim's hands clenched. He'd forced Rooney's decision to give up the wreck and that was good. It had been easy. Next it was essential he destroy the evidence in the cabin, but

Rooney had no intention of diving again. He had to think of a way of persuading him. Then he got it. He asked him to photograph the bell that showed the name *Rosita*.

Rooney demurred, saying his camera was nothing like as efficient as Denny Witherspoon's. He lapsed into technical jargon to describe a problem with the focal length, and then added that his processor was broken. Basically he didn't want to go down again.

'What's the use? She's not the *Gloriosa*.'

'That's exactly it, Mike. You've seen the evidence. I think it's important we record that.'

'You sound like Denny all of a sudden.'

'Maybe he's right. But look, he's photographed everything else down there, it makes no sense to miss out on the clearest indication of her name.'

It took a few more exchanges but in the end Rooney agreed it was worth the final effort of taking photographs of the bell. He managed a weak joke.

'If Drew shows up, convinced she's the *Gloriosa* after all, I'll be able to prove she isn't.' He held out the camera. 'Do you want to do this, Jim? Say goodbye to her?'

Jim said no. He watched Rooney go over the side again. Then he dashed into the cabin, took a tube of sealant from his pocket and tried to fill in the damage the bullet had caused to the panel behind the steps. The hole was ragged and the plastic sealant he'd brought was the wrong colour. Dismayed, he realised it was too light.

Also it needed time to dry. It was supposed to be applied carefully and sanded down and reapplied. He could do none of that. He bodged it, thrusting it into the hole, smoothing it over with a finger, wiping away the excess as it dribbled down the panel.

He'd been wrong, then, about the angle of the shot. It couldn't have been upwards as Drew leaped down into the cabin because that would have sent the bullet on deck or into the sea. No, it had passed through Drew's body and into the panel. But where did it end up? He was desperate to find it and dispose of it.

Opening the floor hatch in the wheelhouse, he looked down into the engine house. Two layers of acoustic lining separated it from the cabin: a lead lining to cut out low frequency noise and a plastic foam layer for high frequency. Neither of them was marked by the passage of a bullet. Well then, it had lodged in there, hidden itself in the acoustic lining and left only the hole in the cabin panelling as evidence of its journey. It would be a long job to recover it, and he would have no opportunity to do so. The best he could hope for was to disguise the hole. He closed the hatch and returned to patching up the hole.

All the time he was mentally charting Rooney's progress. Rooney wasn't on a journey of exploration this time. He knew exactly where he was heading, he had a very brief job to do when he got there and he'd surface again in a very few minutes.

Jim wished he could keep him down there to allow himself time to fill the hole properly. He thought about moving the boat. If he couldn't force Rooney to linger with the wreck, he could prevent him reboarding. He could simply take the boat away.

He stood back and looked at his handiwork. The small hole that originally troubled him was now at the centre of a shining wet patch an inch wide. Not only did it look terrible and terribly obvious, but chemical smells permeated the cabin.

Taking a knife from the galley, Jim scraped at the shiny area. This altered the appearance but didn't improve it. He wiped the knife on a paper handkerchief and returned it to the galley. When he turned back to the companionway, the bullet hole seemed a pale eye staring at him from a greyish patch on a dark wood panel. He groaned.

He could move the boat. He could take it a little way off and give himself time to deal with the hole. When Rooney surfaced he'd have to splash around until he was picked up. Tempting. But as Jim had no solution to the problem of the bullet hole, it seemed foolish to indulge in what amounted to threatening behaviour simply for the sake of doing it. Besides, how long would it take a scared Mike Rooney, abandoned miles from land, to realise that the last time he'd seen Drew, his partner had been on board this boat with Jim Rush and at this very spot?

Jim blotted the hole and the patch around it with a piece of paper, not another tissue because they left wisps of paper fibres behind, but a smooth sheet torn from a notepad. He crumpled the paper, concealed it in his pocket and went up on deck.

The water was undisturbed. A ferry with old patched sails was passing down the chain of islands but no other craft were in sight. He looked down through the pellucid water to see whether he could spot the froggy form of Rooney on its way to the surface but there was nothing except a shoal of green and gold fish.

He returned to the cabin, drawn back to it. The chemical smell was unmistakable. He looked around for something to disguise it. At least he could do something about the odour.

He made coffee. He made it strong, with heaped

spoonfuls of the Colombian brand whose flavour he especially liked. As its rich aroma filled the cabin, he blessed the day he'd upgraded Drew and Rooney from instant.

Leaving the coffee mug on a low heat with its lid off, he went on deck and gulped sea air and then ran down into the cabin again. There was nothing to be detected but the encouraging smell of freshly made coffee. He went back up, the white eye of the bullet hole gazing at him as he passed it.

Before long Rooney surfaced, saying he'd taken several other shots as well as those of the partly exposed bell, and in particular the area where the chest had once stood. He admitted trying to heave the bell free, hoping to bring it up, but also admitted to being nervous.

'I kept thinking everything might cave in, the way the chest did.'

While they drank their coffee, Jim offered to get the film processed, saying he knew a place where he could get it done quickly and without any risk of losing it. Mike Rooney removed the film from the camera and handed him the evidence.

Martin Peters put down his knife and fork and leaned back in his chair. 'Jim. Great to see you.'

'Sorry about the timing.'

'No, no. Sit down.'

Peters pushed one of the rattan chairs across the terrace towards Jim with his foot. 'Have you eaten yet? No, don't lie to me. I can tell you haven't.'

Before Jim could put up token resistance Peters was on his feet and using the hotel telephone. 'They'll be here in no time,' he said afterwards. 'Well, make that their kind of no time. Drink?'

'Thank you.'

Peters poured wine into a spare glass. 'So, what brings you to Bamboo Lodge this evening?'

'This.' Jim put Mike Rooney's roll of film on the table between them. 'I need it in a hurry and I don't want to risk losing it. Can you do it?'

Peters picked up his fork and gestured at the film with it before eating. 'Polaroid transparencies? Easy. I've got one of mine to do, too. You're lucky, mind, to find me here. I only got in this afternoon and I'm off again tomorrow.'

'I know, I met Denny down at the harbour.'

Peters forked another mouthful. Not wanting to ask a question the man might choose to answer while chewing, Jim went on: 'He told me you didn't get what you were looking for.'

Peters took a gulp of wine before admitting he was disappointed with the way things had gone. The ship had passed but he'd seen nothing switched from it to a smaller boat and nothing tossed over the side for reclamation later.

'What do you think went wrong?' Jim asked.

A shake of the head, the twin bushes of hair bouncing. 'Perhaps somebody got a tip-off that the police were on to it. I haven't had time to ask around yet.'

His eyes narrowed. 'Jim, you didn't pick up anything about it from Drew or Rooney, did you?'

Jim said not. 'I'm convinced you're wrong about them, Martin. They're nothing more than a couple of guys who like poking around on the seabed. Some people go along the beach with metal detectors, these two scan below the water.'

Martin Peters made a face that said he thought Jim quite naïve but he wasn't prepared to argue about it. The hotel servant arrived then with Jim's supper and the subject was dropped for a time. When it revived Peters remarked that although he'd found no proof that Drew or Rooney or both were involved in arms dealing, Drew had been behaving very oddly and he'd done so around the time a consignment was expected.

'Denny told me about him going off. Disappearing, was the way he put it. Where do you reckon he's got to, Jim?'

Jim shrugged. 'Mike's come up with half a dozen theories, none of them fit. All we know is Drew stepped off his boat in the harbour and walked away.'

'Denny says . . .' He stopped himself, covered up by taking a sip of wine.

'Yes?'

Peters dabbed his mouth with his napkin, an unexpectedly feminine act. 'Oh, you know our Denny, the way he talks.'

'Go on, Martin. Say what he said.'

He answered leisurely, in what Jane described as his cricket commentator's voice, the softness roughed up by rolling 'r's. 'He's building a big, big mystery out of it. Drew decides to opt out for a few days, that's all. *I* say he's fixing something up with his smuggling pals. Maybe Mike Rooney doesn't know about it, maybe I got it wrong about Rooney. But Drew, he's involved for certain. I'd stake my last roll of film on it.'

'What's Denny's version?'

'He says there's no independent proof, information either comes from Rooney or from you.'

Peters was speaking lightly but Jim noticed the contradictory gleam in his eyes. He imagined Peters and Witherspoon trapped for ages on the little motor cruiser with nothing to occupy them but gossip. Of course they mulled over what might have become of Drew. Of course they swapped opinions about Mike Rooney and Jim Rush. He thought Witherspoon would have been cagey about the wreck, though, because he stood to lose by it if he weren't, but Peters had probably weaseled the truth out of him.

Jim conceded Witherspoon was right, the information had all come from him or Rooney. 'But it's not as though exhaustive inquiries have been made, is it? There could be a dozen people walking around on this island who have a lot more information than we do but nobody's asked them yet.'

After they'd eaten, Martin Peters took Jim's film and developed it in a replica of the magic box Denny Witherspoon owned. A brief whizzing and whirring, and soon Jim was looking at the bell bearing the name *Rosita*.

'So that's the Rooney wreck,' said Peters. 'Is she worth anything?'

Mischievously Jim asked: 'You mean you couldn't get Denny to say?'

'Denny became intriguingly clam-like. Obviously he couldn't deny he dives on a wreck because unless he looks for dumped boxes of sub-machine-guns, then what am I supposed to think he does out there?'

He looked down the strip of transparencies. 'Well, I know now, anyway. Three cannon, half a bell and a load of coral. Bit of a waste of time by the look of it, Jim. Sorry you played?'

Jim laughed it off. 'It was a wonderful dream while it

lasted, Martin, and a terrific excuse to spend time out on the water. And what the hell, I've seen a Spanish galleon!'

The word *Rosita* was legible with the aid of a magnifying glass. Jim had got what he wanted and was happy to leave but Peters made him a present of some mounts to make slides, and poured him a glass of rum.

'This wreck, this *Rosita*,' said Peters, 'where did you say she was?'

'I didn't, Martin. Now tell me about *your* film. If you didn't post it off to a newspaper or a magazine, it's not your usual work. Right?'

'Right. Just a bit of scenery, sunset over the ocean, fishing boats at dusk and whatnot.'

He refilled his glass and settled back in his chair and talked about how he'd always thought he'd be a landscape photographer until, quite by accident, he'd fallen among journalists. One thing led to another and he found himself specialising in celebrity pics.

'I've promised myself, Jim, one day when I'm too old for this royalty caper I'll switch to landscapes. I sell a few now – book illustrations, magazine travel features, advertising . . . There are plenty of outlets. And I've taken some good pictures, I'm not too shy to admit it. That film I developed this evening, I'll be surprised if there isn't at least one shot that pays for the day.'

The day had been one of his more expensive ones. He'd hired an aeroplane. In other words he'd been a spy in the sky, snooping on the secluded islands where the rich and famous sought a privacy he chose to deny them. Landscape photography hadn't interested him until the home run.

'I persuaded the pilot to come down really low over the waves, God knows how we didn't get our feet wet. Still, that's the secret, isn't it? Dedication, in whatever you do. Dedication.'

He mentioned one of the islands he'd photographed, saw-tooth mountains silhouetted against a bright afternoon sky. Jim couldn't place it. Peters said it was a tiny speck of rock near the southernmost tip of the archipelago.

'The pilot was good. Of course, I'll have to wait and see whether he's available to me in future. It gets more difficult. They get warned off, you know.'

When Jim raised a puzzled eyebrow, he explained: 'I used to have a choice, there were several glad of the work. Now they all have their excuses ready. Well, that's OK. I understand their position. If they do a job for a cheeky devil like me once or twice a year, they risk losing their bread-and-butter work as a reprisal. You can't blame them.'

In a while Jim made a move to leave. Peters kept swinging the conversation round to Drew and Rooney and the wreck. Especially to Drew. A wrecked galleon and a disappearing wreck hunter appealed to his sense of drama. Jim felt he'd contributed to the situation himself by shutting down all attempts to probe life on St Elena and the neighbouring islands. It didn't leave them much apart from the weather. At one point it would have come as a relief if Martin Peters had shown his landscapes, but although he'd indulged himself by talking about them, he did not.

Jim asked Peters to call him a taxi and asked the driver to take him to the harbour. This was the easiest destination to give, especially as he had to do it in Peters' hearing. Jim thought of changing it once he was on the move, but there was nowhere better to go.

Once there he spotted Denny Witherspoon on his

cruiser. Witherspoon was less than delighted to see him. Earlier everything had seemed fine but that had been the briefest encounter.

Jim invited himself aboard and started to explain he and Rooney had decided to abandon the wreck.

Witherspoon was sharp. 'Mike already talked to me.' He looked confused and het up. He said: 'The job for Martin Peters falls through and now this.'

'A rotten coincidence.'

'I liked it, I really liked going out there with you all and working on her.'

'I know. It's a big disappointment to all of us.'

Witherspoon realised he sounded self-pitying and changed his drift. 'Jim, I'm really sorry it didn't work out for you. I mean, for me it was a bonus, a bit extra while I was waiting for Martin. But you guys invested a lot in it.'

'You did a fine job, Denny.'

A sudden hope fluttered. 'Jim, that's Drew's boat Mike's got over there, right? What if Drew comes back and wants to go on with the wreck?'

'Oh, come on, Denny. You know he won't do that. Remember how he was always dragging back when Mike wanted to go full steam ahead?'

Ruefully Witherspoon admitted that yes, that was the way of it. He glanced around the harbour. A young couple were cuddling in the lighted cabin of a plastic palace anchored a few yards away. Outside the Green Parrot a handful of people chatted, their laughter brittle across the water. Witherspoon's body trembled as though he were chilled by a sudden breeze. But there was no breeze, the air was cloying.

He looked troubled and cold, the Californian confidence

wrung out of him. He muttered something about feeling tired and went to the cabin, leaving Jim to walk away into the night.

'Martin Peters is a menace, Jim. Can't you lure him away to bother someone else? You must have somebody on St Elena who's more interesting than I am.' Mike Rooney poured scalding water on to Colombian coffee.

Jim dragged his gaze from the pale eye staring at him from the panel behind the stairs. 'Martin? What's he doing to you?'

'First he comes wandering by with his camera and snaps me eating my breakfast. Says he's idling away the morning taking pretty pics of the harbour. Then he hangs around and asks about Drew.'

'So far, so normal. I don't see the problem.'

'The problem is he's been talking to Denny and he's caught a dose of mysteryitis. Everything I said, he wanted to know how I knew it. You know the way Denny's mind works, Jim. Well, Martin Peters was doing a fair impersonation of our Californian friend.'

'Where is he, by the way?'

'Denny? He took off early this morning. I went on deck about eight and saw his boat on the way out of the harbour.'

'Was he alone?'

'From what I could see.'

Rooney took a couple of mugs off their hooks and poured the coffee. There was no milk, he offered a creamy white powder instead. Jim chose to drink his black.

'To get back to Martin Peters,' said Rooney, stirring powder. 'When he'd finished going on about Drew he started on the wreck, trying to find out where she lies.'

'But you didn't tell him?' He was afraid that now Rooney had given her up, he saw no reason to be reticent.

'Not the faintest hint.' He frowned. 'But I got the idea he knew. In fact I wondered whether . . .'

'No, I said nothing about her location. He learned from Denny we had a wreck, and he learned from me she was no good and we abandoned her. I went so far as to say she was collapsing, to put him off.'

'That would put anyone off.'

Content with that, Rooney sipped the coffee but it was too hot to drink so he set the mug down on the cabin table. Jim thought they'd finished with Martin Peters and was surprised by Rooney's next remark.

'Because of Martin Peters I had a visit from that fat policeman.'

'You did? When?'

'Yesterday afternoon. He marched up here with a string of questions about our gear and what we use it for. I said what I usually say, about pipelines and cables, but he wasn't having it. Then I caught on, somebody had told him we'd found a wreck.'

Jim smothered a smile. It was absurd Rooney believed anyone would accept the cables and pipelines cover. A tourist might be fooled but not a man with local knowledge.

Rooney went on: 'He warned me there's a procedure for reporting wrecks and handing over valuables recovered from them. He said it isn't a free-for-all.'

'And what did you say to that?'

'I denied we'd ever struck lucky. I mean, we aren't going out there again so why get involved in any legal hassle?' Laughing he added: 'He was sitting right there, Jim, where you are. If he'd leaned over and raised the lid of that locker, he'd have seen exactly what came off her.'

They were still joking about it when they heard the name of the boat called. Rooney recognised the voice and his smile died. He went up, signalling Jim to stay where he was, out of sight.

Jim heard the lilting cadence of the policeman's island accent, heard him quite clearly, saying: 'Sorry to trouble you again, Mr Rooney, but it's necessary for us to continue that conversation we were having yesterday.'

Then Rooney's voice, a mite petulant, showing nervousness. 'Look, I've got nothing to tell you that I haven't already said. Absolutely nothing.'

'Maybe that's right, Mr Rooney, but we have to talk anyway. My place this time. In one hour, shall we say?'

'If it's *really* important.'

'I'd say it's important, Mr Rooney. One hour. OK?'

Jim heard the man walk away down the quay. Rooney remained on deck for a few minutes before returning to the cabin.

'Did you get that, Jim? More questions.'

Jim had been weighing up what to suggest. He came down in favour of warning Rooney. It was a gamble because genuine amazement at false allegations could be a surer defence than a prepared denial.

He began tentatively, then rushed out with it. 'Martin Peters is convinced you and Drew smuggle arms.'

Rooney's face was the classic picture of stupefaction. Jim knew it wasn't faked. He'd never wanted to believe Peters and now he felt justified. If Rooney could repeat this reaction when the policeman put it to him, he should be all right.

Eventually, when Rooney had run through the gamut of disbelief and indignation, he began to worry. What had Peters said to persuade the police to take the accusation seriously? What had convinced Peters himself?

Jim remembered something. 'He showed me a photograph of you in the forest near the old plantation house.'

'But that's where we store our things.'

'Martin thinks you stash arms consignments there.'

'The man's crazy.'

'He's wrong, OK, he's wrong. But if he's responsible for the police interest in you, this is the kind of thing he's told them.'

He looked at his watch. Fifteen minutes had gone by since the policeman called. Say it took fifteen to walk over to the police station. That gave Rooney half an hour to work out the best way to refute the allegations.

'Let's talk this through,' Jim said.

When it was time for Rooney to set off, he seemed reasonably confident he could produce a convincing denial to any of Martin Peters' nonsense. He and Jim shared the first part of the journey, Jim seeking a boat to ferry him to St Elena. He didn't want to go but felt he ought to. He'd spent yet another night away, and these jaunts outside the magic circle didn't endear him to Guy.

But when they reached the point where their paths diverged, Rooney weakened and pleaded with him not to leave the island. Despite his tanned and olive skin, he paled. And although he tried to keep it light hearted his voice wavered.

'I want somebody here who knows I was last seen walking into that police station. You'd know what to do if I didn't come out, right?'

It was all the excuse Jim needed. 'Don't worry, Mike, I'll stay around. We'd better have a plan though.'

'Meet back at the boat at two?'

'No, make that five.'

Rooney frowned. 'You think it's going to take that long?'

'No, but as I'm staying there's something I want to do today. Make it five at the latest. If you're not back on board by then, I'll go down to the police station and ask why.'

'Thanks, Jim.'

'Good luck.' He strolled away, determined to look relaxed and unconcerned, and wishing Rooney was managing to do likewise.

Although Jim made it appear an aimless amble, a stroll before the frying heat of the day, he knew exactly where he was going. He walked along a beach of pink sand, over a shoulder of rock that made a headland, around a bay and then was brought up short by a fence enclosing tourist villas. By cutting inland and climbing a hill he was able to enter the gardens of Bamboo Lodge.

Concealed by trees he looped behind the main building and the scattered *cabañas*. The terrace where he'd been fed by Martin Peters was secluded and shrouded by shrubs. He began to fiddle the catch on the terrace doors. A sound of running water sent him scuttling for cover. Jim was certain Peters had mentioned going on one of his snooping expeditions. He wondered whether the policeman had asked him to stay, because of the story he was spinning about Rooney and Drew.

Jim was puzzled why Peters was spreading the story because if he had Rooney arrested or frightened off, he was cheating himself of the pictures he'd spent weeks waiting for. The ship would make another passage, he could try a second time for shots of the dumped crates and the men bringing them ashore. Unlike Jim, Peters' faith in the story was undimmed, and so his behaviour was illogical.

It was possible someone else, perhaps a hotel servant cleaning, was in the *cabaña*. Jim went to the main entrance of the hotel and asked the receptionist to check whether Mr Peters was in. Down in the *cabaña*, Martin Peters lifted his telephone.

Jim told him he'd mislaid a gold ballpoint pen and might have left it there a couple of days ago. Peters said he hadn't found it and suggested Jim come and look.

The imaginary pen was described so lovingly that Jim rather regretted its loss. He could picture the engraved initials Jane paid to have done when she bought it, one of her impulse gifts in London.

Peters emerged from a corner where he was exploring beneath a cupboard. He paused on one knee. 'It's always worse when it's a present. I once lost a cigarette lighter my wife gave me, never heard the end of it. You'd have thought it was the Crown Jewels. Each time she mentioned it, it got more valuable.'

Jim had never thought of Martin Peters having a wife, he seemed wedded to his work. He asked whether the lighter had been found and Peters, getting to his feet, said not.

He dusted his trouser legs. 'I'll give you a call if I come across the pen.'

Jim began to make his farewells but, exactly as he expected, Peters delayed him. This time it was with the offer of a beer.

'Time for a quick one? I've got to be off myself in half an hour.'

They opened the doors to the terrace and sat out there again. Jim encouraged Peters to tell him his movements, where he was going and when he intended to return. He carefully avoided mentioning Drew or Rooney, not even Denny Witherspoon.

Peters' eyes were indicating that he too wanted more out of this conversation than a discussion of wind and weather. What he was actually saying was that he was going to visit another island, one where there was black magic to be seen.

'If I can sneak a few shots, it'll pay very nicely.'

'You have to be careful with that, Martin. They don't like anyone messing with it.'

Peters pulled a long face. 'Killjoy.'

'I'm telling you it's dangerous.'

'Oh come on, a few old ladies and some chicken guts? You're not telling me I'm supposed to be scared of them?'

Jim shrugged. 'Don't be scared, be careful. That's all.'

A sly look came over Martin Peters. 'How about you coming along, Jim?'

'Me?'

The suggestion was alarming and then enticing. Of course, he'd be interested to see precisely what went on, and at the same time he'd be preventing Peters stirring up further trouble about spurious arms dealing. While he didn't care deeply about Mike Rooney's fate at the hands of the police, it couldn't be ignored that Rooney being questioned about arms dealing with Drew was virtually the same thing as Rooney being asked about Drew's disappearance. The fewer questions anyone raised about that, the better.

Besides, Peters was turning the voodoo outing into a

dare. Hard to resist, always had been. 'Bet you're too scared' – it was tantamount to saying that.

Jim let Martin Peters talk him round. He finished his beer and rose to leave. 'Can I meet you at the harbour, say on the hour?'

'I'm using a boat called the *Jasmine*. The boatman looks half dead but swears he knows the way.'

Back on board Rooney's boat, Jim wrote a message which he left on the table, using a lump of coral as a paperweight. He didn't spell out who he was with and where he was going, only that he intended to call on Rooney either very late that night or, more likely, early next day. He signed off with his initial, J. Then he went in search of the *Jasmine* and black magic.

8

'"*That old black magic . . .*" Oops.' Martin Peters stopped
singing and whisked a glance over his shoulder. The owner
of the *Jasmine* was negroid with a half-closed eye that made
him seem surly.

Peters slid along the seat towards Jim. 'Looks like a
zombie, doesn't he? Just the chap to take to the party we're
going to.'

And before Jim could reply: 'Hey, do you know that in
Haiti they had a law that said they weren't allowed to raise
the dead to work in the fields?' He looked at his watch.
'God, I wish we'd get there.'

'You said nothing's going to happen until sundown.'

'I want to look around first, get the feel of the place.'

Jim registered the shift, the second the eyes were saying
something different from the mouth. So it wasn't only black
magic Peters was after.

'What we'll do,' the photographer was saying, 'is scout
around the port and then take a taxi up to the village. If we
time it right we'll catch them with the whole kit and
caboodle.'

'Which is?'

'Drums? Goats? Chickens? War paint?'

Jim laughed. 'They're not Red Indians.'

'They're every damn thing. You look at the faces, Jim, the shades of skin tone.'

Jim raised a hand to shield off a lecture. Peters was excited and talkative this afternoon. Perhaps he was always like this when he was on what he called a good story.

Peters lectured him anyway, with a tale about a French official bewitched by his mistress and prevented from sailing home. Then another about a woman whose malevolent stare ruined lives by depriving her victims of sleep.

He said: 'Of course, you can't photograph any of that. Sleeplessness or . . .'

'Superstition.'

'But a ceremony, that's perfect. Mind if I ask you a favour?' He held up a camera.

'You're asking me to take photographs?'

'Just point and click. It focuses and does the rest itself.' He demonstrated by taking a photograph of Jim.

Jim was too slow to obscure his face. He disguised his objection by demanding a second shot. 'Hold on, Martin, I wasn't smiling.'

Later, he thought, he'd destroy that film. It was impossible to allow Peters two portraits of him, tantamount to pasting up a wanted poster.

The island hunched on the horizon, blue and sombre. It didn't look at all like a place he wanted to go to, and his misgivings about gate-crashing a voodoo session revived.

Peters subsided into nervousness. When they landed, he was curt with the boatman. Jim was embarrassed and made a placating gesture but he was on the side of the man's bad eye and it was doubtful he was noticed.

As they walked along the dock, Peters dangled the key to the engine. 'That'll stop him sliding off into the night.'

Jim deliberately misinterpreted the flaunting of the key and took it from him. 'Sure, I'll look after it.'

The dock was a poor place, with old tyres nailed to its beams to protect boats from the roughness. There were only a couple there, fishing boats that had known better days and richer owners. Others were upturned on the sand, men lounging against them. A street of weathered houses ran up into the town. Jim noticed how Peters was checking everyone and everything, searching, always searching.

'Martin, are you looking for information about the voodoo?'

Peters was derisive. 'They don't put up posters, Jim. "Black magic. Eight tonight in the forest clearing. If wet, in the church hall. Dress informal. Entrance . . ." What's the local currency, do you think? Beads? Shells?'

'There's a taxi over there.'

But Peters was striding on, away from the taxi. Then he recognised his own rudeness and turned, saying: 'This event, Jim . . . the Neighbours are supposed to be there.'

'Who?' Then he realised. 'Martin! You can't involve me in . . .'

But Peters was chuckling wickedly. 'Too late, old friend.'

'You didn't say anything about this.'

'Cheeky, eh? Anyway, it's what you might call academic, isn't it? Apart from the boat we came in, there are two old crocks tied up back there.'

The taxi driver refused to take them once he knew where they wanted to go. Peters said what the hell, they'd walk. It was uphill. The road was pale and dusty, the first couple of miles without shade. Women wearing faded cotton dresses sat on the steps of wooden houses and watched them go by. They came to a fort, standard issue for the islands until they got near enough to see it was still in use, as a prison.

'They've probably got him in there,' said Peters. 'The one that did the murder.'

They stopped and wiped the sweat from their faces. Below the fort lay the sea, smooth blue miles to the thrusting peak of a bigger island where the murderer would be taken to be hanged. Unless the voodoo worked.

Peters ran the handkerchief around the back of his neck. 'My contact tells me the family are paying for the witchdoctor to get him off. They aren't saying he's innocent, mind. Only that if they buy the services of an obeah doctor, he'll escape justice.'

'I thought it was all about love potions and revenge, I didn't know this.'

'Interested, Jim? Could be useful, couldn't it?'

The tone was jocular, the eyes deadly. Peters was toying with him. If he'd said at the outset they were going to witness a ceremony carried out to save a murderer from the gallows, Jim wouldn't, *couldn't*, have gone. But Peters had hedged until they were on their way. Jim's head swam. Could Peters be threatening him with secret knowledge about Drew's death? Or about the trouble in London?

He felt a fool to have committed himself to hours of Martin Peters. He was seeing far too much of him. Boredom, he decided, that was why it had happened. All his life things had happened to him because he was bored.

He'd known that feeling when he was too young to put a name to it, that empty, exhausted, unused feeling, a yearning, a dissatisfaction, a restless urge to *do* something, *go* someplace. He'd wanted a proper life, where things happened and people had real conversations and lived like they did on television. In a way, it was still what he wanted.

Peters started talking again, telling him about the more familiar uses of obeah: love potions made from the yellow love vine, *Cusenta Americana*; poisonous plants used to kill or sicken rivals; people frightened to death by discovering a coffin at the door, or a rusty knife hung on it, or a black thread linking nails on the house. Victims committed suicide or lay down to die a natural death.

The glare had gone from the sun but the air was hot and damp. Peters stopped again to get his breath. Then: 'A magistrate summed it up nicely years ago by saying obeah is fraud and sometimes it's murder.' He gave a harsh laugh. 'It's also a money-maker if you can grab pictures of royalty watching it.'

As they passed an isolated house, where a silk hammock was slung from a tree, they heard the drums.

'Shango,' said Peters. The way he spat out the word it might have been a curse. 'African dancers, Jim. That puts them in a trance. Heavy stuff when they send for the drums. Costs more. Mind you, it's a serious business dodging the gallows. You'd pay up and to hell with the extra, wouldn't you?'

There he was again, linking Jim and the murderer. Jim followed him up the road, a step behind, wondering whether Peters was doing it consciously or whether it wasn't his own hysterical reaction doing it. You this and you that – it was a manner of speaking. Jeremy or Guy would have been saying one this and one that, and he wouldn't have been upset at all.

The drums grew louder. A man came through the trees

and blocked their way, saying it wasn't possible to enter the village.

Martin Peters was impressive. He plunged into an act as a camera-toting tourist, waggling his tourist brochure with its crude map and asking after the local brand of parrot.

'How do we get round, then? Is there a path over that way?'

'No path.'

Peters persisted and as soon as the man admitted it was possible to skirt the village, Peters was off like a stone from a sling. When he judged he and Jim were close to the drums, he left the track and made towards them.

He handed Jim a camera, not the one he'd used to photograph him on the boat but another one. 'You shoot from here, Jim. I'm going round to the right. I'll see you on the path.'

'OK, but make it quick.' He disliked the heady rhythm of the drums, he was nervous of being caught.

Through foliage he aimed the camera at a group of men and women. He couldn't see the drummer or any dancers. An old woman filled his lens, unmoving, staring straight towards him. He pressed the shutter.

Her mouth began to work. He pressed the shutter a second time and as it clicked she threw back her head and sank to the ground. She lay there twitching.

He photographed the people who came to surround her, photographed their flying limbs and urgent movements. The drum beat made him increasingly unsteady. There was no victim but there was menace. He backed away to the path and sought Peters.

Peters waved him away. He was shooting a mêlée of figures obscuring the drummer. For him it was pure spectacle.

'Martin, I think we should leave.'

'Like hell. It's just warming up. Look at *her*.'

The old woman Jim had watched came staggering forward. People encircled her, as her body was racked by the rhythm. Her eyes were open but sightless. Peters gestured to Jim to photograph her, as he was doing.

Jim snatched another shot and then tugged Peters' sleeve. 'Let's go.'

Peters jerked free. His eye went to the viewfinder again. Jim had gone about twenty yards before Peters came tearing after him, furious but afraid of being abandoned there.

A woman spied on them from the trees. Peters gasped. 'Did you see that?' But Jim was ahead of him and speeding.

Reaching the roadway, Jim looked in the direction of the village. Three men were coming. He shouted to Peters. 'Quick.'

He was sure they'd be overtaken if they ran all the way down the long hill to the town, so when they reached the house with the hammock, he dashed down the side of it and found a way to the beach below. The sun was low. They waded around a headland and, quite close to the town, regained the road. Women's eyes glinted at them like fireflies from the steps of wooden houses, but it felt safe.

As they reached the street leading to the dock, they saw the men. Half a dozen of them, waiting. Automatically, Jim sidestepped into an alley. Alone, he would have tricked his way past them but with Martin Peters in tow that was hopeless. It was going to be a dash for the boat, nothing elegant.

He flew down a side street and sprang on to the roof of a car parked by a wall. Too astonished to do otherwise, Peters aped him. Jim poised on the wall and gave him a second to accept a hand up. Then they dropped on to the quay. Men were already running towards them.

Jim was aboard, slashing the rope that secured the *Jasmine* and pushing her off. He assumed Peters was aboard too, he had no fractions of seconds to check. Heads appeared on one of the boats moored alongside, but Jim pushed against it and it swung away.

He started up the engine, bringing the *Jasmine* round until she nosed out to sea. Then he looked for Martin Peters.

Peters was on his hands and knees on deck, hunched over his camera bag. He was stashing away the camera Jim had used.

'All right, Martin?'

A breathless nod followed by: 'What did you get?'

Jim ignored the question and opened up the throttle. He couldn't hear Peters until the man struggled to his feet and limped across to join him. Then Jim told him he'd photographed the old woman. They had to shout to each other above the engine noise.

'The witchdoctor, the obeah,' Peters said.

'Was she?'

Peters winked. 'Well, she *will* be by the time those pictures are published.'

Then he remembered something. 'Oh, what about the zombie?'

'You fixed a time and he wasn't there. We can't go back, Martin.'

Peters looked back, though. There was doubt in his voice when he spoke next. 'Jim . . .'

Jim turned. The elderly fishing boat was leaving her moorings. She was at least as fast and her crew had the advantage of knowing the waters.

Shortly after, he glanced back again and saw she was already leaving the harbour. Beside him Martin Peters gave an hysterical laugh.

'Black magic and now pirates!'

'"If they chase the enemy, let them that chase shoot no ordnance till he be ready to board him, for that will let his ship's way."'

'What on earth?'

'Orders to King Henry VIII's sailors, who as you know, Martin, made pretty good pirates. Let as in hindrance, way as in progress, in case you were going to ask.'

'I wasn't, I'm struck dumb by your erudition.'

'You quote Cole Porter, I quote Thomas Audley. It takes all sorts.'

For a few minutes Peters occupied himself by taming his hair which the wind kept flinging into his eyes. He clutched at the twin bushes and held them flat, emphasising the near baldness of his crown. Then he could contain his worry no longer.

'You're going a bit close to those rocks, aren't you?'

'Very. How are we doing behind?'

Their pursuers were closing on them. The fishing boat had a bigger engine, she'd overtake them before they reached the reef and the open sea. But there were rocks, there was a chance. It was ebb tide, it was a devil of a chance.

Peters was frightened, chattering nervous jokes about black magic and piracy being enough without shipwreck as well.

Jim glanced behind. The other boat seemed an arm's length away. On his portside the rocky islets parted and a white-water channel threatened a rough ride. It looked worse than he'd expected. Another glance round. The gap had narrowed to a hand's reach. Jim swung the tiller.

He called to Peters, offering hilarious, spurious reassurance. 'There won't be any shipwreck. I have one eye closed and I'm going for the gap.'

Immediately the yacht was seized by twisting eddies that sent her racing down the gorge. As cliffs cut off the light and the breeze, he wrenched the tiller to keep her in the middle of the channel. The sea was growling on rocks, tossing the boat to shake her free of his control. He fought back, willing her towards the light at the end. Every ounce of him was engaged in the combat, he had nothing left for dread.

Ebb tide, and her keel had a six-foot draught. Any moment she could be grounded, tipped over, battered to matchwood. And there was only the slenderest chance of a swimmer surviving the maelstrom. He'd flung the boat into a tide race at its wildest.

He saw things that weren't there. A yacht battling towards him. The mast of a sunken galleon. A red tartan rug in the snarling water. Each shadow became a threat. But he had no time for dread.

Quite abruptly it ended. The boat was ejected on a tremendous outrush of water into a seething sea silvered by moonlight. And it was quiet. The thundering noise of trapped water battering stone had stopped. It was too quiet. His hand went for the key but there was no response. The engine was dead.

Drifting. Drifting in moonlight. Drifting in moonlight with an enemy chasing the long, safe way around the islets and the coral reef to seize her. The *Jasmine* drifted.

'Can't you fix it, Jim?'

'I'm not an engine man.'

He was struggling with sails. Patched old sails. Peters was no use, a let and a hindrance. He was desperate to help but inexperienced. After a few blunders brought cross words, he demoted himself to look-out and kept watch for pursuers.

'Jim, do you think they followed us down the channel?'

'They wouldn't be so crazy!'

Breeze slapped into canvas and she was suddenly alive, carving a line through silver sheen. Wind and current were with her. Now she could out-distance anything that came out of that harbour back there. She fled for home.

Martin Peters ransacked the cabin for rum, beer, anything to take the edge off his hunger and celebrate his escape from several kinds of destruction. There was nothing.

'What was it anyway?' he asked, coming to sit on deck again.

'Probably a short in the electrics. As we came out of that channel, the spray had the cockpit awash.'

'Me too. I thought I was going to drown without going in.' He stuck out a leg to illustrate wet trousers and shoes. 'I'm deeply grateful that you saved my life again, Jim, but would it be all right with you if we now sauntered coolly back to base? It was great fun while it lasted but if you've got any other novelties lined up, just forget 'em, OK?'

He fidgeted for a bit, then said: 'Wish I'd got one of that woman glaring at us through the trees, Jim. A real black look, that was.'

'Or would be by the time the picture was published.'

Peters smiled, his warm cuddly look firmly in place. 'Reckon I've been bewitched?'

And he sang, picking up the song in mid verse: '"*that same old witchcraft . . .*"'

The tune got stuck in his head. Jim started another conversation, purely to stop it. He preferred the natural sounds of a sail in the wind and the slap of water on a hull. But right then he preferred anything to another reprise.

He said something banal, about how he was looking forward to getting back, but Peters twisted it around.

'Outsiders, Jim, that's us. No, don't look like that, it's true. We don't fit. Me, I'm not supposed to, I'm the fly on the wall, the observer. But you? I get the feeling that place chokes you. All those . . .'

'Classtrophobia.'

'Oh, I like that. Did you make it up?'

'That doesn't mean nobody ever made it up before.'

'Somebody like you stuck with people like them – I see something that doesn't fit.'

Jim changed the subject again but Peters moved on to wonder aloud how soon they'd know whether the murderer was to be spared the gallows. And that led to a discussion of the varying penalties for identical crimes, which led on to Caribbean crime and especially drugs and arms running. They were back with Drew.

By his manipulation of their conversations, he revealed

he'd guessed Drew's fate and Jim's culpability. Whatever his other failings, he was an acute observer and had deduced too that Jim wasn't what he wanted the world to believe. Peters had pierced his armour. Peters was dangerous.

Peters was especially dangerous because he had two portraits of Jim and a hotline to the newsdesks of European and American publications. Jim tried to measure the danger. When he considered it, all Peters *could* have was suspicion. As there was no body and no other evidence of violence, there was no murder enquiry. If ever it came to that, and to Jim being accused, then Peters was in the money. He owned the portraits and had spent much of a day in Jim's company discussing Drew and the use of black magic to dodge a murder conviction. Better, he'd accompanied Jim to a voodoo ceremony held for this very purpose. Of course, none of it was exactly like that, but by the time Peters offered his story for sale, it would be.

'By the way,' said Peters, breaking into his thoughts. 'Those shots of Diana and her kids diving. They've been taken by a weekly magazine.'

'Sounds as though you owe me a drink.'

'You can have a sandwich too.' He put a hand to his rumbling stomach. 'I wish this tub would hurry up, I'm seeing mirages of chicken and chips. Can you have mirages at sea?'

'I don't think you can by moonlight.'

'Oh God, it's even worse than I thought.' He gibbered at visions of chicken and chips.

Jim's note was lying where he'd left it on the table in the cabin of Mike Rooney's boat. There was no sign of Rooney and none that he'd returned from the police station. It was past midnight, more than seven hours since they were to meet.

Although Jim had promised he'd go to the police station if Rooney weren't freed by five, he'd said it as a bit of routine encouragement, secure in the belief he'd be out during the afternoon.

The pale eye behind the stairs was glowing, a point of light forcing him to stare back at it. He shuddered and hurried out on deck. A man on another boat told him he hadn't seen Rooney. In the Green Parrot the barman flashed a smile and pointed out: 'Hey, you've lost Rooney now as well as Drew?'

Jim put on his Southern drawl to reply: 'I'm gettin' real careless.'

But the barman hadn't seen Rooney. Neither had a couple of holidaymakers whose cruiser was moored close to Rooney's old fishing boat.

After that Jim stopped asking. He told himself it was too late to venture into the police station because if Rooney were there it had been decided to detain him until morning. Whoever was in charge this late would have no authority to release him, even if Jim convinced them they ought to. Besides, if he went in there to argue Rooney's case, he might be held too.

He stayed on the boat, stretching out on Drew's bunk. Beneath him lay the meagre haul from the *Rosita*, in front the glowing eye gazed. He was sleepless and uncomfortable, alternately dreaming wild dreams of Martin Peters pursued by Cole Porter and lying awake worrying how to free himself without fleeing. Forced to run, he'd have to give up the *Rosita* and he had no intention of doing so.

Jim lay there, evolving a plan to raise the treasure. Eventually, when dawn lightened the cabin and a breeze rushed down the hill to set the loosely tied ropes flapping, he stirred. Up on deck he saw swirling cloud, a rosy glow to water and rock, a fishing boat coming into harbour, and boats swinging on their anchors as eddies swirled. He ducked down into the cabin and made coffee, wishing he had milk instead of Rooney's dubious white powder. But he tipped in the powder and drank great warming gulps to steady him after the night fears and coax him to face the day. It was to be a difficult day.

The first part was all right. He'd washed his shirt in the early hours and found it dry and not badly creased. When he'd left St Elena he'd packed a spare one and changes of underwear because his outings had a habit of turning into overnight stops. Showered and dressed, he considered his shoes. They needed polish. Some days he wouldn't have troubled but those were the ones when it didn't matter what impression he made. On this day he needed to look expensive.

He rooted around in lockers, hoping for a cloth to buff the shoes. He did better, finding brown shoe polish. When the shoes were shining and he was putting the polish and cloth back where he'd found them, he again felt himself watched by the pale eye. Jim uncapped the polish and smeared a little over the filler in the bullet hole. Stepping back, he considered it. An improvement. He was alone, the eye gone. The new effect was of a knothole, a natural blemish.

Things went wrong immediately after that. First the boat juddered as someone climbed aboard. His hope that it was Rooney faded as he looked up the companionway and saw the feet. The fat policeman's shoes were unlike anything Rooney wore.

The man gave a smile that was a passable imitation of his cousin Claude's. 'Mr Rush? You've come visiting here?'

'Where's Mike?' The policeman's opening was encouraging because whatever he and Rooney had talked about, Rooney hadn't revealed Jim was with him the previous day. The less he was discussed, the better he liked it.

'Mr Rooney's fine, just fine.'

'You know where he is?'

'Sure, he's down at my office right now. We've been having a talk about a few things, you know.'

The man pushed back his cap until it was at the angle he preferred. His eyes were everywhere, taking in the clutter on deck; noticing the shine on Jim's shoes and the creases in his shirt; magically seeing through walls into the wheelhouse where the screen sat blindly, and into the cabin where a bullet hole waited to be discovered, and into the acoustic lining of the engine house where the bullet itself was lodged.

Jim leaned casually against the wheelhouse doorway, his hands in his trouser pockets. 'What's he been up to, then?'

'Not for me to say, Mr Rush.'

'Well, when is he coming back? I have a meeting with him.' He gave his watch a disgruntled glance. It was possible he could persuade the man he'd arrived that morning.

'He'll be back when it's the right time, Mr Rush.'

Jim sighed. He gave a weak smile of resignation. 'Well, I hope it isn't too long. I have to be back on St Elena this afternoon.'

He thought it would do no harm to remind him of his St

258

Elena connections, that it might make the difference between going free and being questioned. The man didn't react but said if Mr Rush would excuse him he must do what he'd come to do. He meant search the boat.

Jim sat on deck for a couple of minutes while the policeman was poking around in the wheelhouse. Then he said he was going to the bar for breakfast. Fetching his bag from the cabin, he was pleased that with his habitual neatness he'd already stowed in it everything of his that was on board.

It crossed his mind to remove some of the *Rosita* things from the locker and whisk them away before they were discovered. But he didn't. They didn't amount to much, but they were proof he and Rooney had been exploring a wreck and not raising caches of dumped arms. It was preferable to let the police see the proof.

When he came out of the cabin he was glad of that decision. With great charm the policeman asked to be allowed a glimpse into the bag. He made a joke of it, stressing it was mere routine, that you never let anyone leave the scene of a search carrying a bag you hadn't inspected.

With a quip Jim handed him the bag. Wrapped in a dirty shirt in the bottom of it was Drew's gun.

He tried to breathe normally, not to delay and not to gasp, to carry on as though it were indeed all one great joke. And he planned his reaction. Whatever he did he mustn't over-react. There was nothing to say the gun was Drew's, the one that went missing with him. Jim didn't know the local rules about carrying weapons, but felt confident his St Elena status would protect him from serious repercussions.

The man peeped inside the bag and was on the point of returning it when he dipped a hand in. He poked around and pulled out the gun. His eyebrows lifted.

'You expecting trouble, Mr Rush?'

Jim used his toughest Chicago accent. 'Just an old American habit of mine. I don't flash that thing around.'

He was waiting for the man to drop it into the bag but instead he put the bag down and examined the gun. Stupidly, Jim thought, because he flipped it around and looked for distinguishing marks, and all without bothering to take the standard precaution of checking whether it was loaded.

At last he offered it to Jim. Jim flashed another glance at his watch, zipped up the bag and was soon walking down the quay. He felt breathless, relieved and yet in imminent danger. The policeman had handled the gun and within the next few minutes would alight upon the bullet hole.

The Green Parrot was busy. Fishermen had congregated there, a sea scent hung over everything. Jim ordered coffee and food, intending to sit outside to see when the policeman concluded his search and left. But the barman detained him, leaning confidentially over the counter and speaking low.

'We heard that bad news.' His face reflected bad news.

Jim floundered. If the man meant Mike Rooney having to answer a few questions, this was going too far. 'I'm not sure I understand.'

'About Drew.'

Jim's stomach tightened. He echoed, feeling as mystified as he looked. 'About Drew?'

'Didn't that policeman just go down to Rooney's boat and tell you?'

A shake of the head. 'So you tell me. Please.'

Bewildered the man said: 'I can't believe this. We saw the man walk down there but you say he didn't tell you?'

'He didn't mention Drew.'

'That's unbelievable.'

'Please . . .'

'Man, he's dead. His body washed up on rocks, way down south of here.'

Jim was numb. '*Dead?*' He said it twice in varying tones of incredulity.

Unburdened of his news, the barman became busy again, whisking a cloth over the bar top, taking down crockery and preparing food and drink. Fishermen came to the counter to pay and he slotted in their transactions in the gaps between telling Jim how a hotel cruise ship had found the body. Holidaymakers who'd booked a day's under-water exploration had been horrified to have a corpse brought on board. Complaints had been made to the travel company.

'When?' Jim asked, once he was able to insert a question. 'When did all this happen?'

The barman screwed up his eyes and did mental arithmetic. Three days ago, he decided. 'That's when the body was recovered but the story wasn't known here until this morning.'

Jim was doing his own arithmetic, calculating how long it had taken for someone to guess the corpse was connected with the big red-haired man missing from a different island. Someone would have had the joyless of task of viewing it and deciding whether it might once have been Drew. He understood now where Mike Rooney had been all this time.

Desperate for the sanctuary of St Elena, Jim forced himself to linger over breakfast. Food was practically impossible to swallow, like cardboard in his dry mouth. Coffee tasted of nothing. He made himself do it, knowing everyone in the bar, from the barman down to the newest arrival among the holidaymakers, realised he was the man who'd last seen Drew alive. There was little enough to talk about, every detail would be savoured, elaborated, lied about. Keen as he was to leave, he dared not hurry.

The gun, he kept thinking. *He handed me back the gun. Obviously they don't know Drew was shot. OK, the bullet went through him, it's in the boat. How can I get it? I can't, not without dismantling the panels between the cabin and the engine house. Not possible, there's no way I could get the time alone there to do that. Doesn't matter, though. The policeman wasn't interested in the gun. They might never know he was shot. So it's all right.*

He bought a second cup of coffee to refute charges of panicky exit. Staying at the bar to drink it, he asked the barman to repeat part of what he'd said about Drew.

'I wasn't taking it all in. I knew Drew quite well. It's come as a shock.'

When they'd talked for a while, Jim checked the accuracy of the clock in the bar and then left a message for Rooney, explaining he'd run out of time. He walked round the harbour and found a boat to take him to St Elena.

The boatman wanted to talk about Drew too, saying he'd known him. Jim let him talk. He didn't learn anything interesting or useful, except that there was at least one person who'd thought Drew a cheerful fellow fond of a joke. But the boatman's acquaintance had been slight, limited to a few words when he bumped into Drew in the harbour or in a bar.

'You see that spanner over there?'

Jim sought out a spanner amidst a telltale scattering of tools near the engine. 'Yes?'

'Drew loaned me that. Ages ago. I forgot to return it.' He shrugged. 'Too late now.'

The hill of St Elena was fast approaching. Servants were dragging a boat along a strip of white sand. Silvery wooden houses peeped through greenery on the slopes above. From this aspect they looked misleadingly like a large village, as though the island was well populated instead of reserved for the use of one rich man and his friends. The boatman curved inshore and set Jim down.

Jim paused on the path to the house, head cocked. It was disconcertingly quiet. Now he craved the camouflage of the group, it had vanished.

Near the top of the path he met Claude. The house servant greeted him with the slightest show of deference. 'A quiet day, Mr Rush,' he said. And implicit in that incontestable remark was a wealth of comment on the antics observed on other days.

'Where is everybody?'

'Most went to an island over that way.' He pointed beyond the house and the headland, off to the west.

'Another party?' The previous one had lasted days. He feared he couldn't spare days, he needed protection immediately.

'Oh no, it's not a party, it's the treasure hunt. You see...' As Claude broke off Jim noticed movement at a window in the corner of the house. Claude excused himself and glided away.

263

The hall was quiet and cool. Jim was on his way to the room he and Jane shared when he heard a door open and footsteps approaching. Guy came into the hall. He was dressed in what had become normal, a long blue jacket with a stuffed parrot attached to one shoulder.

'Aha, you're back, then, Jim, lad?' In spite of the jolly pirate voice he didn't seem the least pleased to see Jim.

Jim said hello.

Guy hopped nearer. 'Spot of bother with the law, is it, Jim, lad?'

Jim treated this as one of Guy's sillier thrusts. But Guy retorted that the police had telephoned, twice, asking for him.

'They said you were to contact them as soon as you turned up.'

Jim looked puzzled and promised to call them right away.

Guy raised a forbidding hand and gave a twitch of his shoulder to ensure the bird quivered. 'And I say ye shan't, my hearty. We pirates make our own law, so we do. We shall have no truck with coarse and common policemen. Do you hear, Jim, lad?'

'But Guy . . .'

'None at all.' He began to hobble away, then spun back and added, in his normal drawl, which Jim hadn't heard for so long it gave him a start: 'It simply isn't on, you know.'

Then he hobbled out of sight. Jim gaped after him, wondering what to make of it. He believed it, he had no hesitation about doing that. It was unfortunately credible that the police were asking for him, and no less credible that Guy was infuriated by it.

He went to his room, planning to make the call immediately and argue with Guy later, if it came to arguing. With luck Jane would return soon and employ her genius for making everything all right. He twisted the door handle. The room was locked.

Jim went outside and round to the window, taking the longer route rather than let Guy have a view of him doing so. The shutters were closed. On the return journey he pushed through a rear door, a servants' entrance.

'Claude, do you know why my room's locked?'

Overcoming reluctance, Claude said: 'Mr Guy did it. He said that room was to be shut up and he took the key and did it. But exactly why, well, I can't explain that.'

'I may be back to use your telephone.'

Jim headed for Guy. 'You've locked my room.'

Guy stood in his doorway, solid, malevolent, clownish and loving every second of his childish triumph. Jim was afraid of hitting him.

'So what?'

'I'd like it *un*locked, please.' His right hand was balling into fist.

The silly pirate voice told him: 'Well now, Jim, lad, your captain's not going to agree to that and you may lay to it. That's Jane's room and Jane's on a voyage. She didn't wait for you and she didn't say anything about letting you into her room while she was voyaging, not one word, my hearty.'

Jim selected the exact spot on Guy's chin to land the blow. He pictured the fool lifted off his feet and slammed to the floor, the parrot falling with him. With any luck he'd land on his damned parrot. He might . . .

What stopped him was the suspicion Guy would love him

to do it. Guy had been taunting him and tempting him for weeks, deliberately provoking a reaction that would make it impossible for Jim to remain there. Guy wanted him to go but played hell every time he went away.

Once he understood the ploy, the danger was dispelled. He pretended to think Guy was joking, and the more Guy insisted and the bitterer he grew, the more Jim treated it as a game. Finally Jim swung it round, putting the pressure on Guy. If Guy didn't get that room unlocked within five minutes, Jim was going to order the servants to force the door. He put on a very good act. Guy produced the key. Then he shut his door in Jim's face. As Jim walked away he heard Guy stumping about and yo, ho, ho-ing all by himself in his bedroom.

The room on which Jim unlocked the door was very unlike the one he'd left a couple of days earlier. The telephone was ripped out of the wall, light fittings hung askew, contents of drawers and cupboards were flung about, and the mattress hung off the bed. In other circumstances he'd have cursed burglars. Here, he cursed treasure hunters.

He knew before checking that the gold cup had gone. The bag that had contained it lay kicked into a corner of the bathroom. He didn't doubt he'd get it back, that whoever had taken it would claim it was only in fun, and he'd be dubbed unreasonable if he betrayed the faintest irritation at the prank.

After a perfunctory search he concluded that everything else including the silver plate with the initials was there, although things were utterly disorganised and some damaged. He jiggled the dead telephone.

Jim asked Claude to have the room put back as it ought

to be. Claude looked scandalised at the mess but restricted his comment to a clucking of the tongue.

'Would you like to use the staff telephone while I have this straightened, Mr Rush?'

But Jim said not. He'd changed his mind about making the call. If he spoke to the police they'd ask him to go and see them. Eventually they'd call again, of course, but there was no need to speak to them sooner than need be.

Claude told him no one but Guy remained on the island. As Jim detested the prospect of his company, he went for a walk. Down to the beach, over the headland, across a bay, up the hill towards the south. And everywhere he went the landscape was changed. The island appeared to have become the habitat of large and energetic moles. Thanks to Guy, a merry band of pirates had dug holes all over it.

At last, when he'd run out of excuses to stay away, he returned to the house. He needn't have worried: Guy had ordered supper sent to his room and was keeping the door locked. Jim ate alone on the huge terrace by the pool and then wandered through the house. It was grand and shadowy and a good number of the rooms were locked. From curiosity he tested their doors, and went away wondering how much damage they concealed.

Then he went to the room they called the library but he couldn't settle to reading, not even those reports about the wrecks that had once entranced him. He'd dreamed up a way of clinging on to the *Rosita* and the treasure that sank with her. But even that happy thought wasn't enough to lift his spirits. He felt lonely and vulnerable.

He stood at the window, the view obscured by a shrub

being choked by yellow vine. The shrub was alive, just, but had ceased to thrive. The vine was already stretching out to entangle the house. Tendrils clung to the windowsill.

Quite early he went to his bedroom, transformed from its earlier state. Claude had said a lick of paint was required; and it wouldn't take long to find a replacement for the broken lock on the cupboard or matching fabric to re-cover the chair that had been ripped apart. In the meantime, the servants had draped a shawl over the chair.

Jim laid the gun on the bed. He had to make up his mind whether to keep it or throw it away. If the police asked for it again, because they'd found the bullet hole in the cabin or because the pathologist carrying out the post mortem had discovered a bullet wound in Drew's body, then possession of the murder weapon would link him inextricably to the killing.

One thing he was sure of: the bullet had passed through the body and then through the wooden panel. It was embedded in the boat, obviously above the waterline or she'd have sunk.

What was important was that there was no bullet in the body, because this denied the forensic science people the chance to match the scoring on it with marks on other bullets fired by the same gun. They couldn't prove the gun was the murder weapon.

Now the body had been recovered, Mike Rooney would doubtless tell the police what kind of gun Drew had owned and say it had gone missing with him. Worse, if they showed him Jim's, he might be able to swear it was the identical one.

The only argument Jim mustered in favour of keeping the gun was that the fat policeman had seen it in his possession. To dispose of it once the body was washed up was to court suspicion. This argument outweighed the rest.

He wrapped the gun and hid it in the cupboard he could no longer lock.

Pirates invaded the island during the night. Jim awoke to cries from the bay below the house and lay listening to this rather threatening merriment getting louder and nearer. Then fists were beating on his shutters, feet were rampaging around the terrace and a chorus of voices was demanding Guy.

Jim dressed. There was obviously no chance of sleep. He squinted through the shutters, saw six people and heard more. Costumes for the raucous comic opera were extraordinary: stripy T-shirts and rolled-up jeans were now *de rigueur*, also hankies on heads, but the cast had acquired false beards, a few eye patches and weaponry. Two of them emphasised their request for Guy by striking the air with cutlasses.

Behind Jim the door moved, a soft thud as someone tried to open it and found it locked. He went over.

'Who's there?'

'Me.'

'Jane?' He turned the key.

'Who else were you expecting?' She was dishevelled, her black hair looping out from beneath a spotted handkerchief.

'Sir Francis Drake? Blackbeard? Yes, it looks like a good night for that old pirate's ghost to go a-roaming.' He locked the door behind them.

'James, it isn't funny.'

'No, that's what I thought.'

He reached out a hand to whisk the cloth from her head but she sidestepped and ran to peep through the shutters. 'I'm afraid it's getting a bit out of hand.'

'Only a bit?' He was thinking of the damage to the furnishings, the cratered island, the way Guy's mad drama had seized them.

She was thinking of something else. 'Yes. Dylan's split the band and brought his party for a showdown with Guy. He's decided the game can't possibly work. What he says is you can't have heaps of different maps and different riddles leading to the treasure.'

'Isn't that what I said? At the start?'

'Yes, but *you* didn't want to play. Dylan was wonderfully keen, he's put his soul into it and now he's livid. In fact, he's actually going to accuse Guy of *cheating*.'

As he didn't doubt Guy was cheating, Jim found it impossible to share her horror at this. Instead he asked why she'd joined Dylan's faction. Usually she sided with Guy if sides were to be taken.

'I haven't joined Dylan, not truly. But I wanted to come back here and it was the quickest way.'

He kissed her and murmured: 'That's cheating.'

Outside, the clamour reached a new pitch as Guy came roaring into sight, parrot bobbing, crutch thudding over the tiles. Jane clutched Jim's arm.

'Come on, we'd better get out there.'

'*What?*' He wanted nothing to do with it and said, in a lighthearted way, that he felt safer where he was.

She tugged him away from the window. 'We can't just watch, we have to try and calm things down.'

'They won't take any notice of me.'

'Oh, come *on*.'

They went round to the terrace. Guy was silenced and encircled, taken aback at what he called mutiny. But that was momentary. He produced his roughest, gruffest voice in his most piratey accent and shouted them down. He made threats of floggings, keel haulings, hangings from highest yard arms, and various other measures equally fierce and unfriendly.

Dylan was no kinder. He bawled back a new allegation, that there was no buried treasure anyway.

Jeremy, who'd been Guy's helper at the planning stage, squirmed. Guy quashed him with a sneer and called him a Judas. At that, Jeremy blabbered that he'd said nothing, nothing whatsoever, honestly he hadn't.

Guy announced that there was indeed treasure to be won. And Dylan, backed by the more intrepid of his followers, challenged him. 'Prove it, then.'

Jeremy, apparently trying to shift his allegiance from Dylan and back to Guy if only to refute the name of Judas, pointed out the obvious. 'He can't prove it, Dylan, if it's buried. He'd have to dig it up and ruin the game.'

But Guy said he *would* prove it. He stumped away in the direction of his room, bidding them, as he queerly put it, to hold fast.

Jane had said and done nothing, hanging back with Jim a little detached from the action. Although she'd confessed she was worried about the acrimonious twist to events, her face revealed nothing of it. She might have been watching a television show she could switch off if it became too violent, rather than studying her circle of friends tearing itself apart. The word bewitched came into Jim's mind.

He tried to make her smile: 'Does Guy keep a spade in his bedroom?'

There was a twinkle of amusement in her eyes. 'Perhaps he hid the treasure in there.'

'If that's true, he's about to reveal its whereabouts and ruin what's left of his treasure hunt.'

Jeremy came sidling up to speak to Jane, sparing the briefest hello for Jim. 'Dylan's frightfully cross about this, you know. He isn't going to let it go. Once he gets his teeth into a thing, one had better look out.'

Jane sighed. 'I know, but what can we do? I've tried telling Dylan that if he keeps on Guy simply won't let him play any more.'

Other pirates were gathered around Dylan and making plotting sounds. Jim yawned. He wished they'd fight it out down on the beach or anywhere except outside his bedroom window. He felt strained, short of sleep.

Then there came a yo, ho, ho and Guy lurched on to the terrace. 'Aha, my hearties, 'tis the treasure you see before your very eyes, the treasure your captain offers to the bravest riddler of you all.'

He hopped forward, managing the crutch with one hand, twitching his shoulder to set the parrot bouncing, and waving aloft in his other hand Jim's gold cup.

'Gold,' Guy cried. 'And emeralds and all the riches of the Spanish Main. And they can be yours, my hearties...'

The rest was drowned in roars of excitement and approval. Guy had made his point, he'd won them over and the rebellion collapsed. Even Dylan joined in the chorus of: 'Pieces of eight! Pieces of eight!'

Jane's hand tightened on Jim's arm. 'That's...'

'Hush.'

Later, when things had cooled down if not actually quietened down, he explained to her how their room had been ransacked, the cupboard lock smashed and the cup stolen. She stared at the cupboard, hopelessly trying to envisage Guy breaking it open.

'James, what will you do?'

'Get it back, what else?'

'But how?'

'I'll think about that in the morning.'

He went to bed and snuggled down and let her suppose he'd fallen asleep, but his mind churned: Drew's body coming ashore, disposal of the gun, the future of the *Rosita*, Martin Peters and his meddlesome curiosity, and now Guy's theft of the gold cup. He wondered what would have happened if he'd said straight out the treasure Guy was flaunting was actually his. It would have depended, he thought, on how strenuously Jane had supported him. But it was hypothetical, he'd done what Guy had willed him to do: nothing.

The house grew quiet. Once he was sure Jane was asleep, Jim dressed again. This time he pulled on jeans and over them a stripy T-shirt belonging to Jane. He stretched one of her dark stockings over his face and tied her spotted handkerchief on his head. Then he took the gun from its hiding place.

There was no light beneath the door of Guy's room, no chink through the keyhole. The door gave at the first kick. Then he was at Guy's side before Guy had properly woken. He wasn't in bed but slumped in a chair, still wearing the jacket plus parrot.

The robbery was carried out by moonlight. Jim thrust the gun into Guy's alarmed face and demanded the treasure. He used his best upper-class English accent, a touch of Jeremy, a tinge of Guy himself, practically any of the St

Elena set except that strange American Jim Rush. Guy gagged and pointed to where the gold cup lay on his bed. Jim snatched it up and disappeared as abruptly as he'd come.

He overslept next day, to be woken by Jane saying Guy was in a foul mood and insisted on seeing him. For a few seconds he questioned whether the armed robbery was dream or fact. Then he puzzled how Guy knew the identity of the robber.

Jane said: 'He's being frightfully bossy today. That business with Dylan upset him more than he cares to admit. He hates disloyalty, you see.'

'Did he give a clue what he wants me for?'

'No, but he seemed to think you'd know.'

Standing in the shower he thought: *Thank God Jane's tidy. Thank God she doesn't leave hairs in the basin and towels on the floor.* He let the day disappear behind a cloud of steam, wishing he could hide there all day, all this terrible day.

He went to see Guy, making a huge effort to appear relaxed instead of cringing as Guy wanted him to. *After all, maybe my tactics were over the top but what about Guy's, smashing up the room and stealing his guest's property?*

Primed for confrontation about his method of reclaiming the cup, Jim was amazed to be lectured about incurring the interest of the police. He thought they'd dealt with this the previous day.

'No,' said Guy in his natural drawl. 'I don't mean the phone calls. I'm telling you they came here early this morning. Nine fifteen, almost a dawn raid. Who do these people think they are? They barged in, no attempt to make an appointment with me . . .'

'Just a minute, Guy. Are you saying they wanted to speak to you?'

'I'm saying they should have done, as a matter of courtesy, don't you think? One doesn't charge on to private property and harass someone's guests without that someone's permission. At any rate, one shouldn't do that. They did, or they would have done if I hadn't sent them packing, I told them you're not here. I've told everyone to say it if they come again. You're not here.'

This was totally unexpected, Jim didn't know how to respond. Gratitude might seem an admission of culpability. Instead, he put a question.

'What did they want?'

'A gun,' Guy said airily. 'They said they wanted to check up on your gun. Naturally I told them that was arrant nonsense, you couldn't possibly have a gun, none of us have. Why should we go around armed to the teeth? We don't look like hitmen, do we? Then I ordered them off.'

'They'll be back. They're sure to be.'

'That's exactly it, Jim, lad. That's why one absolutely never gets involved with them, because if one does they never quite go away.'

'When they come . . .'

'We'll tell them you're not here.'

Jim said that was fine. He left quickly, before Guy could say any more. The rest of the pirates were straggling back to St Elena and soon the two factions had parleyed, come to terms and set about digging up the island again. Everything was back to normal.

During the afternoon the fat policeman and another one Jim hadn't previously seen pulled alongside the dock. He was on the path above, on his way to the south of the island, when he caught sight of their launch. He stepped off the path and into the forest that had once trapped him with its poisonous breath. A handful of pirates shot by him going north. When they spotted the intruders, they raised a hue and cry as Guy had ordered them to do.

Jim melted into the trees and let his imagination convey the rest. He pictured Guy and his gang lying in the name of loyalty; the police searching Jane's room and finding that, like Drew, he'd walked out of his life taking nothing. He thought of them finding the gold cup but not finding the gun. He took the gun from his pocket and handled it. This piece of metal had killed Drew and conquered Guy, and now he was going to bury it.

He continued south, so absorbed in imagined scenes and exchanges that he overshot, halting only when he realised the path was about to emerge from the cover of the trees. Down a steep slope were the servants' houses. Below them a thin ribbon of surf fluttered on the edge of a blue sea.

Jim retreated six paces, took a couple of steps away from the path, knelt and buried the gun in soft earth near the roots of a tree. Then he took a sharp stone from the path and scratched the trunk with an uncertain X.

9

'It's murder,' said Mike Rooney. 'They found a bullet in him.'

Jim felt his jaw sag. Rooney was telling him Drew had been shot in the chest, he was repeating what the police had said. But in spite of the vivid description of the body in the morgue and his secondhand details of the post mortem, the only thing Jim could think of was the baleful eye that had taunted him from the panelling.

They were at the Green Parrot. Rooney had telephoned and begged him to come as there was much to talk about but not on the telephone.

Sailing to meet him, Jim felt the tensions of St Elena lift, the tangles in his web of deceit unravel. When he reached harbour Rooney was sitting outside the bar, an almost empty glass in front of him.

'Free at last, Mike?'

He saw at once that flippancy was out of place. A flicker of irritation crossed Rooney's face. His eyes were dark circled, anxious.

'Another beer?' Jim went to the bar.

The barman said it was nice to see him but seemed surprised he was there. *I'm ruining a good rumour*, Jim thought. *You won't be able to say I ran off as soon as the body turned up.*

He carried the beers out to the table in the sun, nice cool beers unlike the ones Rooney served on his boat. The glass was halfway to his lips when Rooney told him it was murder, they'd found a bullet in the body.

Jim echoed: 'Murder?'

He was bursting with questions about how they could be certain of the cause of death in a body pounded by the sea for days, perhaps bloated and nibbled by fish. And he was recklessly close to challenging Rooney's identification, and saying he knew for a fact the bullet had passed through the body.

His thoughts raced, seeking explanations. *The eye, what was the eye if not a bullet hole? Ah, but it could still be a bullet hole. Another one, the result of another shot. Or it could be nothing of the sort. Forget it, anyway. Forget it. It's irrelevant, it always was. The bullet that killed Drew was found in the body.*

And then: *The gun. The policeman knows I have the gun. He handed it back to me. Why? Incompetence? Lack of imagination? Too complicated to tangle with the St Elena set? Not now, though. Not now Rooney will tell them Drew owned a gun, and the fat policeman knows mine's the same type.*

Preoccupied with his own delicate position, Rooney failed to notice Jim's struggle to understand. He said, with absolute seriousness: 'I thought they were never going to let me go. It was as if they kept running out of questions and had to break off for an hour while they thought up some more. And then when they came back they pretended they'd forgotten the answers to the earlier ones, and so they had me going over it again and again. In the end I was convinced they were trying to drive me mad.'

'But you weren't arrested or charged with anything?'

'With what? Being miles away with Denny Witherspoon when Drew disappeared from the quay here?'

Jim asked whether the police had paid much attention to Martin Peters' story about smuggling arms. Rooney said yes, he'd been asked about that too.

'They searched the boat but they didn't find any evidence to support it. How could they? There isn't any. I kept telling them Drew couldn't have been involved in anything like that because I was with him almost all the time.' He shrugged. 'God knows whether they believed me.' A pause while he drank and wiped froth from his mouth, then: 'That's the problem, isn't it? There's no proof, there's only what I say and if they don't believe me . . .'

As Jim started to reply Rooney broke in. 'I didn't tell them about the old plantation house because I don't want them poking around up there. Do you think I should have done?'

'I don't know but the decision's taken.'

'Look, Jim.' He leaned across, lowering his voice. 'Drew has packages up there I've never seen into. Now I don't know what might be in them but he was a guy with a chequered history. It's possible there's something I'd rather not be associated with. Do you see what I mean?'

Jim nodded. Weapons? Drugs? Unlikely because those were passed on quickly, not hoarded for months. Stolen property?

Rooney said: 'The police didn't mention Martin Peters had a photograph of me near the house.'

'Maybe he didn't tell them.'

'God, I'd love to get my hands on that. If Martin thinks it's incriminating, then so might they.'

Jim was about to tell him he'd tried, when Rooney stiffened. 'Oh, he's here.'

Martin Peters came round the corner. Seeing them, he changed direction. He was chirpy, bouncing along.

'Let you off, then, did they, Mike?' He added a hello to Jim, then pulled up a chair and joined them.

The intrusion displeased Rooney but Jim didn't mind. He'd drained Rooney of information and couldn't be bothered with hand wringing. Drew's criminal background hadn't held Rooney back when he wanted him to invest in the wreck-hunting venture.

Jim asked Peters: 'Where's Denny?' The cruiser was in the harbour but no one on board.

'Took the ferry for Grenada. He said he was going for a spot of sight-seeing but I assume he's looking out for work.'

Rooney said bitterly: 'There goes my alibi.'

Peters treated this as a joke, not knowing Rooney had been warned he was suspected of arms dealing. He framed a shot with his hands, a shot of Rooney. 'The guilty man. They still have the death penalty here, don't they?'

Rooney looked sick. Jim said: 'No idea, Martin, it's not the kind of thing I ever thought of asking.'

Peters chuckled. 'They don't actually mention it in the travel brochures, do they?' The barman came out and Peters gestured for a beer before continuing: 'Mind you, I could be wrong. Easy to get these islands mixed up, isn't it?'

Rooney pushed back his chair and walked into the bar. Peters asked: 'What's up with him?'

'They think he killed Drew.'

'Oh, come on, they can't think that. Not with honest Denny Witherspoon to swear for him.'

Jim reminded him Denny had gone and Rooney had spent many hours in the police station. 'They haven't questioned anyone else.'

'Not even you?'

'They're focusing on Mike,'

Peters looked into the bar. There was a men's room at the end, Rooney had gone in there. Peters found himself watching the barman staring out into the harbour.

'Well,' he said in a reflective way, 'they're wrong, aren't they, Jim?'

Jim said he was sure of it. He gave another airing to the theory that Drew had met someone and gone off on private business not known to Rooney. Only the ending was changed: Drew was no longer supposed lying low, he was dead; and not only was he dead, he was murdered.

Peters listened without comment. Then he changed the subject. 'We got a few decent pictures, Jim.' They hadn't spoken since the evening they dabbled in black magic.

'Yours or mine, Martin?'

'Cheeky.'

He showed Jim some Cibachrome prints made from transparencies. The old woman who'd mumbled and twitched had come out well. There was an especially hideous one of her riveting the camera with a fearful gaze. The intensity was creepy.

Peters was amused. 'I reckon she was putting the evil eye on you, Jim.'

'Or on your camera.'

'*And* I got the black look from that girl in the trees. Well, so far so good. Don't know about you, but I feel fine. Maybe they got the spell wrong.'

They continued to joke about the experience and about the photographs. The portraits of Jim were missing but neither of them mentioned those.

Then Peters hopped the conversation on to new ground. 'Talking of strange rites, are they still reliving *Treasure Island* up at St Elena?'

He loved Jim's look of surprise and gave a triumphant laugh. 'My spies are everywhere, didn't I warn you?'

'Several times,' Jim said drily. 'What was it this time? A boat? Plane? Helicopter?'

'Helicopters are useless, too noisy and too much down draught. Have I ever told you I use a helicopter?'

Jim conceded he hadn't.

Peters said: 'Anyway, it wasn't a snoop-and-run job, not this time. Mike told me. He said he went to pick you up and found himself centre stage in a panto. Well into the second act, is it?'

'Unfortunately, yes.'

As he spoke Jim realised where this was leading. 'No. No, Martin. You mustn't do it.'

Peters was impish. 'I've heard a rumour you've got Dylan Thing out there. Not to mention Lord Dodo Whatsit.'

'As far as I'm concerned we've got the Pirates of Penzance out there. With cutlasses, Martin.'

'*Cutlasses.*' Peters was grinning broadly, a greedy conniving grin. 'Mike didn't say cutlasses.'

'They came later.'

'Real cutlasses?'

'It's a dangerous game, Martin, you wouldn't enjoy it.'

'How about the Neighbours? Any of them togged out as pirates?'

Jim laughed off the crazy idea. But Peters said it was quite likely Jim wouldn't know and he'd have to see for himself. Jim said no, very firmly.

'It wouldn't be out of character,' Peters went on. 'There was that time Diana and Fergie dressed up as police-women. Tried to gatecrash Prince Andrew's stag night party but ended up in Annabel's drinking champagne and orange juice instead. Remember that?'

Again Jim warned him off.

'Talking of the Neighbours . . .' Peters whisked a maga-zine out of his camera bag and opened it at a double page spread of photographs of Princess Diana on her Caribbean holiday. The picture of her diving into the pool took up half a page.

He was glowing. 'Not bad, eh?' He tapped the diving photograph. 'That's the one, the rest will do nicely but that's the one that's making the money. It's going round the world.'

Jim agreed they'd given him a good show. He under-stood now why Peters was so exuberant. He'd just picked up a copy of the magazine and there his work was, two pages of it and his name correctly spelled. A thought struck him.

'Martin, don't you mind everyone knowing you took these pictures? I remember you saying you tried to keep it secret.'

Apparently Peters had forgotten this. His cheerfulness faded for a moment but then he recovered, saying he'd not be around long enough for it to become a problem.

'Time to head for home, Jim. I've been away too long. I

have to keep my face known at the newsdesks because if I don't, where's the next commission coming from?'

Jim hoped that was the end of Peters' interest in St Elena but, once again, he'd underestimated the man. Peters immediately revived the subject. For diversion Jim dipped into a pocket and pulled out an envelope. He tossed it on to the table in front of Peters.

'There you are, Martin. If you really want to play pirates, here's the essential equipment. You can't leave Go without it.'

Peters ripped it open. He spread the map on the table. It showed the outline of a small island, a cross near its northern coast. Written alongside the drawing were six riddles. He recited them as if they were a spell. Mike Rooney came back while he was doing it.

Jim explained to Rooney: 'That's one of the maps for the game.'

'I can see what it is. It's St Elena upside down.'

'*Is* it? We were told they were fictitious islands.'

Rooney said: 'I've been sailing round here long enough. Look.' He spun the map around. 'See?'

The cross was now roughly in the vicinity of the buried gun.

Martin Peters said it was obviously a pity Rooney hadn't stayed on St Elena and joined in, he might have won. Then he put one of the riddles to them. It was hopelessly difficult so he posed the next one. They agreed the answer ought to be the name of the island.

'Doesn't fit,' Jim objected. 'Even if you spell out saint, it won't fit.'

'Hold on,' Rooney said. 'Try Santalina.'

Peters was blank. 'What for?'

Rooney looked to Jim for confirmation as he said: 'It's one of the names St Elena used to have. A mistake, someone couldn't spell or misheard it and for a time it was known as Santalina.'

And this nugget of information carried Jim back to the archive in Seville and the account of the *Gloriosa* sinking, and the pair who'd escaped drowning, to be swept away in a storm and find sanctuary on a small island where legend said they buried gold and silver.

'Jim?'

Jim focused on Mike Rooney. 'Yes,' he agreed, his voice a whisper. And then, breaking into hilarious laughter: 'It's a real treasure island, after all.'

Martin Peters' interest quickened at this. He demanded to know whether the Santalina treasure hadn't been hunted before now, and Rooney said it hadn't been found. And Peters said the finding of it would make a terrific story.

Jim simply thought how he longed to tell Jane. If any of Guy's maps were of practical use, it was probably the one he'd left disregarded in a trouser pocket. Jane might want to use it to seek the real treasure, perhaps she might dig up the murder weapon as well. Suddenly he was very keen to get back to St Elena to see her and to retrieve the gun.

But there was something he'd vowed to do before he left for St Elena. When Martin Peters went to speak to a holidaymaker he knew, a holidaymaker who was going home to England that day, Jim asked Rooney to keep him out of the way for half an hour. He sloped off, trusting Rooney to manage it.

The air was sweet with blossom and spice. He stole a

moment to stare at the scenery, tempted to guess what the appearance and the history of the islands would have been if Queen Isabella hadn't sent Columbus out with cuttings of Spanish vines and sugar cane on his second voyage. No slave trade? Was it too much to imagine that? A parrot flashed green and blue through palms by the shore, making its terrible cry. Jim hurried on.

At Bamboo Lodge, he nicked open the catch on the patio doors and sought out the photograph of Rooney on the path near the old plantation house. He found the print easily but not the negative and he was short of time. Tipping negatives from their envelopes, he held them to the light, racing through the bright images. He couldn't find that or the portraits of himself. Once he spilled out a pack of colour prints instead, a mistake, his hand ready to pluck them up before they finished their flight. He gathered them, shuffled them together, and stopped dead. One of the prints showed a boat with a scanner fitted to the rear of it. The other showed two men grappling on its deck.

He examined them through Peters' magnifying glass. They were hazy, like snatched pictures of royalty. The men's faces were turned away from the camera. Perhaps the thickset one could be taken for Drew, but the other one could be any young man with fair hair.

As clear as if it were happening then, he heard the buzz of a light aeroplane pottering down the chain of islands.

The lump of coral Mike Rooney called a paperweight was still on his cabin table.

He said: 'They even claimed we had a fight and I hit him

with this. They called it a weapon. You wouldn't believe what rubbish they were talking.'

'But then they found the bullet.'

Jim was struggling not to look at the mark on the panelling behind the stairs. He'd called to deliver the photograph he'd stolen for Rooney and now he couldn't get away. Rooney wanted to tell him all over again what had gone on during the police interviews.

'Yes,' said Rooney, 'they found the bullet but not the gun. They said . . .'

Jim didn't like this pause. 'What?'

'They said you had a gun.'

'An old American custom.' He rolled the hunk of coral along the table and weighed it in his hand. 'You know, they could be right about this. You could do damage with it.'

'Not me, not when I was miles away.'

'OK, Mike, I didn't mean you. I meant anyone could.'

Jim got up from the table. The cabin was cramped, he wanted space. He looked down at the photograph of Rooney stepping out of the trees, Rooney looking furtive.

That's why they're doing it, he thought. *He lets himself look guilty as hell.*

Aloud he said: 'I have to go, Mike.'

'To play hunt the treasure?' The remark was rich with sarcasm.

Jim laughed. 'You used to be keen on treasure hunts yourself.'

He bounded up on deck. Rooney followed, saying: 'Jim, when you said keep Martin out of the way, I brought him here.'

'Here?' He'd expected them to stay at the bar, on neutral

ground. They weren't friends and had every reason to distrust each other. But, of course, Peters would have suggested it.

'He asked to see the boat. When we got here he went around photographing it, the cabin and Drew's bunk, the deck, the scanner . . . Everything.'

'I don't suppose he bothered to ask your permission.'

'I couldn't stop him. He said he wanted a record. He called it the scene of the crime.'

'Just the way he talks, Mike. If it *were* the scene of the crime he'd sell those pictures. But the way things are, as Drew left . . .'

His sentence petered out. Rooney was burning with accusation.

'You're the only person who says Drew was ever here that evening. I hadn't seen him for hours, and yet I'm the one spending time with the police.'

'You're forgetting, they checked on my gun and they've spoken to me several times.'

'It's not the same. I have to stay here, for one thing.'

'They know where I am.'

With some bitterness Rooney said that was exactly it, they knew Jim was at St Elena and they dared not barge in there and upset people.

Although this was wide of the mark, Jim didn't contradict. He consulted his watch and moved towards the rail. Rooney delayed him by saying Jim ought to explain what had really happened once he and Drew were left alone.

Jim took a chance. He gambled on Mike Rooney. With a sigh, a show of reluctance, he said: 'We had a bust-up, like Denny Witherspoon guessed we did. Drew accused me of planning to cheat you out of your cut. But at the same time he was saying it wasn't the *Gloriosa* down there. Quite honestly, he wasn't making sense. Well, he got pretty wild, the way he did the time you stopped him throttling me. I shut myself in the wheelhouse to keep him off. He went down into the cabin and I brought the boat ashore. That's why there were no explanations when he disembarked. He hadn't spoken a word for hours.'

Rooney was unsurprised. He'd always suspected there'd been a fight, he said, because everyone had fought with Drew.

After a moment's reflection he suggested they avoid telling the police because he'd been giving them the impression of three young men enjoying a business venture. To admit to squabbling and fist fights would destroy that image. Motives for murder, which had been absent, would become abundant.

'Surprise!' shouted Martin Peters, springing out of the cabin on the *Mariposa*.

'Martin!' What do you think you're playing at?'

The photographer raised his thumb hitch-hiker style. 'Hitching a lift, Jim.'

'You're *not* coming to St Elena with me.'

'Of course I am, you wouldn't deny me that pleasure.'

Jim slapped his hand against the mast, emphasising the words he knew Peters would disregard. 'No, Martin. *No*. I'm not taking you to St Elena.'

Peters stayed in the companionway, half in and half out of the cabin. 'Then you'll have to shoot me and chuck me over the side.'

Jim flicked a glance to his left. A boat was sliding away

from the quayside. He hoped the crew were too occupied to catch Peters' words or the meaningful edge to his voice.

Peters said: 'Come and see what I've got, Jim.' He ducked into the cabin and waited for Jim to join him.

Jim called down to him. 'You're to get off this boat now. I have to go and I refuse to take you with me.'

Silence.

'Do you hear, Martin? I'm not negotiating, I'm telling you. Off.'

Peters repeated in a singsong voice: 'Come and see what I've got.'

Exasperated, Jim jumped down into the cabin. Peters was sitting on a bench with his camera bag open beside him. He waved some prints at Jim.

Jim took them, heart sinking, knowing what he'd see: the boat with the scanner on the back and a shot of two men struggling on deck.

He read the expression on Peters' face. A supercilious smile on his lips but eyes glittering with cruelty. At that moment he hated him.

'Well then, Jim. What do you say now?'

Jim flopped the photographs on to the floor at Peters' feet, a contemptuous gesture that left Peters unruffled. Peters picked them up and put them on the table.

'That's your set, Jim. You can tear them up if you like, it doesn't matter. The negatives are in mid air. I gave them to a friend who's flying back to London today.'

'What are you trying to prove?'

'I don't have to prove anything, Jim. But you must admit that interesting scene raises questions.'

'Such as who the people are.'

Peters conceded it was a pity he hadn't caught the faces.

'But there's no doubt about the boat, is there? With that paraphernalia on the back of it? There's only one boat like that.'

'Martin, that's not evidence that I shot Drew. Do you see a gun in that photograph?'

'I'm not sure.' Peters scrutinised the picture. 'There's something down there on the left. I'm not saying it definitely is but it could be.'

He prodded the photograph as it lay on the table. Jim leaned over it. 'This?'

There was indeed a dark shape to be construed as a gun if one were determined to find one. Jim felt ice touch his spine. He knew, as only he could know, that the gun hadn't been on deck then. Later, he'd brought it on deck to clean it, but by then Drew was dead and Martin Peters' aeroplane far far away.

He met his gaze. Peters was relaxed, giving Jim time to take his decision, and he could afford to be relaxed because he knew what that decision must be.

Jim smarted at being tricked by Peters of all people. He'd played a game against Mike Rooney, confident he could win, outwit him, do as he liked over the treasure of the galleon, even leave him to talk his way out of a police cell. But he hadn't taken on Peters, this was no part of his game.

Jim felt used, felt he'd all along been used by Peters, ever since that first bizarre encounter and Peters' insistent pursuit of him. All that talk of gratitude because his life had been saved, it had seemed exaggerated but he hadn't noticed it was utterly insincere. From the outset, Peters had marked him down as someone he could use.

Abruptly he threw back his head and laughed, alarming

Peters whose body stiffened and arched back against the cushion. Through his laughter he accused him.

'Blackmail, Martin.'

And when he'd sobered: 'Your photographs are evidence of nothing, but as I don't want to waste my holiday talking to the police, I have to let you have your way.'

Peters stayed below as they sailed out of harbour. When they were passing the headland, he came on deck and chatted as though the previous conversation had never taken place, as though he'd never dangled threats. He told Princess Diana stories and Queen Mum stories. He talked about pirates, real and makebelieve, and asked did Jim know that for all his adventures Drake had died in his cabin?

'Dysentery,' said Jim.

After a few miles Jim made him fetch the photographs, tear them up and scatter them in the wake. Then Jim asked him whether he really wouldn't prefer to be set ashore on some other island. Peters declined to be marooned. He reminded Jim he had copies of the prints at Bamboo Lodge and a set of negatives was on its way to London.

'Who's it going to?'

'My secretary.'

'At a newspaper office?'

'No, she calls into my flat and takes care of things while I'm away. She'll file it.'

'Under what? Murder?'

Peters was smug. 'It's not identified, she won't know what it's about. As far as Sheila's concerned it's a pack of negatives she'll stick in a drawer.'

'You're quite sure about St Elena, Martin? They'll kill

you if they catch you. I don't want to force you to go there if you'd rather not.'

Peters gave him a wondering look and said there was nowhere else he was interested in going, not even to see the Neighbours.

'They're over that way,' Peters said, pointing. He'd seen pirates on the hill and now he could hear them. He slung his camera bag over his shoulder and clambered ashore.

'Martin, wait.' Jim was still tying up.

'It's all right, I know the way.'

He did, he'd once rushed off in that direction and spent a night hiding in a farm building. In fact, he probably knew most of the island well.

Jim walked unhurriedly along the dock. Peters was climbing the path. For a man who was fleshy and out of condition, he made good speed. He carried two cameras. On the boat he'd put a fresh film in one and checked there was a nearly new roll in the other. He was primed for action, a predator scenting its prey.

At the top of the path he turned right, to the south, and a moment later was out of sight. Once he'd disappeared Jim increased his own pace and was soon running in the opposite direction, towards the house. He dropped to walking pace as he neared it.

It appeared deserted but he went quietly, afraid Guy was conducting operations from the comfort of his room. He stepped carefully around a ragged hole where tiling had been prised from the terrace. In the hall a window seat had been ripped out. There were plentiful signs of relentless treasure seeking. Jim sought his own treasure. He unclipped the bath panel in the bathroom he and Jane shared and he recovered the gold cup and the silver plate decorated with a Spanish sea captain's initials. Then he went to find Jane.

He hoped, with the slenderest hope, she might be sunning on the beach where they used to be made to play bounce and a changeling Guy had metamorphosed into Long John Silver. Even if she were sharing a beach mat with Jeremy, he'd prefer her to be there than with the others. The bay was empty. With a sigh, he set off for the south of the island.

The thump of spades on earth had become as much a feature of it as the flight of humming-birds, the glow of hibiscus and the tangle of forest. Before long he heard voices arguing about the answers to riddles, amidst much hilarity. But he couldn't put the owners' names to the voices. Jane's friends remained an indistinguishable mass.

And then it all changed. Hubbub, a clamour, a rumbling wave of anger. People were affronted, people were furious, people were shouting and tearing about. A figure flashed across his path and into the trees, a spade trailing in its hand and a knotted handkerchief sloping over one eye. Another figure followed, its stripy T-shirt torn and grubby, its hand on its cutlass.

Jim moved through the trees after them, going south, going to recover the gun. He almost fell into a fresh crater three feet deep. Spotting it late, he jumped awkwardly across. As the rumble of disputation rose and fell, he heard, from every direction, people crashing through the trees. It was the music of Guy's troops closing ranks.

The island was alive with parrots fleeing in ear-splitting annoyance, fat-bodied spiders and snakes disturbed from tranquillity, creepers reaching out to choke and tree roots to trip. And added to the familiar hazards of the forest was the new one, the one that roared like a beast cornered and attacking.

On the fringe of the clearing where the earth was blackened by fire, he held back. Martin Peters stood surrounded by pirates. The man blustered and tussled but was snared by them. He tried to laugh it off as a tease, but that didn't work. The magic circle held, he could neither talk his way out nor force his way through. Without touching him they intimidated and vanquished him.

There were a great many of them, the numbers swelled by newcomers whose pirate outfits were fresh and un-damaged. The older crew, the Jeremys and Dylans and so on, were raggle-taggle after days of manual labour. There were blistered and bandaged hands. People leaned on their spades, making a stockade to deny Peters' escape. Or they gesticulated with them, as they roared at him in piratey fashion.

On the far side of the clearing, Guy appeared. He hopped, jiggling his Captain Flint and forcing the chant, 'Pieces of eight! Pieces of eight!' before he asked what was going on. Jane told him. Jane told him who Martin Peters was and what he did.

Guy shook his crutch in the air. 'Shall he walk the plank, my hearties?'

They screamed that he should. They screamed approval of every one of Guy's threatened punishments. At each scream he banged the crutch down on the sour black earth.

Peters appealed to Guy as leader of the pack. He was trying to create his own role in the pantomime: the cheeky chappie who oversteps the mark but is forgiven for the sake of his entertainment value. No one was entertained. So he resorted to straightforward pleading, begging to be allowed to go, and plucking from his bag an airline ticket to London to prove he was virtually on his way.

Guy was unmoved, except for dreaming up ever more lavish penalties. The crutch thudded.

Someone seized the camera bag and began to photograph Martin Peters. He twisted away and shielded his face. But someone else had his other camera and was behind him. Then all the others were pretending to hold cameras, clicking and snapping away at him, telling him to say cheese and bobbing and prancing around him and driving him crazy. In Jane's hand was the camera Jim had retrieved from the old plantation house. Peters cowered. The crutch thudded, rhythmic and hypnotic.

A change of mood. Pirates grabbed Peters. They wrenched off his jacket, his shirt, his trousers, every vestige of clothing and of dignity. They photographed and derided. Emptying his camera bag, they broke open the rolls of film he'd used and they reloaded the cameras with new ones. Jane had faded away.

When Peters made a dash for a break in the circle, they photographed him and then they caught him. They lashed him to a blackened tree stump by the bins where the servants disposed of rubbish. He was screaming that it wasn't funny and they were going too far, but they refused to hear his protests. They destroyed him, made him weep for humiliation and fear.

Jim stayed on the fringe, where he'd always been in St Elena life. They were playing a game and were bound only by the rules of that game and not by normal rules of decent behaviour. But it was too late to explain that to Martin Peters and the knowledge would have made him no more comfortable. Instead, Jim looked around for Jane.

'Now?' Her face clouded.

'I have to.'

'The wreck?' she suggested, offering him an excuse. He doubted she believed it, she'd always been accomplished at handing him excuses.

'Yes, it's to do with that.'

He didn't want to talk any more. No, he did want to, but there was no time. He gathered her to him and kissed her, hard, not knowing whether it was a goodbye sort of kiss or a promise that it wasn't.

She straightened the spotted handkerchief that covered her long black hair. There was mud on her cheek, a plaster on her calloused hand.

With a wild, preposterous hope he blurted out: 'You could come . . .'

She gave that low, murmuring laugh that he loved, and said with her gentlest irony: 'Do you really think so?'

Behind them in the clearing there was another roar. Someone had been going through the pockets of Martin Peters' clothing and found the upside-down map of St Elena. Peters was being forced to tell them which island it was. They were brandishing cutlasses at him. Dylan was twirling a length of rope, the end looped into a noose.

Peters sobbed that it was St Elena upside down, he promised ancient treasure hidden where the cross was, he said anything he could think of to make them go away and leave him alone. A few scampered off to dig.

How long, Jim thought, *before one of them sees my cross on the tree? How many minutes before they dig up the gun?*

A wind frisked through the tree tops. Jim looked up, to a sky flecked with cloud. The tide was turning. He relinquished Jane's hand, and left her without risking any more words. There was a lump in his throat, a profound sadness as he hastened away through the trees.

He broke from the jungle into light. Sun was turning sea to blood. Silhouettes of islands floated on redness and galleon clouds sailed down the wind. It was a time for Blackbeard's head to fly like a comet, for black magic and wickedness. He rubbed his eyes and saw the fiery gold and green of Venezuelan emeralds beneath his eyelids, all the wrecked treasure he'd one day find a means of claiming.

When his vision cleared, there below him was the *Mariposa*, sucked by the tide. Insignificant, insubstantial, a toy, an ornament for beautiful lives, she was his escape.

Passionate fragrances of the island filled him as he ran down to her. The red stain was spreading, she became a wraith in a crimson bay. He looked at his hands, afraid he was made bloody too, but there was no blood. He was black, the silhouette of a running man, a motif for the cover of a crime novel, a figure dangling between hope and disaster, reaching out for a safety that was forever beyond his grasp.

He heard the screams as he was casting off. They weren't the excited yells of fanatical game players who saw their goal within reach. Nor of diggers whose treasure of gold and pearls had transformed into a gun. They were an animal's agony.

For a split second he havered, the rope slack around the post. Then he whisked it free and pushed the boat away from the shore.